ꟿF ONLY
FOR
THIS
LIFE

If Only
FOR
THIS
LIFE

Robin Hardy

Westford Press

If Only for This Life
Book 1 of The Sammy/Streiker Salmagundi
Contemporary Christian fiction/allegory

ISBN: 978-1-934776-90-2

Westford Press
mail@westfordpress.com

Cover image of Phalaenopsis orchids © Vyaseleva Elena

Unless otherwise noted, Scripture verses are taken from the HOLY BIBLE, NEW INTERNATIONAL VERSION. NIV. Copyright 1973, 1978, 1984 by International Bible Society. Used by permission of Zondervan Publishing House. All rights reserved.

Scripture verses marked RSV are from the Revised Standard Version of the Bible, © 1946, 1952, © 1971, 1973 by the Division of Christian Education of the National Council of the Churches of Christ in the United States of America.

Karen Sigler S.F.O., *Her Name Means Rose: The Rhoda Wise Story* (EWTN Catholic Publisher) 2000

"There Is a Land of Pure Delight" Isaac Watts, 1709

Catechism of the Catholic Church: Communion of Saints
http://www.vatican.va/archive/ccc_css/archive/catechism/p123a9p5.htm

J.B. Phillips, *Ring of Truth* (New York: The Macmillan Company) 1967

To Sandy Huntress
and
Mimosa Stephenson

good friends and great encouragers

"If only for this life we have hope in Christ,
we are of all people most to be pitied."

1 Cor. 15:19

ONE

Upon his approach, the woman's head swiveled toward him. Her eyes flicked from his black hair to his sunglasses and his hazy smile, over his slender hips to his lazy stride. She puckered her lips at him and Sammy thought, *You still have it, old man.* He had lately turned 36.

He passed her without responding, but two of his companions did drool. One was on his shoulder: his 5-month-old son, Clay. She cooed at the baby before turning back to the booth displaying hand-thrown pottery.

Clay's older brother, Sam, Jr., though not yet three, was competently walking the other drooler on a leash: great big Bubba. The gangly mongrel's ears pricked up repeatedly toward other dogs, squirrels on nearby oak trees, and food booths, but Bubba had learned that defying Master Sam Kidman's tentative hold meant submission to Mister Sammy Kidman, whose grip was considerably tighter.

As the first weekend in November always brought

the Cottonwood Art Festival to a suburban city park just minutes from the Kidmans' Dallas home, so every Art Festival saw the attendance of Sammy's wife Marni and her mother Pam, an artist of local renown.

With this year's mild weather and turning leaves, Marni desired her boys' company on this excursion. Of course, once here, she and her mom had disappeared and left the guys to their own devices.

Today, Sammy didn't mind, because an event that drew this many women meant numerous opportunities to be ogled. Behind his sunglasses, he noted all the female heads that turned toward the Kidman Cohort and all the adoring glances bestowed not just upon him, but upon his progeny.

Samuel James Kidman, Jr., was famously a copy of his black-haired, blue-eyed father, who in turn had grown to expect praise for the workings of genetics beyond his control. While baby Clay, mostly bald at this point, could not be exhibited as another Kidman copy, he was certainly the most contented child anyone had ever known. This, too, Sammy claimed credit for, deservedly or not.

Hearing guitar strains in the distance, Sammy veered toward the source. "This way, Sam. Let's catch some music." Bubba, noting the change of direction before his handler, turned to keep abreast of Sammy's legs, and Sam followed.

They departed the dirt path toward an open-air stage where a guy with an amplified acoustic guitar had just begun his set. While he showed good technique, Sammy detected at once "piezo quack"—the annoying distortion from cheap methods of amplification. Apparently, Clay noticed it, too, for he suddenly lifted his head from his dad's shoulder and bawled out his objections.

The heads that spun in Sammy's direction were not smiling, nor were the glances adoring. The guitarist stopped playing to glare at the interruption, so the Kidman Cohort beat a hasty retreat. Clay continued to voice disapproval of the undersaddle piezo transducer that the underfunded musician chose to use.

Sammy had to withdraw clear to a solitary stand of oaks thirty yards away before Clay condescended to quiet down. Bouncing him gently in the shade of the oak trees, Sammy muttered, "Shee, guy, was it that bad? Yeah, I guess it was." They were now on the outskirts of the festival, with a youth-league soccer field between them and the back sides of the nearest booths.

"Ooh, pretty feet!" Sam exclaimed, and Sammy turned to look where he was pointing behind the trees.

A low wooden stage was set in a patch of grass fifty feet beyond the trees, and on it danced a ballerina in a body suit and flowing tulle skirt. With a chortle of delight, Sam dropped Bubba's leash to run toward her. This surprised his dad considerably, as Sam had never shown any previous interest in dance or ballerinas.

Given that there was already a crowd of children sitting on the grass watching, Sammy picked up the dropped leash to follow without concern. Sam stopped on the fringes of the audience to watch, but stayed on his feet in order to see over the heads of taller children seated in front of him. Sammy, holding a quiet Clay, drew up behind him to watch the dancer.

In flat ballet shoes—not en pointe—she was dancing to a bouncy calypso tune that Sammy could hear clearly, though he didn't immediately notice a sound system. He smiled vaguely; something about her exuberance was infectious. The kids were certainly enjoying it.

One or two jumped up to dance in imitation of her, which she seemed to encourage, pointing at them. When one audacious little girl stepped onto the stage, the dancer took her hands to improvise a *pas de deux*. In a graceful arch, the ballerina turned toward the newcomers, and Sam began bouncing to the music.

Then Sammy, a cop at heart (though retired), began looking around, and his smile faded. There were upwards of thirty children clustered in front of the platform, but no adults save himself. Where were the parents? His eyes canvassed the area around the platform, but he still saw no musicians, no instruments, no sound system nor techs. Where was her crew?

The music ended and the ballerina came down from the platform. Holding something small, she began threading through the children. It seemed to Sammy that she arrived at his group in definite haste.

Bending to Sam, she placed something in his hands and kissed his cheek, then she looked up at Sammy with a luminous smile that made his heart thump. She had clear blue eyes and a heart-shaped face, and her blond hair draped unhindered to her shoulders. Because she was pretty, he was careful not to smile in return. Bubba whined, pawing at her foot, and she laid a hand on his head. He fell right down and rolled over, requesting a belly rub.

From the festival area, Sammy heard Marni calling, "Sammy? Sammy!" so he turned quickly.

"Okay, guys, Mom's looking for us. Let's go." He

glanced back at the blonde ballerina, dimly noting that Sam still clutched her gift. So Sammy held the leash.

Emerging from the oak stand, he saw Marni and Pam paused on the path, looking around. Sam ran toward them, extending his prize. Sammy hustled Bubba forward, and Clay lifted his head.

"Hey," Sammy said, drawing up to them. "You didn't have to holler. We were watching the dance show."

"Holler?" Marni asked. "We were looking for the pizza. Have you eaten yet?"

"No, and we're starving. Right, guys?" Sammy prompted. Bubba looked agreeable and Clay stuck two chubby fingers in his mouth.

Sam, meanwhile, presented the ballerina's gift to his mother: a stem of flowers. "Oh, Sam, don't pick the pretty flowers," Marni said, distressed.

"It's not plastic?" Sammy said in surprise. "He didn't pick it. The ballerina gave it to him. She was handing them out to all the kids." The last sentence was meant to assure her that he had solicited no special favors from a dancer for his sons or himself. Not that she had anything to worry about; Marni was as pretty as anybody, even with two kids.

"Oh." Marni handed it off to her mother, who stared at it. Then the young wife asked her husband, "Do you remember where the pizza is?"

"Yeah, down the first path toward the street," Sammy said, gesturing.

Pam held the stem, touching the delicate blossoms of purple and white. "But this is. . . . Sammy, where is the dance show?"

"Just past the trees," he waved, turning with Marni up the path toward lunch.

Pam, holding the stem, hurried toward the trees. She recognized these flowers as Phalaenopsis orchids, which were awfully valuable to be tearing up to give to children. Being tropical, they did not grow in Dallas outside of greenhouses.

Emerging through the trees, she gazed around the grassy patch. There were no orchids here. There was no ballerina. There were no children. There was nothing here but grass.

"Mamaw!" Sam cried from far up the path. "Mamaw, hurry!"

Pensively, Pam turned back toward her family, orchid in hand.

"Sammy," Marni said in disappointment, "it's Saturday. Why do you have to go down to the office today?" In Marni's Prius, they were pulling into the garage of their home following a successful Arts Festival visit—successful in that Marni had managed to acquire a few small pieces that could be enjoyed even on a high shelf. Filling the back seat of the Prius were two small boys and one large dog, asleep.

"A minivan," he muttered, eyeing the crowded back seat in the rearview mirror as he shifted into park and cut the ignition. "Next stop after a minivan is Dotage Village."

She snickered, but he replied to her question, "Somebody has to go pick up the new case files that Pruett left. You want to dodge the cameras?"

"No," she sighed. "But I don't want you to, either."

"Then go chew on Pruett for leaving them there," he grunted, heaving himself out of the seat. He opened the back car door to release Clay's carrier from its base and lift it out without waking him.

While Marni coaxed a drowsy Sam out of his seat, Bubba slid under Clay and past Sammy to hop over the door of Sammy's classic 1966 Mustang convertible, lime green. He sat in the white leather passenger bucket seat, waiting.

Sammy and Marni looked at each other. "How does he know you're going somewhere?" she breathed.

He scoffed, "He doesn't. He's just making a suggestion." Sammy unlocked the door into the laundry room, shoving it open and glancing inside, just like a cop. On her way in after Sam, Marni paused to look back at him, anxiety clouding her almond-shaped eyes.

Handing her Clay's carrier, he reassured her, "Just keep reminding yourself: the checks come for another eighteen years no matter what happens to me."

"Sammy!" she breathed again, rolling her eyes, but it was true: This past July they had received the second annual payment of $1,172,500 from the $35-million-winning lottery ticket that Sammy had thoughtlessly picked up from the ground.

With the proceeds, they had established MK & Associates, a private investigative agency, and had hired Sammy's former partner Dave Pruett as well as his and Sammy's former sergeant, Mike Masterson. (To allay their fears of working for Sammy, Marni was made the agency head.) The investigators occupied themselves with collections on large delinquent child-support accounts on a pro bono basis. Given wide latitude for legal extortion, it was fun work that they all enjoyed.

He leaned down to kiss her lightly. "Be right back."

"Okay," she smiled.

With a half-smile, Sammy turned back to the Mustang, and Bubba shifted in anticipation.

Heading down the freeway toward their frontage-road shopfront, Sammy reviewed the plan at hand to answer a not-unexpected attack. Strangely, he had forgotten to tell Marni this reason for going to the office today. Jan Breemont, a high-powered insurance executive whose office furniture Sammy had confiscated to settle her massive child-support debt, was out for blood again—his, of course.

After seeing her furniture and paintings auctioned off for upwards of $30,000, Jan had come calling on Sammy with a loaded Korth, which she had emptied in his direction over a period of seven hours. That was the same day that Clay was born. Following her arrest, she retained sharp legal counsel which managed to obtain a probated sentence for her.

To assist her in paying his fees, her attorney then put her in touch with his publisher, who threw together a sensational, grossly inaccurate account of her case, which hit the bookstores just a week ago. Since she named Sammy, as well as the address of their shop, the work of MK & Associates had come to a standstill. So he, Mike and Pruett had gathered their brains to initiate a counter strike, which was scheduled to go down this afternoon.

Due to his years undercover with the Dallas Police Department, ex-Detective Kidman had never allowed himself to be photographed, so La Breemont had no photos of him to put in her book except stills from the video of his appearance on "Judge Evelyn." Given the disguise he had worn during filming, the stills were not helpful for identification.

So an assistant book editor made the mistake of attempting to access Texas Driver's License records for his photo and home address. Since such a use of the database is illegal in the Lone Star State, and Sammy's firm had assisted the Attorney General's office with over half a million dollars in collections, he received a courtesy notification about her arrest.

But that had done nothing to stem media interest in his business. So he, Mike and Pruett had discussed alternatives at length, the most likely of which seemed to be moving. But none of them wanted to do this, as they all liked the location and the suite—it was centrally located; it was cheap; and it was finally broken in to resemble the old Big Building Downtown, where they had all once worked as cops.

Besides which, merely moving would not dissuade the press from thinking that there was hay to be made from MK & Associates; someone would eventually discover their new location. Then what?

So a new plot had been hatched with the cooperation of their landlord. Sammy had no doubt there would be an audience for today's performance, because at least one member of the fourth estate had been continually surveilling their shopfront for days now.

In accordance with the detectives' plan, Sammy drove to the parking lot of a shopping center a few miles from their office. "Ah. Good," he murmured upon spotting the Uglymobile parked in the nether regions.

In a former life, the Uglymobile had been a surveillance van belonging to the Dallas Police Department; now obsolete, banged up, and stripped down, it was ideal for Marni's associates. Therefore, Mike had arranged its purchase from the city using agency funds. Today, the interchangeable decals on the van's sides advertised it as a cleaning service.

Sammy parked next to the van and stepped out of the Mustang, glancing around to make sure no one was watching. Bubba stood up on his seat in interest. Kneeling on the pavement, Sammy retrieved a magnetic key case from the driver's side wheel well and extracted a key. Using this to open the van door, he allowed Bubba to hop in before turning to the Mustang to raise the top and lock the car.

Closing himself and Bubba in the van, Sammy shed his sports coat and shirt. He cracked a side window before rifling a duffel bag for a spray can. Positioning himself near the window, he sprayed his glossy black hair thoroughly with the professional-quality silver hair coloring. Bubba backed into a corner during this application.

While the spray dried, Sammy donned a work shirt that sported the same cleaning company logo that appeared on the decals. Should any curious reporters call the prominent phone number, they would hear a recording of Marni's voice expressing gratitude for their call and dismay that the service had no openings for new clients or employees at this time. If they would like to be placed on a waiting list, please leave a message at the tone. Thank you!

After tucking the denim shirt tail into his jeans,

Sammy flipped down the visor mirror and ran a comb through his hair to give it a natural salt-and-pepper shading. Then he fished around in the duffel bag for a small cosmetics purse which yielded a trim gray mustache and adhesive. Referring to the mirror, he applied the adhesive (too much, as usual) and stuck the fake hair on his lip. Placing sunglasses on his face and a ball cap on his head completed his preparations.

"Ready, Bubba? Show's about to start. Sit tight." Sammy plopped into the torn vinyl driver's seat and cranked up the engine; Bubba sat on the bare floorboard near Sammy's knee, where he could see out the front and side windows.

Swinging out of the parking lot, Sammy drove to the strip shopping center which housed the (now famous) headquarters of MK & Associates, its front windows emblazoned with "Great Deal Life Insurance Company" in black and gold letters large enough to be seen from the freeway.

Noting no cars in front of their shop, but several in front of the newly opened Chinese restaurant next door, Sammy drove back to the alley. He left the van idling while he unlocked the back office door. "C'mon, Bubba," he quietly summoned. The dog agreeably trotted inside, then Sammy shut and locked the door on him.

From there, he drove around the shops and parked directly in front of Great Deal's door. Then he leisurely climbed out of the van and opened its back doors to unload a vacuum cleaner and bucket of cleaning supplies.

He noted without looking up when a woman and

cameraman exited a car in front of the Chinese restaurant to advance on him. Unheeding, he closed the van door and began wheeling the vacuum cleaner over the curb to the sidewalk.

"Hello, I'm Dana Peters with EyeWitness News. What can you tell me about the occupants of this office?" She stuck a microphone toward his face while the cameraman aimed a lens at him.

"Nothing. I'm just here to clean," Sammy grunted. Keeping his face away from the camera, he hefted his cleaning equipment to the door.

"But who paid you?" she pressed.

"Owner," he said, unlocking the door. "He always pays for cleaning when tenants vacate."

"Have the tenants vacated, then?" she asked quickly, but at that moment a dark sedan screeched up into the drive and lurched to a stop behind the van.

The three of them looked over as Pruett, natty in a dark suit and sunglasses, emerged brandishing an ID which none of them could see. "FBI. Turn that camera off," he said with the stony calmness of anonymous government authority.

The cameraman hesitated, but Ms. Peters insisted, "We have a constitutional right to film anything in public."

Yes, they did, but Pruett said, "If you turn it off, you may learn something off the record. If you don't, you won't have a job tomorrow."

After a pause, Ms. Peters nodded to her coworker, who lowered the camera. Neither Sammy nor Dave needed to see his smug face to know that the camera was still recording, albeit their knees. This suited their purposes just fine. "Now then," Pruett said, turning to Sammy, "Who is the owner of this shopfront?"

"I don't know; I'm just here to clean. Do you mind if I get to work?" Sammy complained.

"When did you get the call to come out here?" Pruett pressed.

Sammy extended his hands pleadingly. "The work order was waiting for me this morning, all right? Owner always has these shops cleaned when tenants vacate, okay?"

"You irritate me enough and I'll just make you disappear," Pruett uttered.

Behind his sunglasses, Sammy lowered his eyebrows at this comical threat. More ominously, his standing so close to the door without coming in taxed Bubba's patience, waiting as he was on the other side, behind the doorblinds, and he whined. Sammy was sure that the cameraman heard it, glancing to the door the way he did.

But another nondescript sedan had just pulled into the narrow lot to park in front of the shopfront next door on the right. Despite being vacant for almost a year, the space still bore the window sign of its last tenant: "The FreeWay Church." Out of the sedan stepped Mike, wearing a clerical collar.

"Come over here, Father." Pruett gestured.

African-American Mike, weeks shy of his 45th birthday, would have been unmistakable as a cop were it not for his current disguise. "What is it, son?" he asked with overtones of irritation and authority that almost made Sammy giggle.

"Father," Pruett said, laying a hand on Mike's

shoulder that the "priest" glanced at, "is that your church?"

"No, I'm just here to pick up homily notes," Mike said, chafing under Pruett's hand. Mike didn't like people touching him, even his long-time associates. Naturally, his long-time associates knew that.

"You come by often?" Pruett demanded, shaking him slightly.

Mike's jaw worked. "Occasionally."

"What do you know about the occupants of this store?" With the question, Pruett condescended to remove his hand to point toward the Great Deal space.

The Father hesitated in a conflict of conscience. "All I can tell you is that after this last incident, they left."

"Was that when the ambulance was called out?" Pruett asked, pulling a small notebook from his jacket pocket to refer to a totally imaginary event.

Father Mike hesitated in his answer, and the newswoman went over to begin rifling Sammy's bucket, looking at his cleansers. "Hey," Sammy said mildly, but inside he tensed. His laptop, its leather case wrapped in plastic, was sitting right there in the bucket.

But since that wasn't what she was looking for, she apparently never saw it. Partly extracting a bottle, she said, "This cleaner is for getting blood out of carpets."

Sammy reached out to put it back. "It cleans a lot of stuff," he said. "Part of our standard supplies. Listen, can I go in now? The owner left a guard dog inside and I gotta let him out before he craps all over everything."

"Sure, go ahead." Pruett waved magnanimously, and Sammy turned his back, rolling his eyes. But he let himself in, to Bubba's gratification, and locked the door behind him. He whipped off his sunglasses, stuffing them in his shirt pocket, then gingerly lifted an edge of the miniblinds to monitor the sidewalk proceedings.

Father Mike was taking his leave as well: "Excuse me; I can't really tell you anything else." The FBI agent and the reporters watched him retrace his steps to the church, unlock the door, and go in.

"All righty, then." Pruett jotted down some final notations about picking up dry cleaning, then snapped his notebook shut and replaced it in his coat pocket. "You may stay or go. Of course, if we raid the place and you're here, I can't guarantee you won't spend time in lockup. We do get these little misunderstandings cleared up in a matter of days, generally." With that encouragement, Pruett climbed into the rented sedan and drove away.

The newswoman and cameraman lingered a few minutes, conferring over his camera. Mike came out of the FreeWay Church carrying a sheaf of (blank) papers. He conscientiously locked the door behind him, nodded to the pair on the sidewalk, then also departed in his likewise rented vehicle.

As the pair continued to stand around uncertainly, Sammy had to follow through with the charade of cleaning. First, he retrieved his plastic-wrapped laptop from the bucket to place on his desk. Then he debated where to start cleaning—an unfamiliar pastime, to be sure.

Since the vacuum made the most noise, he turned it on and ran it around the gray industrial carpet. But he couldn't do that for long, because Bubba made a game of barking and biting at the vacuum. So Sammy turned it off and went to peek through the front blinds. "Shee, why're they still hanging around?" he muttered. Surely they weren't waiting for him to clean the whole office.

Surely not. But then he thought that they might just be wanting some additional small verification of what they'd been led to believe. He turned to look around the office—it was a wide-open space whose tenants had made no effort to clutter up—

Sammy bounded forward to haul Pruett's desk, and then his chair, across the room to rest against the right-hand wall, where it was partially hidden by unused room dividers. Sammy extended one divider to completely hide the desk and a filing cabinet. Then he moved Mike's desk and chair likewise, after pausing in irritation to unplug Mike's computer. The old sergeant was the only one to still use a desktop.

Leaving tracks, snags and possible tears in the carpet, Sammy pulled the second desk to fit snugly against the first, then upended the old secretarial chairs to rest on the paper-strewn desk tops. With just those four pieces of furniture relocated, the office looked convincingly vacated. Sammy's own desk, sitting forlornly in the back of the room, looked like the piece of junk that it was, only abandoned.

With apologies, Sammy shut Bubba in the bathroom. Then he took glass cleaner and a small squeegee out of his bucket. He raised the far left-hand window blinds all the way up to begin cleaning the window. The newswoman came right over to look inside, as did her cameraman. Sammy pretended not to notice his raising the camera to film the vacant office, but Sammy was careful to keep his face down.

When he judged that they had seen enough, he made a show of seeing them peer inside, and he indignantly lowered the blinds with a bang. Following, he flattened himself beside the window to peek around the edge of the blinds. Without hesitation, they climbed back into the car and drove off.

Sammy waited a few minutes to make sure they were really gone, but there was no place for them to go on the one-way frontage road but away. Nodding to himself, he first set about removing the mustache. Bracing himself, he gripped one corner solidly and yanked. "Ow!"

His inadvertent cry started Bubba barking, so Sammy released him from confinement in the bathroom. Bubba sniffed at the discarded bit of facial hair, which stuck to his nose. Watching him attempt to rub it off on the carpet, Sammy sat on Pruett's desk to pick up his phone and give his coworkers the "all clear" to return to the office. Maybe then they could actually start getting some work done again.

Leaving the furniture for the other two men to replace at their leisure, Sammy strolled back to his untouched desk. He plopped into his chair to unwrap his laptop, squinting with a half-smile at the sprig of flowers on his desk. He picked it up thoughtfully. "These are the same flowers the dancer gave Sam at the Arts Festival today. When did Marni have a chance to bring them down here? . . .

"Wait a minute. She gave those flowers to her mom. Didn't she?" he mused. His phone rang and he picked it up without a thought that the reporters might be double-checking. "MK and associates; this is Sammy Kidman."

He took off the ball cap and scratched his head; the gray hair spray was making his scalp itch something awful.

Pam said, "Hello, Sammy. Marni's busy changing diapers right now, but thought somebody had better let you know that you're eating over here tonight. Dallas plays Jacksonville tomorrow, and your friend Jon Ramey may start. The station is airing a special interview with him tonight—they're sure to ask about his arenaball experience and that wild game you played in that got him the walk-on with the Cowboys."

"You think?" he grinned, twirling the flower stem. "I'd love to see some footage of my one and only arenaball game. Don't know whatever happened to the DVD that Chandler brought downtown. Oh, man—Chris needs to see Ramey play. He told 'im he was praying for him after that game." Chris, 14, was Pruett's stepson.

"Actually, the Pruetts and the Mastersons are coming over for the game tomorrow afternoon," Pam said.

"Really? That's great. Be sure to let Marni know what she needs to bring," he offered. Following Pam's snort, he added, "Hey, didn't Marni give you the flowers Sam gave her? When did you get a chance to put them on my desk? The office has been locked for days."

There was a moment of silence. "The orchids that the dancer gave Sam?" she asked.

"Yeah. I found them on my desk just now, Booger," he teased.

"Sammy, I . . . didn't put them there. I kept the spike Marni gave me to see if I can propagate it," she replied.

They both hung on the phone in silence while Sammy looked at the sprig.

Two

"Well, that's interesting," Sammy murmured, staring at the sprig. On the point of telling him about the deserted field where he had seen the dance show, Pam opened her mouth, but there was a sudden banging on the front door of the office. Bubba sprang up from the floor beside Sammy, barking.

Although the blinds were still down and Sammy couldn't see a thing from the back of the room, he said, "That's Pruett. I'll be at your house by six. Bye, Pam."

"Bye, Sammy," she replied weakly.

As the banging and barking continued, Sammy strode to the door to flip the bolt and swing the door open. Pruett looked at him. "You look so stupid, you should be under arrest."

"Why can't you take out your freakin' key?" Sammy demanded.

"With a doorman, what's the point?" Pruett entered, removing his sunglasses and smoothing his thinning blond hairs back in place.

Sammy paused at the door, seeing Mike pull up. Over his shoulder, he remarked to Pruett, "When was the last time you went to confession? Here's your chance."

"Nothing to confess," Pruett admitted with a modest shrug. He stopped, hands on hips, to regard the displaced furniture in displeasure. Spotting the gray mustache on the floor—and evidently not recognizing it for what it was—he carefully walked around it.

Mike, entering, had removed the collar and jacket, so no longer looked the divine. "Do you think they bit?" he asked Sammy, then also scowled at the unexpectedly open space.

"I think so," Sammy replied on his way back to his desk. Bubba stopped beside Mike, always a reliable dispenser of pats and head-scratchings. Sammy went on, "But I had to give them a peek through the window, and I think I sprained my shoulder moving mostly useless desks." He grimaced, rotating his shoulder on his way back to his chair. But when he scratched his head again, the grimace was real.

Grumpily, Mike motioned Pruett to one side of a desk while Mike lifted the other side. As they two replaced the furniture, avoiding the fuzzy gray thing on the carpet, Pruett advised Sammy, "I'm taking the Clothier case."

"You are, are you?" Sammy smiled, as that file was resting securely in his drawer at this time. Many attributes made this case attractive to Marni's detectives, such as: (1) The amount of past-due child support that Dr. Gerald Clothier owed was almost $18,000; (2) Dr. Clothier, the professor of a much-derided course in Women's and Gender Studies at a local college, was being investigated by the Dallas police for sexual misconduct, battery, and theft of services (don't ask);

and (3) After marrying a woman and fathering two children, Gerald Clothier decided that he was not fulfilled as a man and became Gerdie Clothier, divorcing his wife and moving in with someone else whose gender was unspecified.

As if all this was not enticement enough to jump on the case, Mike had gotten a heads-up from a friend downtown that an arrest warrant was pending for Dr. Clothier, so if they wanted his/her money for his/her family before it went to a defense attorney, they needed to suction it up at once.

This was possible because the professor had been so careless in his online banking, the agency already had the passwords to his checking and savings accounts, and was only waiting on the bank's management to sign off on their credentials. The catch was, while Dave had hacked his accounts to obtain the passwords, Sammy had submitted the paperwork to the bank. Therefore, he had custody of the file.

Still smiling, Sammy picked up the flower stem and started to toss it in the trash can beside his desk, then paused. It was fresh and bright, not wilted at all. How long had it been here? He had no idea, as none of them had been in the office for the last three days (which hadn't impeded business, as they had been checking phone messages remotely. No one was willing to admit that the primary benefit of office space was as a venue for camaraderie and practical jokes).

Anyway, the question of when the flower was left here led to the even more aggravating question of who had left it. It had to have been Marni, although part of the reason she had demanded a chauffeured ride to the

Arts Festival was her pending insanity from being cooped up in the house for weeks taking care of little ones. Maybe one of her friends, or—

His face cleared. There were any number of ladies to whom she might give her office key in order to mess with his head. Well, he was certainly vain enough to play along with that game.

He leaned over to the trash can to pluck up a tall, slender drink cup, which he set on his desk as a receptacle for the sprig. Okay, sprig in the cup. As he contemplated that arrangement, it dawned on him that something else was needed. So he took the cup to the sink in the kitchenette and filled it half-full of water. This he put back on his desk.

Then he rubbed his head again vigorously. "Gah! This hair stuff is driving me nuts. I've got to wash it out." So saying, he headed for the bathroom. Bubba lifted his head to check where he went, then stretched out with a sigh.

Meanwhile, Mike was not happy upon discovering that his computer was dead, and ascertaining the reason for it. So he then had to crawl under his desk to plug it back in. While he did this, Pruett eyed Sammy's desk and the bathroom door alternately, muttering, "I know he's got that file in there somewhere."

"Second drawer on the right," said Mike, sitting heavily and turning on his computer.

Pruett had half-risen when the office phone rang. He picked it up. "MK and associates."

The male voice on the other end said, "Yes, this is Charles Whinnet of The Rivers Bank. I would like to speak with Sammy Kidman."

Pruett leaned forward in his chair. "This is he."

"Mr. Kidman, I've reviewed your paperwork requesting authorization to seize funds from the accounts of Gerald, aka Gerdie, Clothier for nonpayment of court-ordered child support. I am authorizing you to withdraw exactly seventeen thousand, eight hundred and twenty-seven dollars. Would you like us to mail these forms with my signature to you?"

"Sir, if you would, please have your secretary scan them to pdfs and send them to the MK and associates' email address on page one of our request. Dr. Clothier's ex-wife is in dire need of that money, so we'd like to get that to her and her children today," Pruett said, watching the bathroom door.

"All right. Except, I don't have the current master passwords to get into—"

"That's not necessary, Mr. Whinnet; we have Dr. Clothier's passwords," Pruett said quickly.

"You do? Well, then. But the pdfs will have to wait till Monday morning. Only our executives are required to work Saturday afternoon," Whinnet said. Pruett laughed heartily.

Whinnet hesitated. "You . . . collect no fee for this service?"

"That's correct, sir; it goes entirely to the family," Pruett said, itching to hang up.

"I see. All right, consider it done. You have my authorization to proceed."

"Thank you, Mr. Whinnet. Good-bye." Pruett hung up a little abruptly and set the carpet ablaze getting to Sammy's desk. Bubba sprang up and relocated to the other side, out of the way.

Pruett wrenched open the second drawer and rifled files. Finding the one he wanted, he swept it out with such vigor that he inadvertently knocked over the unstable paper cup, which flung water into the trash can and across the carpet.

Uttering an expletive, Pruett caught up the cup and reinserted the sprig before gently closing the file drawer (to avoid telltale sounds reaching the bathroom). Then he swiftly exited the office, catching up the laptop from his desk as he gripped the purloined file.

Never raising his eyes, Mike waited for his outdated computer to finish booting from an unexpected shutdown, which he wouldn't have to do had Sammy taken ten seconds to shut it down before unplugging it. He was still waiting when Sammy emerged from the bathroom a few minutes later, damp and refreshed.

His sigh of relief was cut short when he regarded the state of his desk, carpet and Bubba. Then he turned to see Pruett gone. In apprehension, Sammy leaned over to check his second file drawer, pawing with greater urgency as he did not see what he expected to see.

Closing the drawer with a bang that almost toppled the paper cup again, he flailed at Bubba, "He stole my file! What kind of watch dog are you?" Declining to own it, Bubba got up to lie down beside Mike instead.

Sammy looked at Mike, but it never crossed his mind that Mike might be complicit in this theft. "Eh, I can get it back. He can't do a thing till he gets authorization," Sammy muttered, sitting to open his laptop. Mike calmly opened a browser window to recommence long-deferred research.

"First thing, get a phone number to see if I can

nudge that approval along," Sammy muttered, obviously forgetting that today was Saturday. "That was . . . The Rivers Bank. Cute." He brought up a search engine to type in the bank name.

Glimpsing the top result caused his heart to drop down out of his chest: "Comatose Teller Dies." Swallowing, he clicked on a photo to enlarge it. He stared at the pretty blue-eyed blonde with a heart-shaped face before reading the lede of the accompanying article: "Adair Weiss, teller at the Richardson, Texas, branch of The Rivers Bank, has died of injuries sustained in an alleged assault by former branch manager Duane Minshew. The District Attorney's office has upgraded the charges from assault to first-degree murder. . . ."

Obviously, then, she couldn't be the dancer from the Arts Festival, Sammy reassured himself. The resemblance was just a very unfortunate coincidence. Or maybe she was a relative, a sister. But if that were the case, she'd hardly be glowing with happiness over her sister on her death bed.

Sammy skimmed the article, which recounted the apparently unprovoked choking—in the bank, during the workday—which had left Ms. Weiss in a coma just over a year ago. A coworker who had unsuccessfully intervened in that attack, and who had subsequently spent many hours at Ms. Weiss' bedside, was with her when she experienced the cardiac arrest that resulted in her death.

That unnamed coworker had refused all interviews. There was a photo of the coworker, in huge black glasses, walking away swiftly from the hospital with her head down.

Then Sammy read, "Ms. Weiss, 25, was an accomplished dancer who had been practicing under the tutelage of famed ballet teacher Madame Prochaska—" Sammy closed the laptop and stood in one motion.

When he could breathe again, he casually relayed, "Ah, I'm taking off for home, Mike." Sammy never thought to look for the new files that Pruett had supposedly left.

"Yeah, I'm about to clock out myself," Mike replied, turning up his watch. "Oh, and, you'd better bring Marni's car to work for the next several days, at least. Too many people can probably spot that Mustang of yours."

Sammy turned his head. Marni was 25. How horribly unfair was it for a 25-year-old to die? "Then Pruett can't bring his Firebird."

"I'll tell him," Mike grunted. Glancing up, he assessed Sammy's face. "It's only for a week or so."

Sammy nodded, groping in his pocket for the key to the Uglymobile. "We can't leave the van parked in the shopping center," he said, blinking rapidly.

Mike peered at him. "No problem. I promised Galt he could use it tomorrow, so just leave the key in the wheel well. And . . . I'll shunt the next good case I come across to you."

"Thanks," Sammy breathed. He looked back at the gracefully arched orchid spike on his desk, then turned decisively toward the door, summoning, "C'mon, Bubba." But the dog was right beside him.

When Sammy arrived home in his Mustang, he was inexplicably relieved to see Marni's Prius sitting exactly where it should be in the garage. Entering through the laundry room, he and Bubba walked into an empty house. No one was here.

He stood blankly in the kitchen until he remembered that they were having dinner at Pam and Clayton's house tonight. Expecting him to arrive in the Mustang, Marni had probably just walked her guys the six blocks to the Taylors' house. "She's so lazy," he said, just to hear a voice.

But Bubba went to the back door, so Sammy opened it. Bubba, preferring company on such errands, waited in the doorway for Sammy to go with him.

While Bubba took care of his business, Sammy glanced around at the herb and flower beds that Marni had taken care to water during the long, hot summer. They looked rich and healthy—magenta and yellow mums, brown-green rosemary spikes, red, orange and yellow peppers, and silver-green oregano that had busted through the bed to invade the one next to it. Where did orchids grow? Mulling this over, Sammy turned back into the house.

Within minutes, he and Bubba had arrived at the Taylors' home in his Mustang. Pam answered the door. "Well, this is an honor—you're ten minutes early. Hello, Bubba," she said, bending to pat him. Bubba graciously received her pat on the head, but he did not bother to sprawl on his back for a belly rub because she wouldn't bend down that far. "Come in, boys."

"Thanks." Sammy entered, removing his sunglasses to his shirt, as usual. "Hey, did we ever bring over dog food?"

"No. Never," Pam replied amiably, shutting the door after them.

"Okay. What's for dinner?"

"Marni says it's not cool enough for lasagna, so Clayton is getting Mexican food," Pam explained.

On their way to the gameroom, Sammy observed, "So our only two choices are lasagna or the Party Platter. Gotcha."

"Tonight, I guess so." Pam saw his lingering glance toward the kitchen, but he wasn't looking for food.

In the gameroom, Marni had just finished nursing Clay, who was now dozing in open-mouthed contentment. Since Sam was rolling on the floor, Bubba pounced on him, inciting their usual wrestling match.

Sammy moved the coffee table out of the way for them, then sat close by his wife to regard his youngest son. "Wow, no wonder he's blowing up. You keep stuffing him."

She eyed him sideways. "So where's my Mexican food?"

He raised his hands. "Talk to your dad."

She grinned, then said, "Oh, I keep forgetting to tell you—I found those all-cotton shirts you like for half price, only, all they had left in your size was pink and black. So I got the black."

"Thank you," he said sincerely, as a pink shirt hanging in his closet would remain unworn to his dying day. Then he casually added, "Okay, you got me with the flowers. Who'd you get to run them to the office?" Pam lolled nearby, listening.

Marni looked him up and down for thirty seconds. "There's a joke in here somewhere, but I don't know what it is yet." Then her face brightened. "Sammy! Did you bring me flowers?"

"No," he said, inwardly tensing. "The, uh, orchids that were left on my desk."

She blinked. "It would help if you'd talk in complete sentences."

"Okay. Who did you give a key to to put orchids on my desk?"

Her almond-shaped eyes narrowed in amusement. "Someone left orchids on your desk? How exotic." Marni had grown so accustomed to women making ineffective passes at her husband that she stopped being jealous years ago. Or maybe a year ago.

Sammy glanced back at Pam to remark, "She's catching on," but Pam was watching him.

"Who left orchids on your desk?" Marni asked, lips widening in laughter.

"That's what you're going to tell me, Mrs. Kidman," he uttered, pressing up against her.

"How many guesses do I get?" she asked, grinning.

Tossing his head in mild irritation, Sammy said, "Okay, enough kidding. Who was it?"

Marni looked up at her mother, then back at her husband. "You really think I know who broke into your office to leave you flowers?" She shifted Clay up out of the way as Sam and Bubba knocked into their legs during their death match.

"Hmph," he said, thinking, *It has to be you; you're the only unaccounted-for party who saw the orchids at the Arts Festival.*

Spotting her purse on the end table, he snagged it to set it on his knee. Then he rifled through it to bring out her keys. "What do we have here? Let me see. House key, car keys, filing cabinet key, storage shed key.

What's this? No office key? Where could it have gone to?"

Again glancing at her mother, she said, "So you've forgotten all about changing the office locks after Jan Breemont's book came out? And never giving me a key to the new locks?"

Sammy's mouth hung open. Yes, all that happened, including the part about his forgetting.

The back door opened and Marni's dad called, "Dinner's here! Last one to the kitchen gets stiffed!" Bubba and Sam immediately ceased hostilities to career into the kitchen together.

"Yay! Here." Marni handed off a soundly sleeping infant to Sammy, who had to juggle him a bit to get him situated right. Clay didn't come close to waking. Then Sammy looked up at Pam, who was still standing slightly behind him.

After his wife had left the room, he asked, "You still have the orchid Marni gave you?"

"Yes." Pam nodded. "It's in the studio window." Sammy stood, wordlessly indicating his desire to see it, so she led him back to the studio.

This used to be a screened-in patio until the Taylors converted it to a painting studio because of the abundant light, especially in the afternoon. A few paintings in progress stood on easels, but most of the space was neatly filled with blank canvases, photographs and storage cabinets. The flooring was a cheap, easy-to-clean laminate.

Pam gestured to a small table out of direct sunlight that held a vase with the stem, as well as two jars with small green sticks standing in something like jello.

Holding Clay, Sammy bent to look at them. "What're these?"

"Those are sections cut from the spike. That is a special hormone powder on the nodes, which is supposed to help them grow new roots. Obviously, I got advice from a florist on what to do, but there's no guarantee they'll actually root," she explained.

Nodding thoughtfully, he looked in the vase with the original stem. "What have you got in there? That looks like packing peanuts."

"That's what they are!" she laughed. "My florist friend was just outraged that somebody cut a blooming spike off a plant. All she could suggest was the packing peanuts with sporadic dousings. The spikes shouldn't be kept in water."

"That information is too late for mine." He then regarded the blooms. "Yeah, this has stripes, which is not exactly like the one on my desk. Mine's spotted. Pretty much the same color purple, but with spots."

"Yes," she said. "Phalaenopsis orchids—usually called moth orchids—come in a wide variety of colors and patterns."

"Do they grow here?" he asked.

"Not outdoors, no. They're tropical—they grow usually on trees, not as parasites, just for support. They have these thick air roots to take in moisture and nutrients. The plants do, that is. The spikes obviously won't survive unless they're able to sprout roots," she elaborated.

He nodded, but she had no more to say about it, and he didn't move. Then he saw a tablet sitting on a nearby stool. He handed her Clay, whom she took readily, and picked up the tablet. "Yeah, you saw the dance show, didn't you?" he murmured, opening a browser window on the tablet.

She deliberated, but said nothing as he went on, "I saw . . . I ran across this news item about the girl, the bank teller in the coma, finally dying." Pam's eyes widened.

"Here." Sammy showed her the article with the photo. "Does that look like her? The dancer at the Arts Festival? When I saw the photo, I almost had heart failure. But that's crazy. How much do you think it looks like her?"

Without replying, Pam took the tablet. Sammy reclaimed Clay so she could hold it steady. She read the article and studied the photo. Then she looked up at him as he waited.

"You never saw her, did you?" he said in disappointment.

"No," she said. "When I looked, there was . . . nothing. Nothing there but grass."

"Nothing but—How long did you wait before going out there?" he asked with drawn brows.

"I had looked past the trees before Sam called me to join you," she told him.

"What?" he gasped.

Clayton poked his head into the studio. "There you are! Hurry and get your food; they're about to interview Jon Ramey!"

Pam and Sammy immediately turned toward the kitchen. "We can't miss that!" Pam said brightly as Sammy shook.

THREE

Judging from Marni's and Clayton's reactions, Jon Ramey gave a great interview. They laughed a few times, and once Marni hooted and clapped. Clayton had to get up to refill plates and drinks after chiding Pam for her failure to do so. And Sammy, eyes glued to the big-screen TV, said nothing.

Following the interview, Marni turned around to him and chortled, "Can you believe he said that?"

Sammy gazed at her, his lips parting in a zombie smile. "No, I can't."

She studied him, then glanced at her mother, who had her head down. But at that time, Sam began his "I-need-to-go-to-sleep" yodel. Bubba's eyes were already shut tight. "Um, I think we need to call it a night," she murmured, packing up a plethora of childish gear.

Sammy stood as if to stretch and turned to Pam. "I need to understand this," he whispered.

"I have a book that may help," she replied.

"Give it here," he ordered.

"No. Tell Marni about it tonight, and let me talk to Clayton. I need to reread it, to see if it says what I remember it saying," Pam replied. Marni eyed them whispering but said nothing as she stuffed toys in a large diaper bag.

Sammy bent to pick up Sam, who immediately threw himself backward in a screaming fit, as toddlers do. Caught by surprise, Sammy held onto him only by tripping over Bubba, who yelped and scrambled out of the way.

Marni gasped, seeing her child's head plummet toward the corner of the coffee table. In an instant, Sammy managed to slide his right arm under Sam's head so that when they both hit the table, Sammy's arm took the force of the hit. "Ow," he said quietly.

Pam and Marni were frozen for a moment before moving forward at once. Clayton came in from the kitchen. Kneeling, Pam lifted Sam off Sammy's arm, and he bent over it in extreme pain. Bubba crept toward him, whining. "Sammy!" Marni gasped. "Let me see—" She reached out to take his arm.

"Don't, please," he said through gritted teeth.

Marni cried out at the unnatural dent in his forearm, already bruising. "Sammy! Oh, Mom, it's broken! Daddy, call an ambulance!"

Clutching the arm, Sammy gasped, "No, we'll— Clayton can drive me to the ER a lot quicker."

"Let me get my keys." Clayton darted out.

Eyes watering, Sammy asked, "Is Sam okay?"

Marni wheeled to her mother, who said, "He seems fine. It just scared him." Sam was certainly quiet in his grandmother's arms, watching his dad with wide, frightened eyes.

"Okay. It's okay, Sam; I'm going to be fine,"

Sammy whispered, and Sam turned his face to Mamaw's shoulder, crying bitterly. By now Bubba was pressing against her legs.

Clayton entered by the front door. "Car's idling in the drive, Sammy."

He got to his feet, gently pushing his wife back. She cried, "I want to go!"

"Marni," Sammy groaned, but Clayton said firmly, "Sweetheart, stay here and take care of your children."

Chastised, Marni sat on the floor, tears streaming down her face. While Clayton opened the front door for Sammy, Marni looked around for Clay, finding him nestled on the sofa. She gathered him up, then sat, crying.

They sat there a minute in confused despair, then Pam inhaled deeply. Sam was already asleep in her arms. "He'll be all right, Marni. The hospital is just ten minutes away. They'll get his arm set tonight and he'll come home. Why don't you go get the foam pad we use for sleepovers, and set it up for Sam in here, next to the playpen? Then we can make ourselves comfortable waiting for—"

She broke off, hearing the front door open again. Then Clayton and Sammy walked back into the room.

The women stared at them. Clayton gazed over their heads and Sammy looked at the floor. Marni unconsciously put Clay down.

As she got up, formulating a question, Sammy looked at her and raised his right arm. She stared at it, then came over and took his left arm to look at that, too. They looked the same. Two undamaged masculine arms. Pam watched from the couch, still holding Sam.

Marni looked at her dad, who cleared his throat and said, "Er, half a block from the house, he just said, 'We can go back home now.' And it . . . appeared that we could."

Turning back to Sammy, Marni ran her hands along his right forearm, which was solid and straight. Just to make sure, she felt his left forearm as well. "I don't understand. I saw it broken. I felt it broken." She gazed at her husband.

He shook his head. "Sitting in the car, I just felt . . . this. . . . It was hot for a second, and then it didn't hurt anymore. And, uh. . . ." He left the ineffable unarticulated.

Pam got up to transfer Sam to Sammy, who took him without difficulty. "You four go on home. Sammy can tell Marni what he knows, and I will talk to Clayton. Then everyone can rest, and you come on over tomorrow afternoon."

"That sounds like a plan," Sammy said mildly. He glanced at Clayton. "Thanks for the Party Platter. And the ride." Clayton nodded.

On the front porch with two sleeping children, a dog, and all their gear, Marni looked at Sammy's Mustang. "I thought you'd bring my car," she murmured, still in shock.

"Let's just. . . ." With Sam hanging over his shoulder, Sammy opened the door behind him to start shoving baby paraphernalia back into the foyer one-handed.

As Clayton came over to help him, Sammy said, "We're just going to leave my car and all this stuff over here for tomorrow. We'll walk."

"Good idea," said Clayton.

"Good night," said Pam.

Sammy and Marni started down the lamplit street with their little ones in their arms and Bubba keeping close to Sammy's knees without a leash. "Okay," he exhaled. "At the Arts Festival—today—" Had it been just *today*? "Clay was starting to fuss during the guitar set, so we went over to the trees. . . ."

As he talked, he made the decision to tell her just what he saw and didn't see, and what Pam said she saw and didn't see, and keep the narrative free of speculation or unfounded conclusions. Since the bare facts were sparse, he had pretty much covered them all by the time they arrived at their home.

"Well, no wonder you were so anxious for me to have left the orchids on your desk," she murmured while he unlocked their front door. "I didn't call you, by the way."

"When?" he asked, pushing the door open and looking in.

"At the Arts Festival. You said, 'no need to holler,' but I hadn't. We were looking for the pizza booth."

"But I heard you clearly, just like I heard the music. Sam definitely heard the music, and acted like he heard you calling, as well."

To avoid waking the boys, Sammy did not turn on lights. He carried Sam back to his bed and laid his head on the pillow. Bubba jumped up on the bed and plopped down beside him, as per usual.

Before taking off Sam's shoes, Sammy ran a hand over the boy's head, feeling for lumps or tenderness. But he already knew there was no injury; his arm had been solidly wedged between wood and bone.

In the dim light from the hallway, Sammy sat back and watched Marni change Clay's diaper, who slept through the process. She raised the side of the crib, then she and Sammy stepped out into the hall. He felt his arm again. "I keep expecting to find it still broken," he muttered.

"Then I didn't imagine it," she said tentatively.

"Oh, no," he affirmed. "Man, that hurt."

They entered their bedroom, where Marni turned on the bathroom light to wash her face and Sammy plopped onto the bed. He got his shoes off, then sat there.

"Sammy," she said, toweling her face.

"Uh," he replied.

"Whatever it is, it's good."

"Uh huh," he said, then fell back onto the pillow without even taking off his jeans.

Kickoff for the Jacksonville-Dallas game the following day wasn't till five PM, but the Kidmans were at the Taylor home by two o'clock. They had no compunction about skipping church this morning because it had become such a quandary.

After the first lottery payment last year, Sammy had made an anonymous donation of $120,000 to their small Bible church. The church factions' subsequent bickering over the windfall made for a horrifying spectacle. Then, somehow, someone in the church discovered who had made the donation, and that it would likely be recurring.

So Sammy became the object of intense politicking to earmark the next donation for this or that specific budget item, which proved to be counterproductive. The

Kidmans stopped attending that church and drifted to the Taylors' large suburban church just because Sammy liked the pastor, Dr. Joe Brodie.

When Sammy approached him about making their annual tithe to his church, Dr. Brodie presented him with a spreadsheet listing the church's financial priorities and invited them to choose what, if anything, they wished to support. They did, and nothing more was said of it.

So they began quietly going to hear Joe's sermons, not even telling Marni's parents. But Marni balked at further involvement, as too many members remembered her as a teenager, and she remembered them.

Sammy wasn't keen to join, either, seeing that so many brass in the Dallas Police Department had followed the new Chief, Carson Howell, to this church. So for now, the Kidmans just sat in the back like sinners.

On the Taylors' front porch today, Pam greeted them and asked Sammy, "How is your arm?"

He shook it. "Like nothing happened."

"And how about Sam?" she asked, but the object of that question answered by streaking through the door into the foyer. Bubba, chasing him, lost his footing on the tile and careened into an entryway table.

While Sammy put out an ineffective hand, the impacted table tottered and crashed onto the floor. The pottery that had been resting on it fell with it, exploding into shards and scattering wet marigolds across the foyer floor. Meanwhile, the perpetrators of this destruction vanished into the kitchen in search of snacks.

The three persons still at the front door regarded the annihilation for a moment, then all three spoke at once.

Sammy: "I'm living in a Three Stooges short."

Marni: "Oh, Mom! I hope that wasn't what you bought yesterday!"

Pam: "Don't worry; both the table and vase were thrift-store finds."

Clayton came to the opposite end of the foyer, glanced around, and said, "Oh, good. I'm glad everyone's feeling okay. Mother, you have a call."

"Thank you." Pam stepped around the carnage toward the kitchen, which left Marni and Sammy in a silent stand-off as to who would clean up the foyer.

Finally, she observed, "I have Clay"—which she did —"and besides, that's your son and your dog." Kissing him lightly on the cheek, she made her way carefully over wet tile to the kitchen.

Exhaling, Sammy said, "You know, there might have been advantages to a broken arm." Then he quickly looked around at empty air, amending, "Kidding." Finally, he also entered the kitchen, only to return with a broom, dustpan, and dry rags.

After effecting a clean-up and returning the cleaning implements to their proper places, he came into the kitchen to hear Pam ask Marni, "Do you want to go with them?"

"I do," Sammy said.

Marni nodded to her mom. "Then tell Charisse and Kerry that Sammy will be happy to cart their packages from store to store." Charisse was Mike's wife and Kerry was married to Dave.

"Uhhh," Sammy said.

Pam, bouncing Clay, turned to Sammy to explain, "That was Kerry who called. She and Charisse decided they'd really rather check out the new outlet mall instead of watch another football game, and wanted to know if Marni and I would like to go with them. Mike and Dave are still coming over."

"What about their kids?" Sammy asked, a little pained.

"Oh, the teenagers have plans with their church group tonight," Pam said.

"Teenagers?" Sammy said weakly. (From Pam's shoulder, Clay reached out to Papaw close by, aiming for the general area of his shirt pocket. "Oho!" Clayton murmured, pleased, as he appropriated his namesake.)

"Chris Pruett is fourteen, Sammy," Marni reminded him. "Lacie is seventeen and Todd just turned thirteen." The last two were Mike and Charisse's children.

"Oh. We haven't played Truth or Dare in ages," he said sadly.

"I guess they're outgrowing it," she said in some sympathy.

He snorted, "Well, Mike and Dave aren't. Hey, what about Kelli? She's not a teenager, yet." Dave and Kerry's daughter was almost two years old.

"Kerry's mom has her for the day," Marni explained.

While the adults were thus preoccupied, Sam and Bubba were on the floor in the corner by the food and water dishes that the Taylors had graciously provided for Bubba. As both dishes were currently filled, Bubba was sharing with Sam—or vice versa. Sam fed Bubba a nugget, then ate one himself, then fed another to Bubba, and so forth.

Marni went on: "Anyway, normally, I'd love to go with them, but I think we need to talk about everything that happened yesterday. . . . I guess you're not going?" she asked her mom.

Pam shook her head, so Marni added, "Tell me about this book."

Sammy turned to Pam. "Tell me about this book."

With raised brow, Pam leaned over to a kitchen countertop to pick up a paperback. After hesitating, she placed it before Marni. Sammy leaned over to look. "Solid German stock," he quipped, glimpsing the stout woman on the cover.

Pam's face registered slight surprise. "That's correct. Except she was an American of German stock— Rhoda Wise, a Christian stigmatist who died in nineteen forty-eight. She was credited with many healings, including that of Mother Angelica."

Sammy asked mildly, "You going Catholic on us, Mother Pamela Marie?"

Pam was hemming around a qualified negative when Marni interjected, "I've heard about that. I read Raymond Arroyo's biography of Mother Angelica. It's fascinating. And . . . parts of it are distinctly supernatural."

Pam cocked her head at Sammy. "How did you know that my middle name is Marie?"

He glanced up from flipping through the book. "What else could it be?" Then he stopped abruptly on the shocking photos of Mrs. Wise lying in bed, bleeding profusely from her head and her eyes.

Nodding to the photos, Pam said, "Lines of sightseers would file past her bed while she was suffering. Skeptics would poke at the wounds with pencils or such to try to debunk the phenomena. Her priest finally instituted a 'no touching' rule."

Sammy muttered, "That's . . . incredible. But I don't see what it has to do with, ah. . . ."

"Maybe nothing," Pam said. "But Rhoda credited her healing primarily to St. Thérèse of Lisieux, whom she says appeared and talked to her, as did Jesus."

Sammy's lip curled, but Pam went on to say, "St. Thérèse's calling card was roses, and . . . she instructed Rhoda to take photos of the rose petals she left. Look a few pages over."

Sammy flipped through and stopped. "Is that a rose petal? There's a face on it."

"Yes. You can gauge the size of the petal by the needlepoint it's resting on," Pam said. All this while, Clayton was silent, half-listening while encouraging Clay to go for the pen sticking out of his pocket.

Sammy muttered, "And that was nineteen forty-eight? A little early for Photoshop."

Pam paused. "That incident may have been in the thirties. I'd have to go back and look."

"I dunno." Sammy shook his head. "It just seems . . . incredible."

Marni observed, "Unlike an arm that decides to unbreak itself. That happens all the time."

Eyeing her, Sammy said, "Okay, then. What do you think it means?"

"That someone is watching out for you," she said.

"Why?" he asked. "*Why?* I mean, how can I thank the party responsible when I don't know who that is? I refuse to believe that a dead girl is gifting me with flowers just because I'm so hot. Which I am, but—that's beside the point. Why is all this happening?"

Everyone was silent for a minute, then Clayton said, "I'm not a spiritual man, but I do know that if you expect your purchasing agent to do his job, you give him a budget to work with."

"Equipping," Pam said instantly.

"Equipping . . . for what?" Sammy whispered.

"I think you'll know when the time comes," Pam said.

Sammy exhaled, glancing around, then his eye lit on the two conspirators in the corner. "What're you doing over there, Sam?"

"Nuttin," Sam giggled behind Bubba, who turned to grin at Sammy reassuringly, thumping his tail.

There was a small silence, then Sammy murmured, "Why orchids, I wonder?"

Pam replied, "Well, they're valuable because they bloom all year, and just hold their blooms forever, under the right conditions. I'm exaggerating, of course, but—"

Sammy asked, "How is your orchid doing today?"

"All right. There's no change from yesterday. I checked not long before you came to the door. The sections, too. But then, it's supposed to take several months for a bud to actually form."

Sammy nodded. Marni said, "I'd like to see it, if you don't mind. I hardly glanced at it when Sam gave it to me yesterday."

"Sure. It's in the studio." Pam pointed to the back of the house. Marni, knowing well where the studio was, turned to go. After a pause, Sammy followed her.

Pam caught up to them as Marni was bending over the two small jars. "What are the little plants?"

"The little plants?" Pam echoed.

Sammy suddenly bent to look. Marni said, "Yeah, these little plants. Are those their roots? Should you pot them soon?"

Open-mouthed, Pam regarded the small cluster of leaves and roots on each segment.

FOUR

Sammy scrutinized the jars. The 2-inch sections that were bare yesterday bore clusters of tiny leaves and roots today. "That was fast. I thought you said it should take a couple of months for them to sprout."

"That's what I was told," Pam said carefully. "They . . . weren't like that when I checked earlier this morning."

Marni suddenly started singing, "There is a land of pure delight where saints immortal reign; Eternal day excludes the night, And pleasures banish pain. There everlasting spring abides, and never-with'ring flowers; Death, like a narrow sea divides this heav'nly land from ours." She was singing the old hymn straight up except for the gleam of laughter in her almond eyes.

"Why does this entertain you?" he asked, mystified.

Something in her smile reminded him of the ballerina. "Sammy, why doesn't it entertain *you*? How favored can you get, to draw out new growth?"

"That's the problem: I'm not the one doing it," he complained.

"What difference does that make?" she asked. "All I

know is, last night my husband was seriously hurt in freak accident, and today he's fine." And she kissed him emphatically.

She left the room singing the second verse: "Sweet fields beyond the swelling flood stand dressed in living green. . . ."

Sammy shook his head, remaining to look at the original orchid. Pam said, "You know, what she said strikes me as the correct perspective on all this."

Not hearing her, he observed, "It's still not wilted, or anything."

She scrutinized the original orchid spike, which indeed looked the same. "They don't require much moisture."

"If they have roots," he noted, which she mutely acknowledged. "How long do they live as cut flowers?"

"I don't really know. You could go check—"

Sammy interrupted, "I am *not* driving down to the office on a Sunday to see what the flower on my desk looks like." With that, he left the room. He did take a drive shortly afterward, but it was just to take the Mustang home and come back in Marni's Prius.

Once Marni had nursed Clay and put him down in the playpen, Sammy was drafted to keep an eye on Bubba and Sam so that she could help her mom fix snacks for game-watching. Pam did not buy prepackaged snack foods; she liked to bake, so they did that.

And when Bubba and Sam devised an engaging game to see who could leap the farthest off the back of the gameroom couch, Marni brought Sammy the leash in a subtle suggestion of a walk.

The moment Sammy hooked the leash on Bubba's

harness, he lunged to the front door, almost taking Sammy's right arm with him. But it didn't even hurt that much—not like it had last night.

The three of them—Sammy, Sam and Bubba—got situated in the foyer, avoiding the table, and emerged from the house as a cohesive unit. Sammy held the leash today, as Bubba was invigorated by the cool fall air and the sight of neighborhood cats.

They walked agreeably, and he eyed Janet Greer's house as they passed it. He'd heard nothing from her or about her since she had confessed to witnessing—and photographing—a murder one year ago last July. Since the perp had died by then, the department decided there was no point in charging her with anything.

The walkers meandered around several blocks to the park, but apparently everyone in North Dallas who wasn't interested in watching football had come here to commune with nature instead, so Sammy redirected his cohort a few blocks over, which led them to their street. Glancing down the block, Sammy saw an unfamiliar sedan parked across the street from his house.

The press? More lottery curiosity seekers? He wanted to know, but wasn't about to engage them with his son in tow. And he was too far away to see the plates.

Sam was flagging by this time, so Sammy picked him up for the six-block hike back to the Taylors' house. Even though the leash was only draped over his wrist, Bubba never strained it, keeping pace with Sammy's stride.

By the time they arrived, Sam was asleep on Sammy's shoulder. On their way in (not bothering to knock or ring the doorbell) Sammy glanced in interest at Mike's Corolla in the drive.

Inside, Bubba headed for his water dish in the kitchen and Sammy deposited his eldest son in Papaw's lap as he was getting settled in the lounger.

"You're just in time for the pregame show," Clayton noted, arranging the sleeping toddler to lie crossways across the padded arm rests. That was not only more comfortable for the child, but made it easier for Papaw to reach the snack tray beside the lounger. Clay was still snoozing in the playpen in the middle of the room; Marni was in the kitchen.

"I'm just in time for the pregame show that's been on for the last two hours?" Sammy asked, helping himself to a cheese roll from the plate on the coffee table. "Hey, Mike."

"Sambo," Mike responded, a beer in one hand and a ham roll in the other. "Man, your mother-in-law is a great cook."

"Yep," Sammy said, "In appreciation of which, you can slide down to my street and see who that is in a dark green sedan surveilling my house."

After loading a paper plate from the platters on the coffee table, he plopped into the second lounger next to Clayton's.

"You want me to go now?" Mike screwed up his face in reluctance.

"You're not, like, curious?" Sammy asked.

"Not as curious as you are," Mike grunted.

At that time, the doorbell rang. Either Marni or Pam answered it, for Dave Pruett walked in. Noting the sweats he wore, Sammy said, "Good! Run down to my street and get the number of the green sedan across from my house."

Pruett nodded. "You fix me a plate." And he turned right back out.

"That was suspiciously easy," Sammy observed.

"Someone should fix him a plate," Mike said without moving from the couch.

"That's right," Sammy agreed from the recliner.

Pam, who had just brought in a bowl of spinach dip, asked, "What does he want?"

"Everything," Sammy said, eyes on the TV. So Pam fixed a large sampler plate for Pruett.

She was just bringing a cold beer from the refrigerator to set beside the plate when Dave appeared from the foyer again, smoothing his windblown hairs. "BZB oh seven oh one," he said, sitting briskly on the couch in front of the plate and popping the top on the beer. "Thank you, Mrs. Taylor."

"Pam," she corrected. "You're welcome." Pleased with herself, she returned to the kitchen.

Grunting, Mike pulled out his phone to select a number and speak a few words. A moment later he put his phone away and said, "Company vehicle belonging to Channel Two News."

"Great," Sammy muttered. His memory being a steel trap regarding offenses to himself, he recalled at once that Channel 2 was the station that had aired a defamatory and fact-challenged story about the manner in which he had prevented Terry Sinclair from killing him.

The gameroom occupants were silent, watching excerpts from Jon Ramey's interview yesterday. Pruett suddenly leaned forward, almost spewing his beer, and Mike chuckled, "Can't believe he said that."

"Said what?" Sammy blinked, as he had obviously not been paying attention. Then he murmured, "I want to know how Channel Two got my home address."

Pruett glanced at him. "You of all people should know that anybody can find out anything about anybody."

"Yeah, it's just annoying," Sammy muttered. "Going to be a lot harder to get in and out my front door." When he thought of Marni taking her babies out for a walk while he was at work, his gut constricted.

"Okay, think," he muttered to himself. "Think. What. To. Do." Upon Clayton's broadcast warning that the game was about to begin, Marni hurried in to claim a plate and a place on the loveseat across from the couch.

While Dallas received the opening kickoff and the game watchers debated how their starting quarterback might be eliminated so that Ramey could play, Sammy sat staring vacantly at the big-screen TV, formulating options:

1. He could relocate his family to stay at the Taylors' or a hotel until public interest died down, sneaking into their house at night for essentials.

Negatory, Sammy decided. They had spent time, money and effort to fix their house the way they wanted it, and chose to stay there when the lottery winnings had provided the opportunity to relocate. It was un-American for them to be forced from their home because the local teevee news wanted a scoop.

2. He could stage an evacuation similar to what they had engineered for their workplace.

Not feasible, Sammy admitted. It would be too easy for skeptics to expose the deception at a residence, and in so doing cast suspicion on their workplace "eviction."

3. He could agree to an interview if the reporters would withdraw from his home.

No, he flat-out refused. Besides betraying a weak hand to start with, it was likely to prove futile when the reporters decided they wanted more information. Worse, no matter how he was disguised, enough data points could emerge that would enable off-site identification of him. He would never ever forget that lesson from his supposedly anonymous underwear spread, and the havoc wreaked when Pruett recognized him in it.

4. He could turn the tables on the news crews.

Sammy leaned forward as the room erupted in cheers. This idea interested him. The teevee people wanted a story. Suppose he gave them a story? It didn't have to be real. As a matter of fact, the less real, the better.

Due to the clapping and hooting, Sam sat up with a start, but seeing who held him, nestled back down again in Papaw's lap. Marni got up to move Clay's playpen to a quieter corner. Bubba followed, lying down so close to the playpen that his coarse brown fur protruded through the mesh.

The downside, Sammy considered, was that it couldn't involve Mike or Pruett, who had already exposed too much flesh to the teevee people yesterday, even if they weren't filming faces. So he could only employ himself and—who? Who could he use to put one over on Channel 2?

Anyone in his immediate family was off-limits,

which meant that somehow he'd have to downplay it around Marni, or she'd insist on playing a part in it. Les? Sammy's eyes widened in mild horror at the possible scenarios should the brittle old gumshoe get involved. There'd be gunplay.

Well then, how about Lawdry in Oklahoma City? Sammy wasn't sure he still had his number. But wouldn't it be nice to see Jana again? Assuming they were still married.

Sammy sifted through everyone he knew while a commercial came on and the game watchers stood, debating the starting quarterback's performance thus far in the first quarter. Clayton, commenting on his anemic completion rate, stood to place Sam in Sammy's lap preparatory to taking the standard bathroom break.

The rest of the group gathered up empty plates, cups and cans to throw them away or replenish them in the kitchen. In another minute Sammy was left alone with two sleeping kids and one dog that was watching for the possible deposit of more crumbs on the floor.

The commercials did not distract Sammy in debating every possible accomplice among his former coworkers downtown: Garrett, Chandler, Pierce, Carrie, Geoff, Brickett, Reyna. . . . The problem was, after being off the force for 15 months, he had lost touch with most of these people. Mike assiduously kept in touch with his contacts downtown, but Sammy just hadn't bothered. Now that he needed help, he didn't have a ready ally.

A new commercial came on that began playing Carole King's "You've Got a Friend," sung by James Taylor. Eyes downcast, Sammy listened. It was so . . . comforting, and an unusual choice for an NFL game.

Sammy glanced up at the commercial, which featured a barefoot blonde in a black bodysuit dancing to the music against a bright white background. She was good. She—

His breathing stopped as she turned toward him, or toward the camera, and he recognized the heart-shaped face. Then she gestured to him in a welcoming way, with that same laughing smile.

Panicking, he flailed for the remote beside Clayton's lounger to swipe eight buttons at once, hoping blindly to toggle the power off. When the TV went dark, he began breathing again. "Well, duh." He passed a shaking hand over Sam on his lap. "She recorded that commercial before the attack, stupid. If it was the same girl. Which it probably wasn't."

Marni came back in, then, sipping a cola. "What—? Why did you turn the game off, Sammy?" When she saw his face, she came over quickly to check on Sam, who was still asleep. "What is it?" she whispered. "What happened?"

He could only shake his head as Mike and Pruett came in, but he quickly turned on the television. The station had just cut back to the game. Clayton came in hurriedly, claiming his lounger, and a moment later Pam came to the door of the room. She didn't appear to be interested in the game, but she did want to see that the refreshments were holding out.

Sammy leaned his head back, looking at Pam. She returned an inquiring look. Marni, watching all this, said, "Sammy, I don't want Sam to nap too much longer, or he won't sleep tonight. Can you bring him into the kitchen to eat some dinner?"

"Sure," Sammy gulped. He started to stand with the sleeping child, then paused to ascertain Bubba's whereabouts. The dog was still sitting against the playpen, but had raised up at Sammy's stirring.

So Sammy hoisted Sam to his shoulder and stepped away from the lounger. He followed Pam to the kitchen, and Marni followed him. Bubba trailed them just far enough to keep an eye on both Clay's playpen and the doings in the kitchen.

Pam was placing Sam's booster seat in a chair and drawing it up to the table. Sammy jostled the boy without apparent success in waking him: "Sam. Hey, Sam. Time to wake up, guy; Mamaw's got some good stuff to eat here. Sam."

From the refrigerator, Pam asked, "Would you like chocolate milk with dinner, Sam?"

"'K." He immediately raised his head, and Sammy pursed his lips, setting Sam in the seat.

Pam fixed him a plate of pigs in blankets and apple slices to go with his chocolate milk. Sammy, still weak, sat beside him. Marni sat, waiting. Pam looked at Sammy as Sam began eating the finger food.

"Um," Sammy began. "Everybody went out of the room, and I was wondering what to do about the news crew that's staking out our house right now. I was thinking about some offensive counterintelligence, but I can't use Mike and Pruett because of what we did yesterday, and I'm *not* using you," he directed to his wife.

"So then," he inhaled, "I was thinking, *who can I use?* when this commercial came on of James Taylor singing, 'You've Got a Friend.' You know the song—"

He sang a few lines and his audience nodded. "And I look up, and there's a girl dancing on teevee—"

"You're kidding," Marni breathed.

"She looked straight at me and waved at me like, 'Come on,'" Sammy said, gesturing.

The two women said nothing for a moment, then Pam said, "I suppose it's pointless to ask if you're sure it's the same dancer. With their hair pulled back, in make-up for the camera, it might be hard to tell."

"Good point," Sammy noted. "That's a consideration. She was wearing different dance gear—ah, a black leotard. Her hair was pulled back in a ponytail, when it had been loose the first time. But then she turned, and looked at me. . . ."

Marni suddenly got up to fetch her mother's tablet from a countertop across the room. Opening a browser window, she asked, "What was the product being advertised?"

Sammy rested his elbow on the table to chew on a knuckle. Sam offered him a wienie bite, which he accepted. Chewing, Sammy leaned back in the chair and crossed his arms over his chest to stare at the ceiling. "I have no idea. I never saw anything on screen but the girl. The stage was white; the background was white."

"No lettering? No logos?" Marni asked.

"No. I'm sure of that. Just the girl dancing."

"Was there a voiceover?" Marni asked.

"Just the music," Sammy averred.

Pam asked quietly, "What did you feel that she was saying to you?"

"She was offering to help," he said stonily.

They were silent for a minute. "This," he gulped,

"this can't be good. It can't be of God. The Bible warns us against—communicating with the dead, or spirits. We don't know what they really are."

"But Sammy," Marni whispered, "you were miraculously healed. Ghosts and evil spirits do not heal people. Do they?" She and he looked at her mother.

Pam said slowly, "I've never read, in the Bible or elsewhere, of evil spirits healing anybody. But the question about spiritual unknowns must always be, 'Does this honor the God of the Bible? Does it acknowledge Jesus as His Son and Sacrifice?'"

Sammy blinked. "That's right. Besides, I don't know that she's responsible for that healing," he pointed out. "A dead girl? How can she do anything?"

Pam lifted her chin. "That is an important point."

"Okay, I grant you that," Marni said, raising her hands, "but it also can't be a coincidence."

Pam suddenly left the room, and moments later returned with a thick book. She plopped this on the table and began turning pages. The other two let her search in silence.

A moment later Pam looked up and said, "I hope that I'm not taking this grossly out of context. This is the Catechism of the Catholic Church on the Communion of Saints: 'The union of the wayfarers with the brethren who sleep in the peace of Christ is in no way interrupted, but on the contrary, according to the constant faith of the Church, this union is reinforced by an exchange of spiritual goods.' It says more on the subject, then quotes St. Thérèse as saying, 'I want to spend my heaven in doing good on earth.'"

"The one who healed Rhoda, supposedly," Sammy

murmured, glancing toward the biography still on the other end of the table.

"Yes," Pam said, closing the Catechism.

Sammy sat up. "Well, I'm not Catholic. I don't believe in all that." Marni opened her mouth; although she said nothing, her face was plain: *Well, I do.*

Pam squirmed a little. "I'm not an authority, and I happen to agree with you, Sammy, that we must be very careful with the supernatural. But. . . ." She got up again, taking the Catechism with her.

Sammy and Marni sat in silence. She was thinking back four years ago, when Sammy stepped in the line of fire to prevent a drug addict from shooting her, Kerry, and Chris. The subsequent blood and terror and ambulance ride were all a blurred recollection, except —"He was so handsome," she whispered.

Sammy turned his head. "Who was? Somebody besides me?"

"The doctor," she said. "The one who showed me where you were in the morgue. Everything else from that day is just a blur, except his face. He was so beautiful."

He regarded her. "They told us that no doctor was down there at the time."

She regarded him back. "No, there wasn't. But I found you, didn't I? Yours was the only sheet I pulled away. Did they tell you that?"

Pam reentered the kitchen with another, smaller book in her hands. She cleared her throat. "This is a collection of—thoughts, really, by J.B. Phillips, who was a Canon in the Church of England and a highly respected translator of the New Testament. It is such a wonderful little book, worth reading from cover to cover, but, he says something interesting in one part. . . ."

She began flipping pages while the other two watched patiently. Marni did get up to refill Sam's cup with chocolate milk. "Here it is." Pam cleared her throat again. "Starting on page one eighteen, he says:

Many of us who believe in what is technically known as the Communion of Saints must have experienced the sense of nearness, for a fairly short time, of those whom we love soon after they have died. This has certainly happened to me several times. But the late C.S. Lewis, whom I did not know very well and had only seen in the flesh once, but with whom I had corresponded a fair amount, gave me an unusual experience. A few days after his death, while I was watching television, he 'appeared' sitting in a chair within a few feet of me, and spoke a few words which were particularly relevant to the difficult circumstances through which I was passing. He was ruddier in complexion than ever, grinning all over his face and, as the old-fashioned saying has it, positively glowing with health."

Five

"Glowing," Sammy blurted, as if recognizing the attribute.

Pam glanced up at him, but continued reading:

"The interesting thing to me was that I had not been thinking about him at all. I was neither alarmed nor surprised nor, to satisfy the Bishop of Woolwich, did I look up to see the hole in the ceiling that he might have made on arrival! He was just *there*—'large as life and twice as natural.'

A week later, this time when I was in bed, reading before going to sleep, he appeared again, even more rosily radiant than before, and repeated to me the same message, which was very important to me at the time. I was a little puzzled by this, and I mentioned it to a certain saintly bishop who was then living in retirement here in Dorset. His reply was, 'My dear J——, this sort of thing is happening all the time.'"

Pam closed the book and they sat in silence a

moment. Then Sammy exhaled in exasperation. "Well, even allowing that it may be true—what do I do?"

"Accept her help?" Marni suggested wryly.

"How? I ain't praying to this chick," he said with perhaps more vehemence than necessary.

"Who do you usually pray to, Sammy?" Pam asked quietly.

"Jesus Christ," he asserted.

"Well then." Pam bowed her head and closed her eyes, waiting. Marni promptly followed suit.

Since neither of them offered to help, Sammy irritably braced his elbows on the table with his forehead resting on the heels of his palms. Sam, Jr., looked around, then bowed his head and clasped his hands. He paused to take another sip of chocolate milk through the straw, then resumed an attitude of prayer.

Pruett, on his way into the kitchen for another beer, saw this scene at the table and paused, backing off. But he stayed within earshot. Sammy said, "Lord Jesus, I don't know what to do. Help me know what to do. Help me know whether she's with You or not. Help me keep my family safe. Amen." He sat up, crossing his arms in defiance.

Pam smiled, idly flipping through the book again. Marni watched Sam dunk a wiener bite into his chocolate milk.

Pruett lingered unseen another few beats, then resumed his trek into the kitchen. Opening the refrigerator, he glanced over. "Well, this is a solemn group. What's up?" he asked casually.

Sammy chewed his lip, glancing at his wife. She widened her eyes. *Tell him.*

He looked away. *I can't without telling Mike, too.*

Pam said, "I think Clayton needs to hear the latest."

Sammy leaned back in his chair, shouting, "Okay, anybody who wants to watch Ramey throw touchdowns, stay in there. Anybody who wants to hear about dead dancers leaving me flowers, come in here."

Moments later, Mike and Clayton appeared at the kitchen entryway to stare at them. "What the hell?" Mike said mildly.

"Something new?" Clayton asked.

"Okay, sit." Sammy rubbed his face vigorously. Dave plopped into the chair across from him; Mike and Clayton sat with greater self-control. "Okay. This all started yesterday at the Arts Festival," Sammy began.

Over the next half-hour, he related the events as he had to Marni: just the bare facts, without speculation. Pam retrieved the orchid and the small jars from the studio to show them; Marni had to go get Clay when he called for dinner. (For modesty's sake, and to not distract from Sammy's narrative, she sat just outside the doorway to nurse her son.)

Sammy finished up, "Here's the million-dollar question: If I'm understanding correctly that she's offering to help me, *why?* I don't need her help."

The group sat in silent contemplation of this, then Pruett leaned over for the tablet still on the table. "Maybe you do and you don't know about it yet."

"What do you mean?" Sammy asked warily.

"When was the last time you ran a search on yourself?" Pruett asked, tapping the screen. Sammy hesitated; Marni came to the table to burp Clay over her shoulder.

Moments later Pruett found what he was looking for. He sat back and read out loud: "Hello everyone: last year's lottery winner Samuel Kidman lives at thirty-eight forty-nine El Rancho Drive in Dallas, Texas. His home phone number is two one four, three nine one, twelve oh one. Jesus said, 'Go sell everything you have and give to the poor,' and Samuel invites everyone who needs help to stop by his house or give him a call.'"

The others stared at him, then four people asked questions all at once. Pruett turned the tablet so that Sammy could see it. "It's just—some blogger," Sammy sputtered. "It was just posted twenty minutes ago."

"That looks like a GoHappy blog," Pruett said, pulling out his phone. "We should be able to get them to take it down."

"I don't understand," Pam said. "Does this blogger think they're going to get money from you with that?"

"Blackmail?" Sammy asked. "If that's what they were after, they would've called me before posting it. They have my number."

"Some people just like to screw with other people's lives," Pruett muttered, searching on his phone in dissatisfaction.

"Maybe not too many people have seen it. There aren't any comments yet," Marni said, looking over Sammy's shoulder.

"You have to refresh it," Pruett said. He put the phone to his ear, then made a sour face. "Cretins. No phone number."

Sammy refreshed the screen, then put his head in his hands. "There are, like, sixty comments already," he whispered. Now, moving appeared to be the only feasible course, and one they had to take immediately.

"No telling what this means for our shop," Mike muttered. "We wasted our time yesterday."

"And got on camera," Pruett added, trying another number.

Marni suddenly leaned over the tablet. "Well—this isn't going to help them at all. Dave, you read the number wrong. They have our address as eighty-eight thirty-four El Rancho. There's no such number on our street."

Pruett glanced at her parents before rebutting, "Sweetheart, I learned to read numbers before kindergarten. It said three eight four nine, which, coincidentally, is your address."

Sammy was looking at the screen. "This says eight eight three four. But I looked at it before you refreshed it, and it *was* our address—then."

Marni took it again to scroll through the comments. "All these people read eighty-eight thirty-four, too. Some people must have checked it out already, because they're mad. And—Sammy!" she exclaimed.

Apprehensively, he looked over, then slowly took the tablet. Marni whispered, "Is that her?" Pruett and Mike quickly rose to see. Sammy stared at comment #7, which said only, "Mean hoax." But the avatar was that of a pretty blonde who went by "Adair."

"Yeah, I think so," he murmured.

"Is there a profile of her?" Pruett asked. Sammy touched the screen, then shook his head. He turned the tablet around to show Pam, forgetting that she had not seen the dancer. Clayton leaned over to look.

By this time, Sam was throwing wienie bites to

Bubba, who scarfed them down. So Pam got up to escort Sam to the other room for a fun and exciting diaper change.

"They have our phone number wrong, too," Marni noted. "But I bet it was right when you saw it," she conceded to Dave.

"I've called it often enough to get your lazy-ass husband out of bed," Pruett murmured. Then he got up. "My work here is done. I'm gonna catch what's left of the game." Clayton got up to go with him.

Mike remained in the kitchen. "What're you going to do, Sambo?"

He thought about that. "I . . . feel like I need to go scout out our house, see if it's safe to go home," he proposed to Marni.

"Okay." She nodded. "Make sure you have your phone, please, since your car phone is in your Mustang in our garage."

"Yeah." He stood, patting the bulge in his pocket. "I'll walk. It's . . . easier to run on foot," he joked weakly, and she smiled weakly in response.

Sammy was at the front door when he felt the pressure on his leg, and looked down at Bubba whining to go. Sammy glanced around for the leash, not sure where he'd left it. Then he told Bubba, "All right. But you stay with me." Bubba promised, tail wagging.

They stepped out into the cool night. Sammy had to wait for Bubba to make a pit stop, then they embarked on the six-block trek to the Kidmans' street. Turning the corner onto El Rancho, Sammy transgressed well into a neighbor's yard to avoid the streetlight.

Peering down the block toward his house, Sammy

was at first encouraged to see no crowd of loiterers. But the same car was there, only parked in the opposite direction, facing away from him.

If that was their only lookout, he could get his family in through the rear-entry garage without a problem. But then they'd see lights go on in the house, and know that—

He started. Someone had just come out of his house. A woman in a sleek, pearl-gray business suit stepped off his front porch and began walking swiftly away from him and the green sedan at the curb.

Following cautiously, eyeing the sedan, he stayed in the shadows, hissing at Bubba to stay with him. Absolutely, he was going to find out which publicity-seeking airhead news reader that was, and see that she took a trip downtown for breaking and entering. But he mustn't let the Channel 2 people see him, either.

They unexpectedly decided to help him there; whoever was at the wheel turned on the ignition and pulled away from the curb. Apparently, they were as intrigued by the trespasser as he was, because they began following her at three miles per hour, lights off.

When she glanced over her shoulder, signaling her awareness of her pursuers, the car's driver turned on his lights and accelerated slightly. Sammy broke into a run, which caused Bubba to trot.

The woman began running lightly, which was a feat in high heels and a pencil skirt. At the end of the block was a little corner market, miraculously open on a Sunday evening. Transparently, she aimed for the refuge that the shop provided.

As the sedan sped up to intercept her, Sammy felt a

rising anxiety—not for her safety, but for his purpose: if they succeeding in stopping her, he wouldn't be able to get close enough to identify her. He needed to know who this was; he needed a name for an arrest warrant because "Nosy Blonde Newscaster" covered too many people.

When she was within 100 feet of sanctuary, the hunters closed in on their prey, and the driver turned sharply to cut her off. But then Bubba, disliking the imbalance of the chase, bounded forward with a volley of outraged barking.

As Sammy opened his mouth in dismay, Bubba darted in front of the oncoming headlights, placing himself between the newscaster and the car, and turned back to bare his teeth at the blinding lights, his hackles raised.

The next several events took place in a matter of seconds: the car screeched to such an abrupt stop that the airbags deployed; Bubba jumped out of the way to regain Sammy's side, and he got within ten feet of the woman, illumined by the headlights. She looked back to wink at him, then darted through a side yard to reach the market's small parking lot.

With Bubba quiet and obedient at his side, Sammy faded back into the shadows of a neighbor's trees while the car's two occupants struggled out from under the airbags, one holding his bloody nose. By then, the woman had yanked open the door of the market, and they doggedly staggered after her. But Sammy knew they wouldn't find her.

"C'mon, Bubba." He turned to start back to the Taylors' house, and Bubba trotted happily along. Taking his phone from his pocket, Sammy glanced down at him.

"You recognized her, didn't you?" Bubba grinned, tongue lolling.

Sammy made a call, stepping off the grass onto the lighted sidewalk without a backward glance. When his wife answered, he said, "Hey. It's okay. Adair got us an opening to get back into the house. Get the guys loaded into the car; Bubba and I'll be right there."

When Sammy entered the Taylors' foyer a few minutes later, the occupants of the gameroom were high-fiving each other over Jon Ramey's game-winning touchdown pass. "Good thing for him, after that interview," Pruett remarked.

"What did he say?" Sammy demanded.

"Only that—" Pruett's explanation was cut short by Marni's lugging a tired, restless toddler while carrying a tired, restless baby into the foyer.

"You have to take him," she explained.

Sammy leaned down to pick Sam up, but he began winding up for a repeat performance of last night's acrobatics. So Sammy just took him under arm like a sack of flour, reaching out with the other hand for his diaper/toy bag.

"What happened?" she asked in a low voice.

He gestured toward the driveway. "Let's get home; I don't know how long we have. Then I'll tell you and you can call your mom."

They said hasty goodbyes and loaded up Marni's Prius. Sammy drove watchfully to El Rancho and looked down the empty street before bypassing it to the rear alley.

He turned in their driveway and hit the garage-door

opener, all the while watching Bubba in the rearview mirror.

But the dog was docile, even sleepy, from the excitement of the day and the abundance of wiener bites, and there were no strangers lurking about the house to excite him. (In fact, Sammy saw no more surveillance of his house for the whole week following. But there was a reason for that.)

Once inside, they had bedtime routines to perform before they could talk. So while Sammy bathed Sam and brushed his teeth, Marni sponged off Clay in the sink and allowed him to nurse woozily until he fell asleep, which took about five minutes. Then they put the three boys to bed. Bubba laid his paw over Sam's midsection to watch the grown-ups leave the room, then he shut his eyes.

Sammy turned out all extraneous lights and peered out the front window blinds to see a peaceful, empty street. Closing the blinds again, he exhaled, "Okay. Here's what happened." He put his arm around her while he talked on their way to the bedroom.

The following morning, Monday, the investigators at MK & Associates conferred via text messages about how and where to get back to work. They unanimously agreed to return to headquarters, reporters be [consigned to the nether regions]. Since Mike still had the rental car, he would drive it today, redonning the clerical garb just in case, and park in front of the church. Pruett intended to come in Kerry's car, also parking in front of the church.

But Sammy did not want to deprive Marni of her

Prius for the day, as she disliked taking her children in his Mustang (and also showed an alarming tendency to ride the clutch). So he decided to take his car and leave it in a strip center a half-mile up the frontage road, then walk to their office. As punishment for Bubba's darting in front of a car to save somebody who likely did not need saving, Sammy went and found the leash.

He checked out the front windows again, but saw nothing suspicious. Heading out, he told her, "I've got my phone on me, as well as the car phone. So if you see anything—*anything*—you call me."

"All right," she said mildly, bouncing Clay, and Sammy noted her complete lack of fear.

"Bye, Sam." He looked back at his son playing with blocks and ignoring Dad in perpetual pique that he took his playmate to work with him everyday. "All right, then. Bye, Clay." He leaned over the baby to kiss his mother, then stepped back.

"Let's go, Bubba." The dog slipped past Sammy's knees through the laundry-room door into the garage and hopped over the side of the Mustang into the front passenger seat as per usual.

After they had left, Marni made out a grocery list and got her children's gear together for a trip to the store. She just decided that Jan Breemont had disrupted their lives enough with her book publication, and if there had been an army of reporters outside her door, Marni would still be compelled to go get diapers.

A new store had recently opened that was a little out of her usual circuit, but, given that they were advertising great sales, she wanted to check them out. So she loaded her boys into the car to go. They were sleepy enough from a busy weekend to cooperate but not so tired as to throw fits.

And they left. Driving to the store took 20 minutes —longer than Marni had counted on and too long to make it part of her regular routine. And when she arrived, it was way too crowded for a Monday morning. She had to park far down the row and walk Sam by the hand while carrying Clay in his carseat. It was not fun, especially with cars speeding down the row or backing without warning.

But for some reason, she didn't mind. She didn't really know why she was so cheerful, but she was. Strangely, the closer she got to the store, the happier she became, although she wasn't thinking of what to buy. She just suddenly felt very happy.

At the front of the store, she found an empty cart and swung Clay's carrier into it. As she lifted Sam to the child's seat in the front, she noticed the potted plants on display on the deep front walk of the store.

Gravitating toward them, she saw arching clusters of flowers that looked very much like the stem that the dancer—Adair?—had given Sam at the park. Marni scanned the plants, which seemed to be waving to her, calling, *"Pick me! Pick me!"*

Impulsively, she put a pot of solid pink orchids in her cart. Her home being dominated by males, she just felt the need to stake out a feminine corner here and there. As she lingered over the orchids, she glanced up toward the parking lot. Approaching the store were two women, one largely pregnant and one a blonde. Marni squinted.

As the women reached the front walk and headed for

the door, Marni's face cleared in recognition. "Jill!" she screeched.

The blonde woman swung around, and the pregnant one looked over. "Jill!" Marni pushed her cart over to throw her arms around a very surprised Jill and hug her in unfeigned joy. "Oh, Jill, how are you doing? You look great!" This was Marni's first roommate when she had moved away from home and had first met Sammy over four years ago.

"Marni," Jill said in shock.

"I love your hair cut! It's so sweet! and it fits your face perfectly. I bleached my hair—can you tell?—but it will never be as pretty as yours! Oh, tell me what you've been up to!" Marni exclaimed.

"Uh, Marni, this is my—sister-in-law, Candace," Jill said, tentative but polite.

Marni turned to the wary Candace with a little gasp. "Mark's wife?" Candace nodded, glancing at Jill in some apprehension. "Oh, you lucky girl!" Marni cried, and there was no hint of sarcasm or dissembling. "Mark is such a wonderful man. He's everything you could want in a husband and a friend. He'll be such a good dad. Is this your first? When are you due?" she asked in radiant excitement.

Both women were gaping at her, but Candace's mouth began to form a little smile. "Yes, it's our first. Three weeks, the midwife says."

"Oh, you're going to a midwife? Good for you! I had Clay, my youngest, at the Carrington Birth Center in University Park," Marni confided.

"That's where I'm going!" Candace exclaimed.

"Oh, they were wonderful! It was such a great

experience! Imelda was my primary midwife and Sasha was her assistant," Marni explained. Jill was watching her fixedly.

Candace cried, "Sasha is mine!"

"She's *great*," Marni emphasized. "So calm and reassuring, and so knowledgeable. Listen, she's going to make you drink tons of raspberry leaf tea, so just do what she says and drink it. I really think it helped with Clay, because his birth was so much easier than my first, with Sam." She nodded toward the restless toddler.

"I will," Candace promised.

In glancing at Sam, Marni noted the signals of an upcoming toddler tantrum. "Okay, I see I'd better go get my shopping done. Oh, I'm so glad to meet you! And to see you again, Jill! I sure would like to hear how the birth goes," she said wistfully.

Candace whipped out her phone. "What's your number?"

Marni gave it to her. "Good luck!' she called, pulling out a toy for Sam as she pushed the cart through the entrance.

Left settling in her wake, Jill lowered her head and Candace put her phone away. "Well. She's a lot different than what I expected, from what you told me," Candace said.

"She's changed a lot," Jill murmured, unaware of how red her face was.

As they entered the store, Candace groaned, "I have to pee again. Sorry. Be right back."

"No problem," Jill assured her. Sighing, Candace went into the store's restroom.

As soon as the door closed behind her, Jill pulled out

her phone and made an urgent call. "Mark? Sorry, I'll make it quick. I need for you to call that show's producer and tell him I changed my mind. I've got nothing to say about Sammy Kidman. . . .

"I know; I know, but—no, I'm not. And if you do it, Candace won't be speaking to you for a long time. We . . . Candace and I ran into Marni today, and—oh, I'll tell you about it later. Just cancel the interview. Okay. Thanks. Bye."

Six

It was a little dicey, walking with a dog for a half mile down a freeway frontage road during morning rush-hour traffic. But Sammy and Bubba had no difficulties, for two reasons:

First, Bubba had spent so much time riding with Sammy in the Mustang that traffic did not spook him. Second, the way Sammy was unconsciously holding the leash, combined with Bubba's confident leading and the style of Sammy's sunglasses gave drivers the impression that they were a blind man being led by a guide dog. Since most people are not psychopaths at heart, this made them a little more cautious passing the pair.

Entering the narrow shopfront parking lot, Sammy was gratified to see Mike's rental in front of the church. The door of "Great Deal Life Insurance Company" was locked, so just as Sammy was pulling out his keys, Bubba put his nose to the crack of the door and whined. It was unlocked from the inside, and Mike stepped back to let them in, then locked it again.

"Yeesh," muttered Sammy. "I sure wish all this would blow over sometime soon."

"Well, we have new deadbeats to annoy, so let's just turn our attention to that," Mike grunted.

Glancing around, Sammy confirmed that Pruett hadn't made it in yet. Bubba ambled over to his water dish. Discovering it to be empty, he looked back at Sammy. When Sammy didn't see him, Bubba issued a sharp bark. So his purported owner refilled it at the kitchenette sink and Bubba had his morning drink, then flopped in the middle of the industrial carpet until he should be needed.

"Yeah," Sammy belatedly agreed with Mike. Given his own propensity to leave his phone in random places, he made a point to leave his laptop, which he needed for work, AT work. He went straight back to his desk to flip open the laptop. Before checking messages, he scanned the news. A breathless headline from Channel 2 caught his eye: "Mystery Woman Causes North Dallas Accident."

Sammy clicked on the article and and read: "A news unit scanning a North Dallas neighborhood was involved in a one-car accident precipitated by a woman in a business suit walking a large, wolf-like dog at night."

In growing amusement, Sammy read how she suddenly stepped off the sidewalk into the path of the cruising car, which narrowly missed her by hitting the dog instead. The occupants of the car were bewildered to discover that, upon emerging, both the woman and the dog had vanished.

The article went on to describe the news team's pursuit of the woman into the corner market, and their subsequent failure to find her. Moreover, the clerk on duty and the lone customer in the store at the time both insisted that no one entered before the news team, and surveillance footage verified that.

The crack Channel 2 team, suspecting subterfuge that was possibly drug-related, promised to keep a steely eye on the suspiciously innocent-looking corner market.

Accompanying the article were sketches of the woman and the dog. Sammy grinned at the depiction of the ferocious beast with fangs that, in reality, slept with a toddler at night. Looking at the sketch of Adair, he shook his head slightly. They got nothing right but the hair, barely.

He sat back, pondering, then saw the paper cup on his desk with the orchid sprig, fresh and bright. If he were to evaluate last night's episode by the results alone, it looked like she—or someone—really did provide the diversion he needed. . . .

He looked down, refusing to contemplate such imaginings any further. Time to get to work. So he navigated to his inbox to start scanning messages.

"What—?" He was staring at the fresh new message from The Rivers Bank, verifying in writing the verbal authorization granted Saturday to Sammy Kidman of MK & Associates to seize $17,827.00 from the accounts of Dr. Gerald (Gerdie) Clothier for delinquent child support.

Sammy yanked open his side drawer before remembering that the file was gone. Then he turned back to his laptop to open the record for disbursements to date, and did indeed find that, as of the day before yesterday, Dr. Clothier's ex-wife was almost $18,000 richer.

"That sectional coelenterate posed as me to work the Clothier file!" he exclaimed.

"Sambo," Mike uttered, turning in his chair, "which was harder: filling out the paperwork or getting the account numbers?"

"Mike, what are you talking about?" Sammy cried. "We don't have to get account numbers! Authorization means they hand us the numbers!"

"Not if they don't know the names on the accounts, El Stupido," Dave said, entering through the back door. In lazy acknowledgment, Bubba's tail thumped on the carpet. Pruett came in to toss his laptop on his desk, park his posterior in the chair, and throw his feet up on the desk victoriously.

"Names," Sammy repeated mechanically.

Twining his fingers behind his head, Pruett said, "The genius Gerald Clothier has a dummy account at that same bank under the name Gordon Clothier. He left the passwords right on his desktop! I emptied that account for his ex."

Sammy gazed at Pruett for a solid minute. Mike looked over uneasily at the silence. Then Sammy cleared his throat and said, "Gordon Clothier is Gerald's brother. He doesn't owe Gerald's ex-wife anything."

Pruett paled, slowly withdrawing his feet from the desk to the floor. "Uh, that can't be. The personal information is all the same—address, employer, even the birth date."

Almost detached, Sammy said, "Gordon Clothier is Gerald's fraternal twin. He works at the college part-time as a teaching assistant and tutor. Because he has acute bipolar disorder, he's been living with Gerald, who also has power of attorney for him. And that account represents his life savings."

Pruett stared at Sammy in utter dismay. Mike said, "Can we put that money back into his account?"

"Not *that* money," Sammy said, glancing at the disbursements file on his laptop. "The agency can reimburse him, if—" He was interrupted by the ring of the telephone.

Sammy picked it up. "MK and associates. This is Sammy Kidman."

There was a pause. "Is that Sammy Kidman?" asked a male voice.

"Yes, this is Sammy Kidman."

"Mr. Kidman, this is Charles Whinnet of The Rivers Bank. I spoke to you Saturday about seizing assets from Gerald Clothier's account to pay delinquent child support. You tapped his brother Gordon's account instead, which you were distinctly not authorized to do. Gordon Clothier is extremely upset—he's pressing charges against you and your firm for felony theft."

"Yes, Mr. Whinnet, I'm sorry about that. It was an error for which we're prepared to reimburse Mr. Clothier immediately," Sammy replied.

"Well, good; that's the least you can do. But I understand you're going to be served with a warrant this morning," Whinnet said.

Sammy swallowed. "I understand. Thank you for the heads-up." Whinnet hung up, as did Sammy.

In the utter quiet of the room, he said, "I think you both better leave, and take Bubba. Your former coworkers are on their way over with a warrant for my arrest for violating Section 31.03(e)(4) of the Texas Penal Code," he said, grimly humorous.

"State jail felony," Mike said heavily. Pruett was

struck dumb, because they all knew what this charge meant:

The agency would lose their license and be forced to close. The owners, Marni and Sammy, would be liable for punitive civil damages far exceeding the $17,827 taken from Gordon Clothier. As their liability insurance would not cover criminal acts, Clothier could, and probably would, claim the remainder of the lottery payout.

Sammy would be arrested, fingerprinted, and photographed, all as a matter of public record. Until posting bail, he would be placed in lock-up, which, as an ex-cop, put him at the mercy of anyone there who held a grudge against any police anywhere. Cons always knew when a cop was dropped in their midst; they could smell it.

Should MK & Associates repay Gordon Clothier immediately, the case could still take years to resolve, with the arrest hanging over Sammy for the rest of his life. His image and personal information having become a matter of public record, he would remain forever exposed.

"I'll explain everything," Pruett croaked.

Sammy said mildly, "I'd really rather you get out and take Bubba. When they cuff me, he's going to go nuts, and I don't want them to shoot him."

Pruett turned to put his face in his hands and sob. Mike lowered his head, elbows on his knees.

The phone rang again. Sammy had to clear his throat before answering, "Ahem. MK and associates. This is Sammy Kidman."

"SAMMY KIDMAN?" screamed a voice. Wincing,

he removed the receiver a few inches from his ear; Mike and Pruett stared.

"MISTER Kidman, you—thief! You—evil, flesh-eating maggot in the corpse of humanity! I will ruin you! I will make you pay for the remainder of your days for this outrage. You will rue the day—RUE THE DAY, sir —that you ever chose to cross swords with me. I will hound you forever. I will hound your family. I will haunt your doorstep and make your life a living hell."

He went on and on in this vein; as soon as Sammy could wrangle an opening, he said, "Mr. Clothier, I'm very sorry about the mix-up; we're prepared to—" Clothier terminated the conversation by screaming in his ear.

Sammy quietly replaced the receiver. "Yeah, he's ticked." Regarding Pruett's tear-streaked, bloodless face, Sammy searched for some crumb of comfort to offer him. "Hey, you know, Marni thinks Sam and Kelli are going to wind up dating. He tried to kiss her at their last play date." Pruett put his head down on his arms.

As Sammy turned back to close his laptop, his eye landed on the paper cup with the flowers. But instead of one sprig resting in the cup, there were now three. There was the original mottled purple, a white one, and one that was yellow and pink. All three looked fresh and new. Idly regarding them, Sammy thought, *If you really want to help us, now would be a great time.*

Long minutes passed as they waited in silence for the axe to fall. Normally, the wisest course of action for someone who knew that a warrant had been issued for his arrest would be to turn himself in. But as long as there was any chance that Sammy could rectify the situation from the office, he needed to remain here. He just had to think through what to do.

"Yeah, Mike? Unlock the door," Sammy requested. Mike got up and did so. They did not wish to provoke the arresting officers into using force. The new recruits, the ones most likely to serve routine warrants like this, tended to draw down unnecessarily. There seemed to be a lot more shootings of unarmed civilians—

Sammy started. "Pruett, you got your sidearm? Mike? If you do, for the love of God, get rid of it."

Mike shook his head. "Not today."

Pruett sat up, sighing. "Kerry made me put it up."

Sammy nodded. "Good, good."

A moment later he turned around and picked up his phone, speed-dialing home. "Answering machine," he muttered.

He did not waste time calling Pam to see if Marni was at her house when the office door might open to the arresting officers at any moment. He merely left this message: "Baby, I need you to do a few things as soon as you hear this. Make the largest tax-free gifts you can to your folks, the Hawkinses, the Pruetts, and the Mastersons—all of them. Everybody. Transfer owner-ship of our investments to your dad, if you can do that without a massive tax burden. Check with him. Send a chunk to Joe Brodie's church.

"I'll explain the reasons as soon as I can, but right now I just need for you to unload as much of our available cash as you can. I love you, baby." He replaced the receiver.

He then looked at Bubba, still stretched out in the middle of the floor. "Bubba," he summoned quietly. The dog raised his head, then picked himself up with an effort and ambled over.

Sammy took the massive head to stroke it with both hands. "You've been a good riding buddy, guy. I'll miss you." While he told his four-legged friend good-bye, Mike and Pruett stared off into space, numb.

The ringing of the telephone startled them violently. Sammy had to take a breath before picking up the receiver with a trembling hand. His eyes watered as he said, "MK and associates. This is . . . Sammy Kidman."

A torrent of unintelligible, weeping words answered him. Closing his eyes, he began, "Mr. Clothier, again, I'm so sorry—" A blinking light on the phone console indicated that a call was waiting. As neither Mike nor Pruett made a move to answer it, Sammy said, "Mr. Clothier, I'm so sorry; I have to put you on hold. Excuse me, please."

He pressed a button on the phone, then gulped and said, "MK and associates. Thank you for waiting; this is Sammy Kidman."

"Mr. Kidman, this is Charles Whinnet again. I wish you had told me you knew Fletcher."

"Excuse me?" Sammy said weakly.

"Fletcher Streiker just called me. He has personally made Gordon Clothier whole," Whinnet said.

"Fletcher Streiker?" Sammy repeated blankly. "The billionaire?" Mike and Pruett leaned toward him.

"Yes; surely you know him; he owns The Rivers Bank. He has satisfied Mr. Clothier so that he's dropping the charges. I understand you're in the clear," Whinnet said.

Tears streaming down his face, Sammy turned away

from the receiver to tell his coworkers, "The owner of the bank has paid Gordon Clothier back. He's dropping the charges."

Mike and Pruett stared at each other. Sammy said into the receiver, "Ah, Mr. Whinnet, do you have a phone number for Mr. Streiker?"

"Sure," said Charles, and gave it to him.

Unable to see the keys on his laptop, Sammy scrambled for a pen to blindly write the number down. "Thank you for calling, Mr. Whinnet."

"You're welcome."

Breathing out, Sammy clicked on Clothier's line again. "Mr. Clothier? Thank you for waiting. I understand . . . Mr. Clothier, if you'll let me. . . . Sir, I can't understand you."

Neither could Mike and Pruett, though they could hear his continued outpouring from where they sat. He was no longer berating, it seemed, but Sammy couldn't discern exactly what he was saying now.

Giving up, Sammy put him on hold again. After taking a moment to wipe down his wet face, he keyed in the number he had just written down.

"Hello."

Sammy sat up. "Hello. Yes, this is Sammy Kidman with MK and associates. I'd like to speak with Fletcher Streiker, if that's possible."

"Speaking."

"Mr. Streiker, I—ah, Charles Whinnet of The Rivers Bank just told me that you paid Gordon Clothier back the monies that my firm had—mistakenly taken from his account to satisfy a debt owed by his brother. I, uh, wanted to thank you for intervening on our behalf, and, ask you for an account number so that we can reimburse you for that," Sammy said unsteadily.

Streiker considered that. "I'm glad to hear that. But, I don't really need the money."

"No sir, I'm sure you don't," Sammy said, cracking a smile.

"So instead of your reimbursing me, I may ask you to do a small service for me from time to time. Would you be willing to give me a little time and effort rather than cash?" Streiker asked.

Sammy grinned in relief. "I'd—would I ever. You call me any time, and I will hop to it."

"All right. Good. Well—"

"Mr. Streiker? If I might ask—how in the world did you know about this fiasco? And, sir, why would you bother to pull our fat out of the fire?" Sammy asked.

"My wife requested it," he said.

"Your wife?" Sammy repeated.

"Yes, and if you'll excuse me, she's waiting on me. Good-bye," Streiker said.

Sammy regarded the dead line. "His wife asked him to help us." Then he looked at the flowers.

"Let me get this straight," Mike said in his sergeant's voice. "The owner of the bank intervenes to pay off Gordon Clothier because his wife asked him to, and in return, he wants—what?"

"He wants us to do something for him from time to time," Sammy said, looking at the orchids.

"What, specifically?" Mike asked.

"He didn't say," Sammy said thoughtfully.

"I don't believe it," Pruett said in a hard voice. "Anybody can say they're Fletcher Streiker. We don't know the man, and we don't know that was him. For all we know, a warrant could still walk in the door at any minute."

"Well, that's easy enough to find out," Mike said, turning to his phone.

"What we need is to find out if Gordon Clothier is satisfied," Sammy said seriously, then his eyes widened and he looked at his phone, where the light still blinked. Cautiously, he picked up the handset. "Mr. Clothier? Yes, sir. Are you—sir, please let me just ask you if. . . ."

He broke off, squinting in the effort to decipher: "And it just restored my faith in the goodness of the created realm, whence the waters flow in healing mercy to souls in torment—"

The change in Clothier's tone was startling; only his passion remained at the previous elevation. Sammy broke in desperately, "Mr. Clothier, are you pressing charges?"

"Oh, no. Mr. Streiker didn't like that idea," Clothier said.

"Good. And you got your money back?" Sammy asked hopefully.

"Yes, with interest," he said.

"I'm so glad; I'm so glad," Sammy breathed. "Good-bye, Mr. Clothier." And he hung up.

Mike hung up. "There are no warrants issued or pending for you," he told Sammy.

The three sat there looking at each other. Bubba, since he was no longer being petted, walked back to his favored spot to flop down again.

Watching him, Sammy said, "I feel like Lazarus, raised from the dead."

"And I'm the one who almost killed you," Pruett said bitterly.

Sammy scowled at him. "Don't be stupid. That was a mistake any of us could have made at any time."

Mike suddenly looked at Sammy's desk. "Those are the flowers somebody left you? Looks like a bouquet."

Sammy leaned back in his chair. "There was one stem this morning. As of an hour ago, there were three."

Mike and Pruett both got up to come look at them. Pruett cleared his throat. "The door's been locked. Even the landlord doesn't have a key yet. It hasn't been forced."

Sammy said, "Yes, but that's irrelevant. Someone waited while we were distracted with Gordon Clothier to bring in two more sprigs."

Mike noted, "There's no water in this cup."

"I spilled it Saturday," Pruett admitted.

"Killed it," Sammy said blandly. He rocked back in his chair, and they looked at the flowers.

The telephone, when it rang, caused all three of them to jump. "MK and associates. This is Sammy Kidman." He listened, then said, "He's right here," looking up at Mike.

Mike took the phone. "Masterson. Galt! Yes, what?" He listened for a few minutes, then said, "I owe you. Good-bye."

Reaching over to replace the handset, Mike said, "Yeah, they just served Gerald Clothier with warrants. He's in custody now."

Sammy's face clouded. "Man, I hope that doesn't send his brother into a tailspin."

"Apparently," Mike paused to chuckle, "ah, Galt

says the brother was considerably comforted by Gerald's live-in, who owns the house they were all staying at. Galt says neither of 'em was particularly torn up over his arrest."

"Okayyy," Sammy said slowly.

The phone rang again. Clutching his chest, Pruett threw himself back down to his desk. "Make it stop."

"MK and associates. This is Sammy Kidman."

"Sammy! What's going on? I got the gifts disbursed to our friends, the church, and my parents, but my dad just refused to touch the investments and wants to talk to you about it asap," Marni said.

"Oh. Hi, baby," Sammy said mildly, then told his coworkers, "She got your gifts out." Mike and Pruett exchanged glances as he told her, "Okay, well, that's enough for one day, I guess. I'll tell you about it when I get home."

"Okay," she said dubiously. "Oh, I saw Jill Reid today with her sister-in-law. Mark got married, and she's due in three weeks."

"Good. That's good," he murmured. "We'll . . . send 'em something."

"Yeah, I thought we should. Okay, see you tonight. I love you, Sammy."

"I love you, baby."

The three sat there a moment longer, then Pruett got up. "I can't take any more of this. I'm going home. Look for me tomorrow. That is, if you still want—"

Sammy stood abruptly, scattering papers. "If you go full-on drama queen, I swear I'm sending you to the Clothier residence. In. Pieces."

"Sheesh," Pruett muttered, exiting by the front door.

Mike went back to his desk to pick up a few articles. "Me, too, Sambo. Today took five years off my life." And it wasn't even noon yet.

"Tell Charisse hey," Sammy muttered, and Mike left.

Bubba lifted his head to eye Sammy from the floor. "Yeah, we're not hanging around, either, Bubba." He got up to turn off lights and make sure the back door was locked. Bubba got to his feet, shaking himself, and Sammy geared up for a half-mile walk back down the frontage road during the lunch rush.

SEVEN

"His wife asked him to help you?" Marni whispered.

Sammy, splayed on the couch, nodded. Clay was balanced on his chest, trying to raise up, and Sam was lolling on the floor with Bubba at their feet.

"Who is his wife?" she asked.

"I don't know." He shook his head. "Oh—and get this." He sat up, readjusting Clay. "There are now three sprigs on my desk."

"What?" she frowned.

"The first flower I found Saturday, the one with purple spots, I had put in a cup of water, but Pruett spilled the water. Today I find that one and two more—a white and a yellow one—in the cup, all fresh and new and still no water." He lifted Clay by the belly, making him roll and dive in the classic Aviator Baby style. The little guy cackled.

"One for you, Mike and Dave," she said. He glanced at her. "And all three of you were helped today," she added.

"Yeah, 'helped' is not really strong enough—'saved from the flaming pits of Hades' is a little closer, but—"

He lowered Clay back to his shoulder. "The funny thing I didn't notice at the time was that, when I started talking to Gordon—the manic-depressive brother—about what Streiker said to him, he got coherent all of a sudden. He said Streiker didn't like the idea of having me arrested."

She studied him. "He knows you, somehow."

"Today was the first time I've ever talked to him in my life," he maintained.

"I give up. This is too strange," she murmured, leaning into him.

"Yeah." He exhaled restlessly, his mind now far past the events of the morning. All he knew right now was that he and she hadn't enjoyed any decent lovemaking for months, and he was feeling it acutely. He reached down to kiss her warmly, and she responded. Lowering Clay, he pressed her harder—

Then he paused, remembering the demon Vane's influence on him, and the way he had been dogged with fantasies about his weird secretary when he only wanted to enjoy his wife. That was pure evil. Was the same thing happening now?

"Hang on," Marni murmured. Clay, exhausted from exercising, was rubbing his face on Sammy's shirt. Marni gently lifted him to place him in the playpen. Bubba and Sam were cuddled up on the floor. Sam was already asleep because it is almost impossible to lie down next to a sleeping dog and stay awake.

Then she knelt on the loveseat, out of sight of the sleepers but still in the same room, and began taking off clothes. Sammy silently vaulted over the back of the sofa and tiptoed across the room, unzipping his pants.

For the next forty minutes they didn't think about

anything but how good it felt to get together again.

Afterward, lying on his back with her curled up on top of him, Sammy wasn't even cognizant of the fact that there had been no oppression, no hint of outside interference in his quality time with his wife. He wasn't ready to think about that yet. As Sam suddenly sat up, blinking, Marni had to get clothes back on without drawing his attention.

"Mommy?" Sam got up to peer toward the bathroom. Tail thumping the floor, Bubba looked back at his hormonal parents pulling themselves together on the couch.

"Hey, Sam." Sammy, barefoot but dressed, caught up with him in the hall.

"Dada!" Sam lifted eager arms for Sammy to pick him up.

Bouncing him, Sammy said, "Hey, listen. I was just going to the potty. I need help. Want to go potty with me?" Obviously, Sammy was ready to get Sam out of diapers.

"Uh unh," Sam declined. Then, because his diaper was askew, Sammy felt the warmth cascade over his arm and down his shirt front to complete the journey by soaking into his pants.

Sammy lifted his face to the heavens in exasperation. "Okay, let's go change," he sighed.

After cleaning up Sam and putting him in fresh clothes, Sammy walked him to the bedroom where Marni was freshening up.

Coming to the door of her dressing area, he said, "Hey, you know that—" His eye landed on the pink orchids and he jumped. "Gah!"

Sam went into fits of laughter, mimicking him: "Gah! [*jump*] Gah! [*jump*]"

Marni grinned reassuringly. "I bought that at the store opening today. See, it has leaves and roots and everything."

Puckering his lips at her humorous condescension, he bent to examine them. "First time I've seen one of these as, you know, a whole plant. It is pretty." He touched a glossy green leaf.

She sighed, "Oh, you're home, and we're not bankrupt—let's go somewhere, just to get out of the house for a little while."

"Sure," he said, straightening. "Where do you want to go?"

They both stood there looking at the orchid. Then she said, "Let's go look at plants."

"A nursery?" he asked. "Or, like, the arboretum?"

"Oh, I'd love to see Fall at the Arboretum," she said.

"Let's go," he gestured.

So Marni gathered all the necessary gear for the guys, then they started through the house to the garage. Bubba fell right in with them, waving his tail.

Sammy paused. "I don't think they allow dogs in the arboretum."

Marni tossed her head. "Well then, let's just go to a park."

Sammy whispered, "You're great."

"So are you," she purred with her sidelong glance, and he felt a tingle shoot up from his loins.

They packed everybody in the Prius, then Sammy just started driving around looking for a dog-friendly, kid-friendly, hoodlum-free park in Dallas (other than the one near their house, which they had seen enough of). After fifteen minutes of meandering, he pulled into the parking area of a listless but benign-looking green place.

But Marni touched his arm and pointed toward a billboard advertising the Fletcher Streiker Arboretum, just a few minutes away. Sammy regarded the billboard, then swung the car back down the road. "Sure. Why not?"

A few minutes later, he pulled into the parking lot of Streiker's Arboretum. It was well-paved, clean, and not too crowded. "Before we all get out, let's see if we can bring Bubba in or not," he murmured.

"Look." Marni pointed to a sign highlighting Arboretum rules, one of which read, "Leashed dogs are welcome with the purchase of poop bags. Please use them."

"Gah! Where's the leash?" Sammy exclaimed, searching around small storage areas that could not contain a leash.

"Gah!" laughed Sam in the back, and Bubba barked, waking Clay.

"Ha ha," Sammy threw over his shoulder, but Marni opened the glove compartment and found the leash.

Sammy hauled out the stroller for Clay alone, as Sam would not condescend to be placed in a conveyance that his baby brother required. Then they ambled up the path to the admissions booth.

The general park area was free to the public, but special exhibits required paid admission. Sammy paid for everything, including the requisite poop bags, and they entered the central plaza.

Marni caught her breath at the trees that covered

acres of sloping hillsides around the arboretum. Flaming oaks, ginkgos, sugar maples, sweetgum and American smoketrees provided a glorious backdrop to the smaller evergreens such as pine, yaupon and holly trees. These were set along trails lined with beds of chrysanthemums in every color, as well as marigolds, Copper Canyon daisies, fall asters, and oxblood lilies.

The Complete Kidman Cohort began rambling up one trail, just walking and looking. Sammy held Bubba's leash (when he remembered to) in case the squirrels proved too great a temptation, and Sam skipped alongside while Marni pushed Clay in the stroller.

There were niches along the way with whimsical statuary, fountains, or huts made of gourds, pumpkins and vines. Squealing, Sam darted in and out of these little houses.

They were too small for grown-ups, but Sammy leaned down and stuck his head in one or two, just to confirm that it did not house something that might object to sharing its space.

For Sam, the walk became an adventure to see what lay beyond the next curve of the path, in the next niche. One corner contained a large koi pond not only with benches around it, but a food dispenser. The dispenser was equipped with a timer so that only a preset amount of pellets would be released within a 4-hour period. It just so happened that there was an abundant supply available for Sam to toss to the fish, who jumped and thrashed to snap it all up.

His parents sat to watch, and since there was no one else around, Marni got Clay out of the stroller to nurse him. It was such a nice spot that they lingered for quite a while, not getting up to leave until Sam attempted to wade in and Bubba proposed to go fishing.

They resumed their walk along the path. Since they were so leisurely about it (as Sammy tended to stop and throw up his hands when he talked, especially about Pruett) Sam found a sturdy stick to dig for bugs to fill his pockets with. The times that Bubba attempted to dig with him, Sammy would yell at him and reclaim the trailing leash.

If Bubba felt discriminated against, he didn't complain. However, he did hunch up and drop a pile, so Sammy had to pull out one of the poop bags. He held the full bag in some disgruntlement, as he didn't remember seeing any trash receptacles. But when he turned around, there was one at his elbow.

Sammy and Marni walked, and looked, and talked while the outside world of concrete and exhaust faded from view, then faded from mind. He rediscovered her intellectual acuity and she was amazed by the simple, overriding need he had for her to believe in him.

"Man, you know," he said, "when I was looking at the End of Everything—the business, the lottery money, my privacy, your security—the first thing that went through my mind was, *How will Marni take it?* When I got it settled in my head that you'd stick it out with me, then I started thinking about contingencies—that's when I called and left the message on the machine. Pruett was blubbering, but I didn't cry until Whinnet told me we were in the clear."

"His wife requested it," she murmured, leaping ahead to his conversation with Streiker. "If you're sure you haven't met her, then she must have read something about the agency. Maybe she saw the 'Judge Evelyn' episode we were on."

He shrugged. "Yeah, but that doesn't explain how she knew about Gordon Clothier." His fleeting request upon first sight of the orchids at his office, not counting as a prayer, remained firmly locked up in his mental compartment of Things Disallowed, Therefore Ignored.

At length they paused and looked around at the waning light. They had been following the path deeper and deeper into the park while giving no thought to getting back out again. "Where did we get to?" she asked.

"I thought it would circle back to the beginning," he replied in something of a non sequitur.

"Pretty feet!" said Sam, pointing through a break in the landscaping.

Sammy and Marni looked where he pointed. In another area of the Arboretum stood an octagonal gazebo at least thirty feet in diameter. It was lit with strings of tiny lights that glowed in the late afternoon shadows. Steps led up to its wooden floor, on which a man and a woman were dancing together.

They were just having fun, obviously; it wasn't a choreographed routine. But the skill and grace of the woman was apparent, even dancing closely to her partner with her arms around his neck. Sammy's hands went clammy.

She looked toward their group and waved, whereupon the man turned around. He said something to her and kissed her, then she departed the gazebo on the far side while the man came down the steps toward them.

They watched him cross the narrow strip of lawn around the gazebo, then scramble up a gentle embankment bordering their path. He drew up to them, asking cordially, "Are you enjoying yourselves?"

Neither Sammy nor Marni could reply at first, but Bubba fell down at the man's feet and rolled onto his back. The man knelt to give him a very satisfactory belly rub. Sam reached out grubby hands to hug his neck, and the man hugged him warmly in return. Holding Sam in one arm, he wiggled Clay's exposed foot, then replaced the sock that had been kicked loose.

Standing again, he regarded them genially. Marni said with a slight quaver, "It's lovely. We just seem to have gotten ourselves lost."

"Oh, well, you just keep following the path," he said, turning with a gesture for them to follow.

As he began walking away at a rather fast clip, Sammy swung up Sam, who was yawning. Marni leaned down on the stroller handles to elevate the front wheels, allowing for greater speed. Clay waved his arms in glee. Bubba, tongue lolling, trotted at the man's side with the leash trailing in the dirt.

The man led them briskly up the path, rounded a corner, and suddenly they were back at the central plaza. Sammy and Marni blinked at the people posing in front of masses of hyacinth blooms and the children thronging the concession stands on their way out. Since twilight was imminent, the Arboretum was closing for the day.

"Here you are," he said, glancing around in satisfaction. "Good turnout, for a Monday." Turning back to the Kidmans, he added, "It's good to see you again, Marni," and kissed her cheek. Then he reached out to shake Sammy's limp hand. "I hope you'll come back."

"We have to; we bought poop bags," Sammy blurted. The man laughed, patting his shoulder, then walked away.

In shock, the Kidman parents walked their family back to their car. Neither said a word while Sammy loaded the stroller in the trunk and Marni got the boys strapped in. Bubba jumped in, squeezing himself into the available space on the floor of the back seat. Then they sat; Sammy wiped his mouth and started the car.

As they waited in the line of cars to exit the parking lot, Sammy glanced at her. "When did you see him before?"

She cleared her throat. "At the hospital. I assumed he was a doctor, because he was all in white." He nodded as if that were a perfectly reasonable explanation. She barely turned toward him. "That's him, isn't it? Streiker?"

"Yeah," he said softly. "At least, from the voice, I'd say it's him."

They said nothing else for ten minutes, while Sammy gained the thoroughfare and headed for home. Marni reached up to flip down the visor mirror and check her reflection. "What a mess," she muttered, fluffing her scattered blonde bangs with their dark roots. She added, "I'm thinking about coloring it darker and just letting it grow out. I'm tired of having to get it touched up all the time." He nodded without replying.

Then she casually said, "Then that must have been his wife with him."

"Must have been," he said, barely audible.

Marni faced the issue head-on: "Was that her? The dancer from the park?"

Stopped at a red light, he parted his lips and breathed out, "Yes."

Ten seconds passed. "Adair?" she asked.

He barely shook his head, mouthing, *I don't know.* Marni did not broach it again.

Sammy got burgers and chicken nuggets at a drive-through, but Sam was too sleepy to do more than suck on his chocolate shake. Unnoticed by the people in the front seat, Bubba assisted him with the nuggets that fell from limp fingers.

Sitting in Monday evening rush-hour traffic, Marni and Sammy ate their burgers quietly, then Marni pulled out her phone and called her mom to bring her up to speed on everything. Sammy listened without adding anything or correcting her on anything.

After giving her mom a synopsis of the day, Marni listened quietly for a few minutes, then said, "Okay, thanks. I'll call you tomorrow. We're just bush-whacked. . . . Love you, too. Bye."

Turning down the alley behind their house, Sammy asked, "What did she say?"

"She said the only thing she knows to tell us is to look at the results—see what happens, and if it draws us deeper into obedience to God or pushes us away. 'By their fruit you will know them,' and all." She broke off in a yawn.

"Yeah," he agreed with a nod.

Sam would not wake up for a bath, so he got a sponge bath and a fresh diaper before being tucked in with Bubba. Clay got the same treatment before being laid down in his crib. Then Sammy and Marni looked at each other and fell into bed.

The following morning, Sammy was up long before anyone else in the house to go on his standard 5-mile run. When he returned from running, he shut himself in the third bedroom to work out with his free weights and do push-ups and sit-ups. This was all part of his morning routine, because he never knew when he might need decent upper-body strength. It was the mindset of a cop that would not go away.

Mindful of the cases that MK & Associates had pending, and chafed at the various delays in providing relief to families who were owed it, Sammy got himself coffee and closed himself in the bath/dressing area before turning on the light, so as not to disturb his wife.

After showering and shaving, he found the new black shirt that she had considerately hung up in his closet. So he put that on. Fashion-impaired as he was, he figured that as his good gray slacks were at the cleaners, the only thing left in his closet that matched were his black pants. So he put those on, with black socks and loafers. Fortunately, he eschewed a tie. Then upon leaving, he grabbed up his new favorite sports coat, which also happened to be black.

He paused at the door, thinking about Bubba. So he tiptoed back to the guys' room in the dark and peeked in. All was still and quiet. Knowing what would befall him should he wake either guy in extracting his dog, he wisely let them be and left for work in his Mustang without said dog. Sammy also forgot his phone.

He stopped at a drive-through for more coffee and a

breakfast muffin, then drove to the office and opened up. Defiantly parking his conspicuous car in front of the door, he unconsciously did everything to advertise his presence except open the blinds. Then he opened his laptop and got to work.

First, he checked the news, and discovered to his delight a follow-up on the Mystery Woman story. It seems that Channel 2 suspected that one of Channel 7's aspiring newscasters was, in fact, the Mystery Woman, and that she refused to come forward in order to make their competitors look like fools. So now Channel 7 was in on the hunt, desiring to find the woman first to prove that, yes, their competitors were fools.

The amazing thing was, such a woman had apparently been seen late yesterday near a recreation center not far from the corner market down the street from the Kidmans' house (which had been long forgotten by the news crews). A blonde woman in high heels and a pearl-gray suit was spotted walking a large dog, but turned a corner and disappeared when a Channel 7 reporter attempted to hail her. Sammy digested this bit of savory entertainment, then sighed and pulled out case files.

He was in the midst of researching three cases simultaneously. Given the recent Clothier disaster, he went back over the notes he had made on all three, just to make sure all his information was correct. This review process ate up an hour, but it was well worth it.

"Aha," he murmured, seeing the hitherto unknown address of a delinquent dad pop up from the most recent search. He was noting the details when the phone rang. Neither Mike nor Pruett was in yet.

"MK and associates. This is Sammy Kidman," he answered, writing rapidly.

"Sammy, this is Fletcher Streiker. If you really want to help me, now would be a good time."

Sammy almost dropped the phone, but Streiker went on: "A friend of mine is in trouble in the alley behind the convenience store in the shopping center behind you. He needs your help right now. Don't take your car, that will slow you down. Go on foot."

"But—what do I need to do?" he asked.

"You'll see when you get there," Streiker said, and hung up.

ЕIGHT

Sammy gaped at the phone, then paused over the hot lead on his desk. He sure didn't want to walk off and leave it hanging. But if Streiker said somebody was in trouble in an alley, Sammy dare not dismiss that. Knowing exactly the area Streiker was talking about, Sammy got up from his desk and left through the back office door without taking the time to lock it.

He started off at a brisk walk, then began running. He recklessly crossed in the middle of the street, eliciting honks, then bypassed the storefronts in the shopping center to swing around the south corner and look down the alley. And he saw a group of guys clustered around somebody, beating him. Sammy's hackles rose and he bared his teeth, advancing.

At times like this, fifteen years' experience as a cop pays off. Sammy did not rush in blindly and emotionally; he studied the situation to ascertain critical facts as he trotted toward the group: First, how many did he have to contend with? Three, he noted.

What were they armed with? Since they were beating, and not stabbing or shooting, they were using fists, blackjacks or brass knuckles. Catching the glint of metal, he knew that the latter was probably in use.

The emblem on the backs of their denim jackets pegged them as gang members, so this was likely an initiation to gain membership for one of the three. That is, it's easy to hurt somebody with a knife or a gun, but how much damage could you do with your fists? That was apparently the test here. To insure optimal results, a prospective member got as many ordained members as he could to help him.

Speeding up toward them, Sammy noted a few additional details: these were teenagers, probably 16 to 18 years old. Therefore, he must not hurt them badly enough to kill them. It was just a fact of human nature that once you got started on a good beating, it was hard to stop. Finally, as he closed in on them while they were yet unaware, he framed out his strategy.

One hood with his back to Sammy had a sap raised over his head preparatory to striking, not for the first time. Sammy grasped his left shoulder with one hand and the long, braided hair on the back of his head with the other, jerking him to the left and slamming him face first into the brick wall of the alley. The young man tottered, blood gushing from his nose, but Sammy did not wait to watch him fall.

The youth to his right, now aware of his presence, made the classic defensive error of opening himself up in order to raise his weapon. Sammy, proficient with both hands, hit him in the gut with his left fist, supported by his entire body braced on concrete. The teenager fell to his knees, vomiting.

Sammy turned to the third hood, who was now in a

quandary. Letting go of his victim, who fell to the pavement, the gangbanger glanced toward the north end of the alley, where a group of frightened kids was calling for help. Deciding against that route, the youth chanced to dart around Sammy to the south end of the alley, where he had entered.

Executing this move successfully at first, the young man was betrayed by his adherence to fashion. His sagging pants entwined his knees, causing him to spread-eagle on the pavement.

Catching up to him at a walk, Sammy saw the array of bulky rings he wore on his right hand. Unlike brass knuckles, rings weren't illegal, but they were just as effective in causing injury. Moreover, they advertised one's status and wealth.

Noting the victim's blood on the adorned fingers that were spread on the pavement, Sammy raised his face, lifted his foot, and stomped on the hand. He felt the crunching of many bones as the hood cried out sharply. It would be quite some time before he used that hand to beat on anybody else.

With the attackers rendered inert, Sammy looked back to their target, who was being helped by adults into the convenience store, followed by the kids. Since the victim was mobile and attended, Sammy didn't see what more he could do. So with one last bounce on the hand, which provoked fresh cries, he departed the south end of the alley.

Arriving back at the office, he glanced around to ascertain that it was just as empty as when he had left. Locking the back door, he thought about how urgent it had been for him to act at once on Streiker's request without knowing all the details. He also noted that it was a request, not a demand.

Why didn't he tell me somebody was getting a beatdown? Sammy wondered. *So I wouldn't rush in half-cocked*, he knew. Sammy needed to see the situation for himself in order to devise the best response. Amazingly, Streiker trusted him to do that.

Then, sniffing, Sammy looked down in disgust at the blood, sweat and vomit splattered over his clothes. "Eh, I'll have to go home and change," he groused. But inside he was deeply satisfied, not only at the chance to rescue somebody—which was his rationale for becoming a cop in the first place—but at having been useful to Streiker.

Before he would touch his Mustang, however, he had to wash the odorous hair pomade off his hands. Then he locked up the office and drove home.

He arrived to find Marni's Prius gone, but thought nothing of it until he noted that Bubba was gone, too. Thoughtfully, he went to the bedroom to wash up and change.

Despite standing over the clothes hamper, he did not notice the buzzing of the phone that he had left in his jeans pocket last night before throwing them in with the other dirty clothes.

When clean and composed, he returned to the garage to hear his car phone ringing. He opened the car door and sat before picking it up. "Yo."

"Sammy, where are you? I've been calling and calling!" Marni cried.

Since he had never heard her truly hysterical before, he started shaking all over. He would have collapsed had he not been sitting already. The absurd thought crossed his mind, *That's why you always tell people to sit before you deliver really bad news.*

Forcing himself to speak calmly, he said, "I had to come home to change. What happened?"

She cried, "Oh, Sammy, Chris is in the emergency room! He was beat up by a bunch of thugs just a few blocks from your office!"

Sammy's chest almost blew wide open. "Chris? *That was Chris Pruett?*" he shouted.

Strangely, his blow-up served to calm her a little. "Yes. Dave Pruett just called from the hospital."

"Where are you?" he asked.

"At my parents'. I brought the guys over here and called you one last time before heading down there myself," she replied.

"Don't. I'll be right there to pick you up," he said, starting the engine.

She could hear it. "Okay," she said in relief, and he put the phone down.

He thrust the gearshift to reverse, then slammed on the brake so that the Mustang rocked and died. Grasping his head with both hands, he uttered, "I would have killed them. I would have killed them. I would have killed them." In horror, he repeated that certainty over and over. Had he known it was his best friend's son getting pummeled in that alley, he would have not stopped until those three boys lay dead.

"Manslaughter, for sure. Maybe even second-degree murder," he whispered. Even now, he did not know how badly they were hurt.

But Streiker, in his mercy, did not tell him that it was Chris receiving a beatdown. Carefully, Sammy restarted the engine and backed into the alley.

When he pulled up to the Taylors' house, he saw Marni waiting on the curb. He had barely stopped before she jumped in, instructing, "Go." He nodded, pulling away again.

"Baylor Medical Center downtown?" he asked.

"Yes."

"Okay."

Once on the freeway, he shouted over the wind, "What happened? Chris should be in school today."

She leaned toward him, holding her hair back. "He played hooky from school with some friends just for fun. They went driving around, then stopped at the convenience store for snacks. These—thugs cornered Chris in the back of the store and forced him out into the alley, then started beating him up for no reason at all. They didn't even rob him." Sammy nodded grimly.

In minutes he turned into the medical center complex and parked near the emergency entrance. They both ran inside, where he stopped at the desk to inquire after Christopher Pruett.

"He's been moved to an inpatient bed," the clerk said briskly.

"What room is that, please? We're family," Marni explained.

After a pause, the clerk replied, "Room one oh four, down the hallway past these doors. But you probably can't get in." Sammy glanced at her vaguely guilty demeanor.

"Thank you," Marni said over her shoulder as Sammy had already pushed open the hallway doors.

Room 104 was easy to locate for the crowd of

teenagers clustered around the door. Pushing past them, Marni said, "Excuse me. Excuse me, please." Thus they were able to squeeze into the room.

When Sammy saw a television news camera, he melted back behind the kids. Now he knew why the clerk looked guilty, and he wondered what she had been bribed with to let the media in.

But Marni pushed forward until she arrived at Chris' bedside. Dave stood to hug her. "Is Kerry all right?" she asked anxiously.

"She will be." He nodded. "I wouldn't let her come because we're bringing him home in just a little while."

Then Marni looked down at Chris, taking his free hand, and he grinned up at her. Both his eyes were blackened and his nose broken. A cheekbone was badly bruised, and his right hand bandaged.

"Aw, don't cry, Bosslady; it was the greatest thing ever." His words were slurred, as he probably had some dental damage, as well.

A woman standing beside the news cameraman said, "Can you tell us what happened, Chris?"

Pruett turned in alarm, evidently just now noticing the reporter in the room, but Chris wanted to talk: "Yeah. Me and my friends were in the store, and one of those freaks started nudging me out the back. I was pushing back pretty good, but those other two grabbed me and dragged me out to the alley. They just started laying into me, all three of 'em. So I started praying—I prayed to Jesus to help me, and then this black angel came—"

"A black man, Chris?" the reporter interrupted.

"No, I don't think so; he was all in black. He just

appeared and started laying them out like you see in the movies. I looked up and they were all lying there in the alley. He looked back at me in the sunlight, and then disappeared," Chris said.

"He disappeared?" the reporter said skeptically.

The kids standing in front of Sammy chimed in, agreeing vehemently with Chris. While Sammy pressed his back to the wall and ducked his head, the camera focused on the girl directly in front of him, who said, "It happened just like he says. This guy all in black appeared out of nowhere and grabbed them one at a time and tore them apart. Then he vanished."

Other voices seconded this, and it was revealed that by the time the cops and ambulance arrived, the mysterious black avenger was nowhere to be found. Not only that, but despite numerous phone cameras aimed at the fracas, no one captured anything of the man but blurry black images. Unanimously, the witnesses asserted that it was divine intervention, even the adults who were watching from the back door of the convenience store when the black avenger struck.

As it turned out, there was one witness who maintained that the rescuer was human. The reporter pulled this witness in front of Sammy to interview him. With their backs to him and their faces to the camera, the interviewer said, "Your name, please?"

"Lucian Marlowe," the man replied. He was a credible-looking 50-year-old in a nice sweater and slacks.

With surprisingly good interviewing technique, the reporter requested, "Tell us what you saw, please, Mr. Marlowe."

"Yes," he said. "I was in the back of the store when I saw the young man here being forced out the back door. That did not look right to me, so I went to see where they went. They remained almost right in front of the door. One man grabbed this boy's arms and pinned them behind his back so that the other two could could hit him with their fists and a baton, it appeared. I called out to the store manager and phoned nine-one-one immediately. Then we watched the boy get beat up."

"No one tried to intervene? Not even in a group?" the reporter asked.

"Oh, no," he said, as if that was out of the question. "But moments later the man in black came running up. He promptly grabbed one and bashed his head into the wall. Another he punched very hard, it seemed. The third ran past him, and he pursued him out of my line of vision." Listening, Sammy unconsciously nodded. It was a remarkably accurate account.

"In your opinion, was this an angel?" she asked, smiling.

"No," he said, smiling as well. "It was a real man. He had black hair, and was dressed completely in black —slacks, shirt, coat—all black."

"Do you think you could identify him if you saw him again?" she asked.

"Yes, certainly. At one point, I was no more than five feet from him, on the other side of the door, of course."

"Well, thank you, Mr. Marlowe." She began moving away to address someone else, and Marlowe turned to exit. Sammy involuntarily met his eyes.

Marlowe glanced at him, then stopped and said,

"Excuse me, please." Sammy hastily moved out of the way so he could leave.

Still in Chris' room, the reporter began interviewing someone else. Speaking to the camera, which was now pointed away from Sammy, she said, "Here with me is Dallas Police spokesman Frasier Witt [whom Sammy did not know]. Corporal Witt, do you have the beating suspects in custody?"

"We certainly do," he said tightly.

"What are their injuries? Are they in this hospital?" she asked.

"I can't comment on that other than to say that all three are receiving medical treatment under the supervision of their guardians or relatives," he replied.

"Were any of their injuries life-threatening?" she asked.

"No," he replied, and Sammy sank against the wall in relief.

"Are any of them minors?" she asked.

He paused before answering, "One, I believe."

"What will they be charged with?" the reporter asked.

Frasier demurred, "We'll have to get with the district attorney and the accused persons' attorneys before we can announce that."

So she quickly asked, "Will they sue the black angel?"

"I don't know," he replied, "but we are intensely interested in hearing from this man, so we ask anyone who has any information about him to please come forward."

Unknown to the interviewer or the police corporal—

but visible to many in the room and everyone watching the broadcast—Dave Pruett had turned around to regard them at the beginning, and his expressive face registered unmistakable contempt, anger, and disgust as the interview progressed. Finally, he turned back to his son with a one-word opinion of the carefully worded departmental stance.

The nurse finally began ushering everyone out, and the news crew left. Marni leaned down to kiss the air beside Chris' cheek. "We'll come see you as soon as your folks can handle Sammy," she promised.

"Gee, why couldn't he come, Mrs. K?" Chris asked. He called her what Mike and Pruett called her.

"Chris," Sammy said from beside the door. He was obliged to wait until a half-dozen more bodies exited before he could make his way to the boy's beside.

"Sammy!" Chris reached up to grab his hand. "I prayed, Sammy, and I know God heard me."

"I guess so, Chris," he said with a slight smile.

"And did you see Jon Ramey throw the game-winning pass against Jacksonville?" Chris exclaimed. His excitement brought on a little pain, and he sank back down.

"I didn't let anybody forget that you prayed for him, too," Sammy said, smiling.

"Yeah," Chris murmured.

He was looking woozy and uncomfortable, so Sammy squeezed his uninjured hand lightly. "You go home and comfort your mom, and we'll check on you later." He gripped Pruett's shoulder momentarily, and Dave nodded.

On their way back to the Mustang, Marni exhaled, "I

feel so much better after seeing him. Sammy, do you think this really was supernatural?"

"That's a good question," he murmured.

"Don't tell me you think Adair was the black angel," she said.

"No, I don't know that she had anything to do with it." He opened the passenger door and she sat, sighing. Then he went around, sat behind the wheel, and turned the ignition.

When he looked over his shoulder to back out, he saw her watching him. "Streiker?" she asked. "Was he involved?"

"Probably," he muttered.

"Sammy, what do you know about this?" she demanded.

"Let's get to your parents' house; I want to hear what they say," he deflected her. They rode in subsequent silence to the Taylors'.

Upon answering the doorbell, Pam asked, "How is he?"

"Ah, okay, I think," Sammy said, stuffing his sunglasses in his shirt pocket and then pausing in slight dread. "It's awfully quiet in here. I don't hear furniture crashing to the floor. Where are the guys?"

"In the back," Pam laughed, gesturing.

He and Marni followed her back to her studio, where she had obviously been painting while keeping an eye on Clayton keeping an eye on Sam, Bubba and Clay in the back yard. While Clayton was reading on his laptop, Clay was doing push-ups in the playpen and the other two were digging jointly in Sam's own corner of the flowerbed.

Sammy observed them, then came back to join Marni as she regarded Pam's work in progress. She was painting the orchid spike, which looked as fresh as it had been three days ago when Sam received it from the hand of the dancer. The leaves and roots on the sections in the jars were continuing to grow. "That's very good, Mom," Marni murmured. Sammy glanced at the orchid, then plopped into the nearest seat.

"Well, I have a three-dimensional photograph to go by," Pam laughed. "So what's up?" she asked carefully.

Surreptitiously, she clipped a blank sheet to her easel and took up a soft pencil. Sammy had unknowingly sat on her portrait sitter's stool to watch the guys outside. When she had live subjects, the comfortable high stool with its padded seat and back, positioned in good light, was her preferred seat for them.

Since she had maneuvered Sammy into only one portrait ever, she was not above taking advantage of what openings were provided her, by accident or stealth. She began sketching him.

Marni, sitting in a wicker rocker that commanded a view of everybody, replied, "Sammy knows something about what happened to Chris, but he wouldn't tell me before we got here." She then informed him, "We're here."

"Yeah," he said, absently gazing outside. "You know that black shirt you bought me on sale? Well, I wore it today. . . ."

ᴺINE

Pam paused in her sketching and Marni sat up with a gasp. "Sammy! You were the black angel! How did you ever—?"

He waved her down. "Listen, my children, and you shall hear—but you can't tell anybody except Clayton. Not Mike, not Charisse, and especially not anybody in the Pruett household."

"Why not Pruett?" Marni asked. Filling in lines, Pam glanced up at him.

"Because—" He grimaced. "Coming on the heels of his Clothier blunder, it's just—too much. Why did Streiker call me and not Chris' own dad?"

"He called you?" Marni asked.

"Sorry. Let me start at the top." Beginning with his inadvertent costuming, Sammy covered the events of the morning: Streiker's call, his short run to the alley, and his takedown of the gangbangers.

Gesturing to Marni, he observed, "Lucian Marlowe's eyewitness account was correct down to the details. But when he turned around and we were eye to eye, he didn't know me from Adam."

"And you didn't know that was Chris in the alley," Marni murmured.

"Oh, no. It gave me heart failure when you told me. Had I known, I'm sure I would have killed them. So instead of looking at assault charges, I'd be facing manslaughter, at least."

Pam faltered only slightly in her sketching, but Marni turned white. "Are you facing charges?" she whispered.

"If they find out who I am, yes, I'm sure they'll press charges. Doesn't matter if they're founded or not; they're a prerequisite for civil suits."

Marni's jaw dropped. "Do you mean you're liable to be sued by the thugs who put Chris in the hospital?"

"Sure," he said. "Repeat after me: 'excessive force.' And I don't even have the official immunity that comes with a badge."

They were silent a moment, looking out to the back yard where Sam was shoveling dirt onto Bubba's back, who was shaking it off. Pam added some finishing touches to her sketch, then covered it with another blank sheet before turning both face down on the easel and clipping them that way. It was the same easel that held her orchid painting, only that sat farther down and to the right. Neither the sketch nor the cover sheet was touching the 11-by-14-inch canvas.

Marni finally said, "Okay, I understand your reasons for keeping quiet. The only thing that bothers me is, Chris thinks that God really sent an angel in response to his prayer."

Sammy looked off. "That is an interesting point. It makes me wonder how many things we think are supernatural have a very ordinary explanation."

"Like the dancer?" Marni asked. "Adair?"

"If it's Adair, she can't be dead," he said.

"But—they published her obituary," she noted.

"Have you ever read a fake obituary?" he asked pointedly.

Her eyes shot up. "Yours."

"Exactly."

They were quiet a moment longer, then Sammy looked at Pam. "I haven't heard what you think about all this."

She hesitated, then said, "I'm just watching."

"Oh, well. Be that way," he muttered.

"What are you going to do now?" Marni asked him.

He got up off the stool, rubbing his neck. "Eh, going back to work, I guess. We've got a ton of backlogged cases. Pruett won't be in today, and I'm not sure about Mike. There's nobody else to get the work done."

There was, actually: Marni had hired Les Hawkins some months ago on a part-time basis, but as his health was failing, he rarely came to the office without being called. His wife Sarah cleaned it for them on a weekly basis—or did, until Jan Breemont's surprise threw them into turmoil.

Sammy paused by the back door, a hand on the door lever. "I'd like to go say hi to Sam, but I already changed once today."

Marni got up quickly to look. The toddler had discovered how to turn on the garden hose, and was gleefully spraying Bubba, who cowered in a corner. Then the wielder of the water turned an ominous eye to the porch, where Clayton lay snoozing and Clay lay trapped in the pen. "Yikes. See you later," Marni said on her way out.

Smiling, Sammy paused by Pam, still seated in front of her easel. He glanced at the painting of the orchid and she smiled at him, as the sketch was safely hidden. "Yeah," he breathed tentatively, looking outside, which meant, *I'd like to take the dog with me, but not a wet dog, and neither am I willing to dry him off and clean his muddy feet.* Then he went on out while she threw a cover over the easel.

On his way to the office, he got tacos and a soft drink at a drive-through, which he didn't attempt to eat on the road. Pulling up to their shopfront, he found so many cars in the lot that he had to park in front of the church. He believed that they were all patronizing the new Chinese restaurant for lunch, but, taking no chances, he walked around to the alley and entered his office through the back door.

It was empty, as he expected. Placing his fast-food order on his desk, he pushed the blinking message button on the phone and heard Mike say, "Hey, Sambo. I'm helping Kerry rearrange Chris' furniture to accommodate the adjustable bed they rented. He should be home in a couple of hours, so better look for me tomorrow."

Sammy nodded in agreement, then sat and opened his laptop to begin an internet search on his latest target. He typed industriously (with two fingers) referencing the information from the file at his elbow. Then he looked at the fields in the online application to see that he had filled them with gibberish.

Closing the laptop, he picked up the phone and

scrolled to a recent number, which he auto-dialed. In a moment the other party answered: "Hello."

Sammy straightened. "Mr. Streiker, this is Sammy Kidman. I . . . don't know if you've seen the news. I attempted to do what you asked; I hope it was the right thing."

"Well, was Chris satisfied with your help?" Streiker asked.

"Yes, although he doesn't know it was me, and I don't think I should tell him," Sammy said.

"All right," Streiker replied.

Sammy sat there, knowing that the man was too busy to hang on the phone while he worked up the courage to ask him questions. Teeth chattering, Sammy said, "M-Mr. Streiker, was that your wife you were dancing with at the Arboretum?"

Streiker laughed easily. "Sure. She's a dancer, so she thinks she can turn me into one."

"This is going to sound crazy," Sammy said, his voice unnaturally high, "but, is she—Adair?" He changed the question at the last second.

"Yes," Streiker said. "I understand you met her at the Arts Festival in Richardson. She's taken a strong liking to your family."

"I'm very appreciative of that, sir," Sammy said. Another call lit up his phone, and he said, "Okay, I'd better get that. Thank you for talking with me, Mr. Streiker."

"Any time, Sammy."

Pressing the blinking button, Sammy said, "MK and associates. This is Sammy Kidman."

"Where's your phone, idiot?" Dave asked.

"I have no idea. I probably dropped it in the toilet," Sammy replied. Mercifully, it never occurred to him to worry that he might have lost it in the alley. "How is he, Pruett?"

"Okay, considering." Dave's voice cracked. "Mild concussion, broken nose, cracked cheek bone, fracture of the fifth and sixth ribs. Would have been a lot worse had that guy not showed up when he did. Do you know—Chris is sure it was an angel. I watched the video uploads, and—"

"There are video uploads?" Sammy asked in alarm, opening the laptop.

"Yeah, gone viral. Anyway, we're going to get him settled at home this afternoon—I'm waiting on the doc to discharge him now—and then I'll be in tomorrow," Pruett said.

"Okay," Sammy said, searching online. "Marni wanted to come see him tonight."

Dave balked, "Eh, let's give him a chance to rest. He's in a lot of pain, and the doc hasn't given him anything but ibuprofen. Have her call Kerry tomorrow about a good time."

"Right," Sammy said, and Dave clicked off. Meanwhile, Sammy entered a search for videos under the key words "black angel." The first three hits were indeed videos from this morning. His gut coiling, Sammy clicked on the first.

It was jarring to helplessly watch somebody get a beatdown. The video itself was understandably jerky and blurry, as the girl recording it was crying. But suddenly one of the hoods beating on Chris turned around and ran into the back wall of the convenience store, then dropped. There was a black shadow, and the second guy fell out of the picture frame. The third guy let go of Chris to run away from the camera, and the blackness pursued him until he fell.

Sammy chewed his lip, then replayed it. He checked the other two uploads, but neither was as clear as the first. So he went back to it, replaying it with frequent pauses. His face was at no point visible. It wasn't even apparent that he had a face. But the faces of the gangbangers, and that of another boy who inadvertently got in the camera frame, were reasonably clear. Even Chris' battered face was visible at the end, when somebody helped him up to bring him inside. Sammy clicked on all other possibly relevant videos, but they showed nothing more, and much less than the first.

However, there was one video that gave him very valuable information that none of the others contained. This video, filmed through the convenience-store door, started the moment after Chris had been forced outside —it actually caught the biggest hood shoving him out. From that point on, the video was unfocused and partially blocked by people rushing to the door to look out. But the filming was continuous until the black shadow appeared and hoods started falling. From the very beginning to the point of Sammy's appearance was exactly 2 minutes and 14 seconds.

He sat back, absorbing this, while his tacos and soft drink sat untouched. If there were no other videos or photos, no one could identify him as the black angel. There was no evidence linking him at all to the scene, except—

Sammy suddenly shut the laptop and pushed back

from his desk. He went to the front door, unlocked it, exited, and locked it behind him again.

On his way to his car, he did an about-face to return to the agency door. He unlocked it again, then went back to his desk to look at the orchids. There were the three of them, arching gracefully over the sides of the tall cup, unwatered, unwilted. He blinked at them for a moment, then took up the laptop and left the office, again locking the door behind him. The tacos and soft drink remained untouched on his desk.

Arriving home, he noted that Marni's Prius was still gone; the house still vacant. Shedding his jacket, Sammy went to get the clothes hamper and lug it to the laundry room. There, he began unloading his black slacks, shirt and sports coat into the washing machine. He paused over the sports coat, then stuffed it into the machine. If it got ruined, too bad. He wasn't about to take it to a dry cleaner's.

When he extracted his jeans from the hamper, his phone fell out. "There you are," Sammy said conversationally, fishing it out of the pile of dirty clothes. When he turned it on and saw the number of messages, he winced and turned it off again. He finished loading the machine, added detergent, and started it.

Half an hour later, Sammy was eating a sandwich and deleting phone messages at the kitchen table. The laptop sat beside his plate. He heard the garage door open, but before he could bestir himself to get up and go help Marni with the guys, the door opened to the marauding hordes.

He barely had a chance to grab onto the edge of the counter behind him before Bubba leaped into his lap.

The swivel chair rocked dangerously backward.

"Dadadada!" exclaimed Sam from somewhere behind the great furry body that Sammy was trying to dislodge from his lap while keeping the chair upright.

"Well!" Marni's voice said, and he was dimly aware of a diaper bag coming to rest on the table. "You could have told me you were home!"

"Help," he said, smothered in coarse brown fur. Bubba sniffed his sandwich.

"What's that?" she said. "Did you say, 'I'd love to help you bring in all this stuff since I'm just sitting here'?"

"Sure," he said, muffled. Bubba jumped down, preparatory to taking the rest of the sandwich with him to eat in the family room. Sammy yelped at the clawed feet pushing off from his groin. Sam, dirty and damp, climbed up in the newly vacated lap.

"Did you just put on a load of laundry?" she asked in disbelief. She lifted Clay out of the carrier and sat him in her lap.

"Yeah," he squeaked, then cleared his throat. "Washing the black clothes I wore this morning. Look at this." Opening his laptop, he found the black angel video and turned the laptop around to her.

While she intently watched the screen, he bounced his firstborn. "Hey, Sam. What've you got there? Ah, more bugs. Yummy."

"Is that you?" she glanced up, astonished. "That— shadowy movement is you?"

"Interesting, isn't it?" he said, cocking his head. "Anyway, once I saw that, I wanted to come make sure there was no other evidence linking me to the scene."

"Your clothes?" she asked, brow furrowed.

"Yeah, there was blood, and, other bodily fluids," he explained.

"Ew," she said. "Thanks for washing them yourself."

"Yeah," he laughed halfheartedly, receiving the remains of insects which Sam pulled from his pockets to show him. For lack of any place else, he put them on his now-empty plate. Bubba returned to the kitchen, tail wagging, to see what else might be on the table.

"Oh, Bubba might be hungry. I don't know that anybody fed him at Mom's," she said. Clay started fussing and thrashing, as well.

Lifting Sam off his lap to get up himself, Sammy groused, "Well, he's not as hungry as he was." Nonetheless, he filled Bubba's bowl so the dog could eat legitimately.

Sitting again, Sammy said, "I called Mr. Streiker back this afternoon."

She quickly looked up from unbuttoning her shirt. "And?"

"I . . . just wanted to touch base with him about this morning, to make sure I did the right thing," he said tentatively.

"Sammy! What else could you have done?" she exclaimed.

"I dunno," he said uneasily. "I was pretty rough."

She sneered, "What, would they have stopped beating on Chris if you just asked them nicely?"

"I know, I know." He gestured hazily.

"So what did he say?" She opened her shirt front to Clay, who quickly latched on.

Sammy was a little distracted watching them, then blinked. "Streiker. Well, he seemed to say that if Chris was satisfied, then he was, too. I told him that Chris didn't know it was me, and I wasn't going to tell him it was, and he seemed okay with that, too. Then I asked him if that was his wife he was dancing with at the Arboretum, and he said, yeah, she was trying to make a dancer out of him. And he knew about my seeing her at the Arts Festival."

She listened quietly while he explained all this. "And?" she asked, sensing more.

"I asked him if that was Adair, and he said yes," Sammy related. He had to move the plate of bug pieces to the middle of the table to keep Sam from eating them. "Are you hungry, too?" he asked, getting up with him.

While Sammy hoisted his son over the sink to wash his hands and arms, Marni asked, "Did you ask . . . ?"

"If that was the same Adair who died?" he said with curled lip. "I just couldn't get the words out." Leaning into the refrigerator, he brought out a cheese stick which he unwrapped and handed to Sam.

"Okay, there are only two possibilities," she said over Clay. "Either she survived and they ran a fake obituary to keep the press away, or it's not the same Adair."

"That makes sense," he agreed. "But it doesn't explain the weird stuff, like my broken arm that suddenly wasn't."

She grew still. "I forgot about that," she said in a low voice.

"Here's the *coup de grâce*," he said, leaning back. "I found another video that doesn't show much except for the total time of the attack before I arrived: two minutes and fourteen seconds. Not counting the seconds that elapsed while he was shoved outside and arms pinned, Chris was beaten for exactly two minutes and eight seconds. Now, it took me at least six to seven minutes to get from my office to that alley—"

"He called you before it happened," she whispered.

"Bingo. If I had hung up right away without asking any questions and run to that alley, I would have arrived just about the time they pushed him outside," he added.

They sat there looking at each other. "Who is he?" she whispered.

"I don't know," he said, with a wary shake of his head, "but he doesn't operate under the same constraints as the rest of us." Then he got up to open the freezer and pull out some fish fillets.

While Marni bathed Sam and Clay (Bubba having already been bathed, so to speak, at Mamaw's), Sammy fixed them dinner of baked fish, french fries and cole slaw. They enjoyed a quiet dinner, although Sam was heartbroken over the mysterious disappearance of his bug fragments.

Marni and Sam took Bubba out back for his bathroom break, then she tucked all three guys in bed while Sammy loaded the dishwasher. He answered the phone when it rang, so she unloaded wet clothes from the washer into the dryer. She shook out the sports coat and hung it up to dry, hoping to salvage it.

When she came out of the laundry room, he was just hanging up. "Pruett says give him a few days before we come by—he's feeling it now, and Kerry is being ultra conservative with the narcotics."

"Poor Chris. Poor Kerry! A mom feels things like that," she murmured.

Sammy blinked. "That reminds me of something else Streiker said. He said that Adair had taken a strong liking to my family. Not to me, mind you: to my family."

Marni looked away, smiling. "I like her," she said softly. "Some people sing when they're happy; some people dance. She's dancing because she's so happy. And, she's crazy in love."

"Not with me," he disavowed.

She looked at him, her almond eyes slitted in fond amusement. "No. Not with you."

After his customary 5-mile run and workout the following morning, Sammy showered and dressed in comfortable slacks, blue cotton shirt, and sports coat to go into work. All of Marni's associates had stopped wearing ties except on days that they knew they had interviews. For surprise visits, they kept a motley collection of ties at the office, all of which were freely appropriated by any one of them as was necessary.

"I have *got* to get some work done today," he vowed. Before leaving, he made sure to take his phone. He didn't give a thought to the laptop because Marni, knowing him, had put it in the front seat of the Mustang the previous evening.

Stopping in the kitchen where Sam was having cereal, Sammy opened his mouth to call Bubba. Sam, seeing that, dropped his spoon and threw himself on the dog. "Don't take the Bubba!" he cried. Bubba looked at Sammy, his tail thumping the floor, but he did not move, apparently interested in whatever might be left in the bowl whenever Sam abandoned it.

Marni came into the kitchen with Clay. "What?" she asked generally.

"That's up to Mom," Sammy said. "Sam doesn't want me to take Bubba. What do you want me to do?"

She looked torn as the toddler stubbornly clung to the dog. "Well . . . Sam, will you mind me about him? If you don't mind me, I'll ask Daddy to come back at lunch and get him."

"I mind," Sam pleaded.

"Okay," she said, rolling her eyes. "Just check back with us at lunch. Do you have your phone?"

"Yes," he murmured, reaching over to kiss her. Clay turned his head to look at his dad, and Sammy caressed the smooth, sparsely covered head. "Okay," he said, bending to look Sam in the eye. "Here's your chance to prove you're big enough to have Bubba all day."

"K," Sam said tentatively.

Sammy leaned over to kiss his head, then with a glance at Marni, turned out to the garage.

He was so distracted driving to work that he neglected to stop for his customary coffee and breakfast biscuit. And he was hardly surprised to be the first to arrive at the office. But he was very pleased with himself for remembering his laptop.

He unlocked the office and turned on lights, but did not raise the blinds. Then he went straight back to the kitchenette to make coffee. While that brewed, he went to his desk to lay down the laptop and look at the orchids. They were just the same, all three of them.

Then he blinked at the soft drink and tacos still

sitting on his desk. He dumped the flat, watery drink in the sink, but ate the tacos and drank coffee while he scanned the morning headlines.

Regarding yesterday's incident, he saw that all three gangbangers were to be charged with aggravated assault, one as a juvenile and the other two as adults. The police department again requested information on the identity of the black angel, but had found no useable photos of him from any video. The parents of the injured boy, a minor, had refused further interviews, requesting that his name and address not be published. (The television interviewer had identified him only as "Chris.")

Sammy's eye lit on another article that made him laugh out loud. There had been a *third* sighting of the Mystery Woman and Her Wolf Dog a mile farther away from the Kidman house than Sighting #2. This time, the blonde in high heels and pearl-gray suit was spotted in a north Richardson park. Since the dog with her was unleashed, a bike rider who had experienced previous encounters with unleashed dogs called the cops.

He knew nothing about the Mystery Woman, but his dead-on description of her was picked up by a stringer for Channel 7, who arrived at the park at the same time as a team from Channel 2. While the rider pointed out where he had seen her, the subsequent fight by competing news teams had to be broken up by the cops when they arrived, so the opportunity to catch the woman was lost.

Shaking his head over that, Sammy spotted something else: a photo of Adair Weiss' coworker leaving the the Richardson branch of The Rivers Bank, her head down in the midst of the cameras. She had seen something at the woman's bedside upon her death, but consistently refused to say what. Sammy studied the bulky black glasses that she was about to push back on her face.

Seeing nothing further of interest in the news, Sammy closed the browser and dug in his side drawer for the file on the case he was working yesterday. He located the new address, then ran a search on it to determine if it was rented or owned by the delinquent parent.

All this time, his heart was pounding and his mouth dry. While pretending to concentrate on tracking down this particular deadbeat who may have good reasons for being delinquent, Sammy was waiting on a phone call that might or might not come—a call that might require him to act immediately to save someone's life, possibly someone close to him.

The office phone rang, and he plucked it up. "MK and associates; this is Sammy Kidman."

"Hello, Sammy. Will you do something else for me today?" It was Streiker.

TEN

Sammy stood so abruptly that his desk chair shot back six feet. "Yes, sir."

"Okay, great," Streiker said. "Relax; it's not quite as time-sensitive as the surprise I dumped on you yesterday. Sit down."

"All right," Sammy said, flailing behind him for the desk chair. He finally turned around to locate it and drag it under his posterior at the desk. "I'm sitting down."

"Good." There was a pause. "Sammy, do you remember Jessica Threlkeld?"

"Dolly's granddaughter? Sure," Sammy said. Dolly Threlkeld, widow of Dallas pioneer and oil magnate Morgan Threlkeld, was the matriarch of one of Dallas' wealthiest families. Sammy and Marni had worked undercover as chauffeur and maid with the Threlkeld family almost four years ago, before she had become pregnant with Sam.

Then Sammy's dad had gone to work for Dolly as chauffeur, eventually becoming her lover and second husband (in that order). He had died in a car accident last January, leaving her a widow for the second time.

Streiker said, "I need you to find Jess and bring her to the Officina Gentium warehouse in Fort Worth."

Sammy blinked. "All right. Do you have any information to get me started?"

"No, my people lost touch with her entirely," Streiker said.

"I'll get right on it," Sammy said.

"Good," Streiker replied, and hung up.

Sammy replaced the receiver, muttering, "Offuh-keena what? In Fort Worth? Eh, I'll clarify that when I find her."

He mulled this over, clicking his tongue. Jess was just a couple of years younger than Marni. She had gone to Radcliffe to please her grandmother, but he didn't think she ever got a degree because she didn't want an education; she wanted to go into the theater. Then she had come home again—he remembered hearing before his dad died that she was pregnant (not by him, thank the heavens above). Obviously, if Streiker couldn't find her, then she was no longer at Dolly's.

And that was all he could remember. So he picked up the receiver again and speed-dialed home. "Hello?" Marni answered.

"Hey, baby. Everything okay there?" he began.

"Yes. What happened?"

"Nothing bad, only—Streiker called me with another job. He wants me to find Jess Threlkeld and deposit her in one of his warehouses in Fort Worth."

"Okayyy," she said slowly.

"Baby, I—I'm going to give this assignment

priority, so I don't know when I'll be home. I may have to go out of town. I will definitely have to go to Fort Worth when I get her. Are you okay with that?" he asked.

"Sure, Sammy. My parents are right here, and Sam and Bubba are keeping each other company. Besides, it would be kind of stupid for me to get petty after what Streiker did for us, wouldn't it?"

"You sure are smart, for a girl," he said, smiling. He listened to her snort, then said, "First thing, I've got to get some background information. Do you still have Dolly's number, by any chance?"

"I bet so. Hang on," she said, and he could almost see her going to the desk in the front room.

Hearing a faint crash on her end, he asked in alarm, "What was that?"

"Nothing. Bubba and Sam. Here it is," she said, and read the number to him. As he wrote it down, she asked, "What do you think Dolly can tell you?"

"Nothing much helpful. But I'm not going to talk to her. Okay, thanks, baby. I'll check in later."

"Okay. I love you, Sammy."

"I love you, baby."

He hung up, eyeing the number, then lifted the receiver and dialed. "C'mon, I'm counting on you to still be there," he breathed, listening to the phone ring on the other end.

"Threlkeld residence."

"Hellier! You are there! This is Sammy Kidman."

"Sammy, it's good to hear from you," Dolly's longtime butler said warmly. "I'm sorry that Mrs. Threlkeld is not in."

"She's not the one I want to talk to, Hellier; you are. But how is she doing?" Sammy asked.

Hellier paused. "Fair, Sammy. She was crushed when Miss Threlkeld left."

"Yeah, I need to hear all about that, Hellier."

"Well, I presume you knew that Miss Threlkeld was pregnant. She came home and had the baby, a girl, August fifth"—a little over three months ago. "Mrs. Threlkeld hired a full-time nanny so that Miss Threlkeld could join a theater group in Dallas—it was the, ah, Prometheus Unbound group in what used to be the White Mountain Theater," Hellier related.

"Uh huh," Sammy said, writing. Yes, he knew the place. "Then what?"

"Mr. Threlkeld [Dolly's son and Jess' father Stan] did not approve of this arrangement at all. He stipulated that Miss Threlkeld must either go to school full-time or get a paying job. Oh, dear, the arguments were terrible to overhear. Mr. Threlkeld accused Mrs. Threlkeld of interfering, and she insisted that she was merely trying to provide stability for her great-granddaughter."

"What's the baby's name, Hellier?"

"Augusta Mellon Threlkeld."

"Do you have the father's name?"

"Oh, dear," Hellier murmured. "All I remember is Ethan. Ethan something."

"Okay, then what?" Sammy asked, writing furiously.

"It all came to a head a week ago—yes, it's been exactly a week, last Wednesday, that Miss Threlkeld decided that she'd had enough. She left, and left Gussie," Hellier said.

Sammy paused in dismay. "She left with the baby?"

"No, excuse my poor wording. Miss Threlkeld left Gussie here. Oh, Mrs. Threlkeld was beside herself, that she would disappear like that. Miss Threlkeld called her that evening and told her not to worry, but we've heard nothing since. Mrs. Threlkeld has engaged a private detective agency to find her."

"Which one?" Sammy asked.

"Ah, I do believe the name was Dunbar and Smith," Hellier related.

Sammy covered his eyes in aggravation, then sighed deeply, looking over his notes. "Have they reported back?"

"Nothing positive, from what I hear," Hellier said.

"Okay, Hellier, this is why I'm asking. Someone who is deeply concerned about Jess has asked me to find her. I think I can do better than Dunbar and Smith, but I'll need your help. Will you help me?"

"Absolutely, Sammy."

"Great. First thing, I need clearance from your security guy to get in," Sammy said.

"Oh, Mr. McConnico is no longer here," Hellier said.

"No? Why not?"

"Mrs. Threlkeld fired him after he was found in bed with Miss Threlkeld," Hellier related.

"The security guy tried to lay her?" Sammy asked in astonishment. *The stupid: it burns.*

"Actually, there is considerable evidence that Miss Threlkeld set him up in order to dispose of him, but—as he was indeed caught in bed with her, that was rather beside the point," Hellier sniffed.

"So who's there now?" Sammy asked.

"He has not been replaced yet," Hellier replied.

Sammy suppressed a groan, then shook it off. "Okay, here's how you can help: I need every scrap of information about Jess: any forms, documents, charge receipts—I want to see anything that has anything to do with her. If you can start gathering these, I'd like to come photograph them. The right piece of paper could lead me directly to her."

"I believe I can find what you need. When will you be out this way?" Hellier asked.

"I'm on my way, Hellier," Sammy said, standing.

"I'll open the gate for you," Hellier replied.

"Thanks." And Sammy hung up. Before leaving, he made sure to store the Threlkelds' number in his phone —and, for that matter, Streiker's.

Minutes after he had climbed into the Mustang, exited on to the frontage road and accessed the freeway, a dark green sedan pulled up to Great Deal Life Insurance Company and parked. Two men got out; one knocked on the office doors, peering in through the tiny holes of the blind slats, while the other did the same at the church next door. A minute later they met back at the car. "It's empty," one said, looking back at the forlorn Great Deal.

"Same here," the other said, gesturing to the church. So they shrugged, climbed back into the car, and departed.

Within 15 minutes Sammy was pulling up to the scrolled iron gates of the Threlkeld estate, now standing open. It was painful driving up the cobbled driveway again, knowing that his dad had found a very comfortable life here and then stupidly threw it all away.

Firmly shutting down that part of his recollection, Sammy drove to the back of the house so that his bright green Mustang would not alert Dolly to his presence, whenever she came home. And he took care to park beyond the view of the sunroom windows.

Hellier met him at the delivery entrance. "Hello, Sammy. Come to the library."

"Thanks, Hellier." Sammy shook his hand and patted his shoulder on his way into the house. "How's—Mary!" he said, looking into the kitchen as he passed.

Hellier's wife, the Threlkelds' cook, looked back in surprise as Sammy came into the kitchen to give her a warm hug and kiss on the cheek. "Jim Brandon," she murmured, referring to his alias.

He grinned. "Don't give me a reason to spank you."

"Oh! Go on now! Ha ha ha ha!" she tittered, and Sammy turned out, smiling.

"She needed me to do that," Sammy explained to Hellier, who merely sighed.

They entered the library and Hellier shut the door. First thing, Sammy noted that all the electronic surveillance equipment remained, although it was presently shut off. "First," Hellier said, presenting Sammy with a file folder, "here is everything that we gave to Dunbar and Smith to begin their search."

"Excellent," Sammy said, leafing through the forms, receipts and printouts. "How long have they been on the case?"

"Mrs. Threlkeld called them day before yesterday, I believe," Hellier said. "They came out yesterday to interview her."

"Ah," Sammy said. *Streiker would have known that,*

he mused. *But apparently he doesn't have much confidence in them, with good reason.*

He started to take out his phone to photograph the records, but Hellier said, "You may take that file, as long as it's returned at some point."

"You're a good man, Hellier," Sammy said, tucking it underarm. "Now that you've given me the official records, I need the unofficial ones."

"What would those be?" Hellier asked.

"Notes that no one thinks important, especially those with the names, phone numbers or addresses of people in her theater group. Any phone messages, letters or photos of the people in this group. Any information about people she went out with or brought to the house," Sammy said. "And if you don't care to dig through trash cans looking for such notes, I'd be happy to."

Hellier's brows drew together as he thought about this. "It's been a week, so I'm afraid that all trash cans that contained such notes would have been emptied. But I will confer with the maid."

He started to step out, but Sammy stopped him. Moving over the security system, Sammy pressed the power icon to turn it on. "And I want the passwords for your system."

Hellier leaned over a niche to bring out a black operating manual. "Everything should be in here."

"Excellent," Sammy repeated, flipping it open. "Did Dunbar and Smith happen to look at your surveillance?"

"Oh, no. No one's touched that equipment since Mr. McConnico left," Hellier stated.

"Ah. Virgin material," Sammy smirked as Hellier left.

Referring to the notebook, Sammy entered the passwords and watched the system boot up. He knew quite a bit about this system, actually. After glimpsing it during his very brief employment at FirstPlace Bank Tower, he had lusted after it so that when he and Marni had opened their own agency, he had desired to install one in their office.

But Marni had balked at the cost—over a million dollars—so had required him to justify it in writing to her. Researching its vast capabilities convinced him that it was indeed overkill for their four-man operation, and he dropped it.

Today, he leaned over the monitors to note their coverage zones. Outside the house, there were cameras on the front entry, back entry, garage, pool, gardens, gazebo, tennis court, and back patio. Inside the house, the entry hall, dining hall, reception room, kitchen/laundry area, back hallway, gameroom *and library* were covered.

Sammy looked up quickly to locate the surveillance camera in this room. After a moment, he found it in a high corner. Smiling to himself, he returned to the console.

McConnico had told him that the bedrooms were not monitored, and that appeared to be the case. But just out of contrariness, Sammy explored all options on the control panel.

Toggling a switch, he suddenly found himself staring at what used to be Bobby's—and his dad's— bedroom, now empty. Toggling the switch again brought up the gameroom, as was labeled in the notebook. But the unlabeled toggle unmistakably showed the bedroom.

"You liar, McConnico; you *were* watching the bedrooms. No wonder Jess wanted you gone," he muttered. He took out a pen to begin noting the hidden surveillance in the notebook, and which rooms they piggy-backed.

Hellier entered, and Sammy looked up. "I'm sorry, Sammy; the maid says that all trash cans have been emptied since Miss Threlkeld left."

"That's okay, Hellier; I'm going over your surveillance. Listen—it may take me a couple of hours, so I'll come find you if I need anything else, and I'll let myself out the back door when I'm done. Also . . . Dolly doesn't have to know I'm here. I don't want to resurrect painful memories for her." Despite the 19-year age difference between Sammy and his father, the resemblance was startling. Or, had been.

"Certainly, Sammy. I . . . hope you find her," Hellier said.

"Oh, no fear," Sammy uttered, and Hellier withdrew smiling. *But I'm not to bring her back here,* Sammy thought uneasily.

"First things first," he reminded himself, returning to the monitors. The electronic log enabled him to go straight to videos of occasions that Jess had entertained visitors. Zooming in on these brought up name tags on faces as well as context of acquaintance, such as "Jarrod Bathe, Prometheus Unbound" on one clear facial shot of a bearded young man. And Sammy had to print nothing or write nothing to save these photos; with a touch and number entry, he could send them to his work email or phone.

Among Jess' guests, he recognized several members

of the old White Mountain Theater Group, including Alex, the director, and Tony—was he the stage manager? Sammy couldn't quite remember.

"Prometheus Unbound," he muttered. "That sounds a little highbrow for this group." Opening the internet browser connected to the security system, he discovered that the original *Prometheus Unbound* was a play written by Percy Bysshe Shelley, the title of which had been appropriated, knowingly or not, by Jess' group.

A further search revealed that this group was formally established shortly after her return to Dallas (with Threlkeld money, no doubt). Jess was listed as a founding troupe member, as was Jarrod Bathe. Sammy copied all this information to his phone.

Then he returned to the surveillance videos. Since he didn't spend any time ogling Jess in her underwear (because Marni had a better body), Sammy had loads of information about her acquaintances after watching just forty minutes of tagged video. And the next place he needed to go, definitely, was the theater.

He started to shut the system off, then paused. Just to see what might be there, he opened the electronic log for his dad's movements. Mostly, the motion-activated cameras caught him going and coming, usually very late in the evening or early in the morning. Remembering their last conversation, Sammy felt his chest tighten.

Noting an afternoon entry in the log, Sammy brought up that video. And he watched his dad enter his bedroom, shutting the door behind him, and bring out a cell phone in some agitation. Sammy frowned; he never knew that his dad had acquired a phone. Sam placed a call and put the phone to his ear. By turning up the volume on the monitor, Sammy was able to hear him clearly:

"Hi, Carla. I've made up my mind. I'm gonna divorce Dolly so that we can be together like we were always meant to be. I . . . I've been prayin', Carla— yeah, I've been talking to God, trying to figure out how to make my life right, and—yeah, it's gonna be okay. I have somethin' to take care of tomorrow, then I'm coming out to your place. Okay. Bye." Carla was Sammy's birth mother, a mere seventeen years old when she got pregnant with him. Her parents had Sam put away for rape for ten years upon the discovery of her pregnancy.

Sammy continued to watch the monitor impassively as Sam made another call. Sammy leaned forward to hear him say: "Heather? Yeah, it's Sam. Listen, I . . . we gotta call it quits, babe. Dolly's gettin' on to us, and there'll be nothin' for either of us if she gets wind of it. . . . Yeah, now—oh, don't. C'mon, don't start that. I hate it when you cry like that. . . . No, really, we can't. . . . Well, I suppose. . . ."

Sam sighed deeply. "Okay, I'll be over. But this is it. This is the last time." He put the phone away, shaking his head in shame or disgust. Then he looked up to the ceiling, almost directly at the hidden camera, and said, "God, this is the last time. I promise. I'm going to toe the line and walk the straight and narrow after tonight." With that promise, he took up his jacket and left.

Seeing the jacket Sam had slung over his shoulder, Sammy's eyes narrowed in recognition. He remembered that jacket . . . covered in blood. So he tapped the panel to bring up the date of this recording: January 18. The day before Sam's death. He'd had a girl in the car with him at the time of the crash. She had walked away.

So Sam's promise proved true: it was the last time. "What's that verse?" Sammy murmured. "That if you make a vow to God, you better pay it, because He'll require it of you one way or another." Watching his father die had knocked Sammy into a catatonic stupor, but once he came out of it, he was done grieving.

Again he reached out to shut the system down, then noticed the remote-access icon on the master panel. It was green, which meant that the system was being remotely monitored. Someone was operating the system remotely to continue recording the family. And the only one who could be doing that was McConnico.

Pulling out the black operating manual again, Sammy searched for a code that he couldn't remember, but knew was there. "Aha," he muttered. "There you are." Accessing the system registry, he entered this code and restarted the system. Then a dialog box opened that said, *Preparing to execute Domesday. Continue or Quit?* Sammy elected to continue.

Remote files quarantined. Continue Domesday or Quit? inquired the dialog box. Sammy pressed *Continue.*

Remote files permanently erased. Continue Domesday or Quit? Sammy chose, *Continue.*

Trojan.Centrifuge.A downloaded to remote system. Continue Domesday or Quit? Sammy instructed, *Continue.*

Sammy had to wait a few minutes at this point. While waiting, he went over his notes on Jess thus far, whistling. Then the dialog box informed him: *Remote hard drive wiped. Domesday completed.* Sammy pressed, *OK*. "Don't be evil, McConnico," he advised.

He shut down the system and got up, pausing to write the passwords in his notebook, just in case. Then he took up the file folder and went on out to his car. After starting the engine, he leaned over to stuff Hellier's file on Jess in the glove compartment.

Wanting to get away from this place, both spiritually and physically, he left the grounds and turned on to Royal Lane before calling his house on his car phone. The answering machine came on, so he thumbed the button and called his in-laws' house.

"Hey, Pam," he said when she answered. "Is my gadabout wife over there?"

Pam laughed, "She just got here. I'll call her." Sammy heard her put down the phone, walk away, and call her daughter.

Entering the studio, Pam said, "Oh, I thought you were in the gameroom. Sammy's on the line. You can pick it up right there." She pointed to an extension on a side table.

"Oh, thanks, Mom. The boys are back in their mud hole," she said in some exasperation, gesturing to Sam and Bubba digging in his corner of the flower beds.

Pam glanced at Clay in the carseat at her feet before looking out to the back yard, where Clayton was standing over the pair. At first she thought he was scolding his grandson—something she had never seen the softhearted grandpa do before. Then she saw him present Sam with a more efficient hand shovel than the spoon he had purloined from the kitchen. Sam accepted it gratefully and put it right to use. Chuckling, Pam went back to hang up the kitchen telephone.

When she returned to the studio, Marni was asking over the phone, "So how's it going?" She listened, glancing outside, then said, "Oh, good, I hope you find her quickly. We're going to spend the night here, so if you miraculously finish up before ten tomorrow morning, you'll know where to find us. . . ."

Idly listening, Pam turned to the half-finished orchid painting, still covered from yesterday. First she checked the orchid spike in the packing peanuts, which was fresh and new as ever. The budding leaves and roots on the sections in jars were growing and healthy. With a mild shake of her head, Pam uncovered the painting—

And drew in a quick breath. There was the pencil sketch she had done of Sammy—except not on the separate sketch sheet, but on the same canvas as the orchid, behind it.

ELEVEN

Pam stared at the canvas while Marni chatted to Sammy over the phone. The sketch sheet was still clipped to the corner of the canvas where Pam had left it yesterday. Tentatively, she unclipped it and turned it over, removing the cover sheet to find it blank. Baffled, she looked at the front and back of both sheets, which were blank. The pencil sketch in its entirety had been transferred to the orchid background.

Marni hung up. "I told you that Streiker asked Sammy to find Jessica Threlkeld, didn't I? He feels like he's making good progress. He found video footage of some members of her theater group, so he's going out there to talk to them."

She came up to look at the canvas. "Oh, Mom! What a great composition! I had no idea you were going to put Sammy in the painting with the orchid but it makes sense. When did you—oh, you sketched him when he was on your sitter's stool yesterday! You sneak. Gosh, that's great. It looks like you planned it that way all along. He'll kill you when he sees it. It'll be worth it." She glanced outside to see some transgression in progress which required her attention, and hurried out.

Hesitantly, Pam began mixing paints to get the right shades for Sammy's skin in the painting.

Meanwhile, the model for the sketch was pulling into the upscale shopping center that housed the newly formed theatrical group. Since there was a sale in progress at the flagship department store nearby, Sammy had to park in the hinterlands and walk. As he always did when parking in uncertain regions, he raised the top and locked the Mustang. Some people just couldn't resist doing stuff to a white leather interior.

On the long trek to the door, he thought back four years ago when, newly saved and newly married, he had been given the assignment to audition undercover for *As You Like It* in order to uncover credit-card fraud. The millionaire perpetrator of that penny-ante scheme never did time, or was seriously inconvenienced in any way for his activities.

But that was the first of a long series of stupid assignments that the department saddled him with, to try to get rid of him. After his premarital mental breakdown, they would never entrust important cases to him again.

And he wondered, why had they punished Mike and Pruett as well—both quality cops? Because, he decided, those two would never kiss up to Lt. Kerr. Pruett didn't even try to make sergeant until Kerr had been discredited, partly because of that crazy arenaball assignment that so nearly blew up in Sammy's face— would have, had not Marni and Dolly laid down some quality investigative work of their own.

This reminiscing carried him to the theater door, and

he paused to regard the sign advertising, "NEWLY OPENED: Prometheus Unbound Artistic Group presents 'The Importance of Being Earnest,' Opening Dec. 26. Tickets On Sale NOW." He vaguely wondered how they would promote the play if the group decided to put on *Prometheus Unbound*.

The door was unlocked, so Sammy went into the theater, ambling up a side aisle to the stage. *Wow, it feels strange to be back here*, he thought. Three people were on stage, apparently blocking out a scene around a couch. Jess was not among them.

One bearded man holding a script turned to glance at him, then paused. "Why—Chase! Chase Carruthers. Where have you been?"

Sammy made the instantaneous decision to play along using his old alias, even though he knew that the reporters had outed him as a cop after his rescue of a kidnapped newborn. What he did not know was that the cast and crew paid no attention to anything but reviews.

"Alex! Hey." He reached up to shake the director's hand. "Aw, I was just passing through, curious to see if the theater was still going. Looks like you're doing a new play."

"Yeah, we are. I'm sorry that we've got the principals cast, but you could understudy for Algernon," Alex said.

"You know, I might do that," he said, nauseous at the thought of learning another leading part, no matter how clever.

"Oh, that'd be great," Alex said. "This is Jarrod, our Algernon, and this is Olivia, our Lady Augusta. Chase was Orlando in *As You Like It* some years back."

"Really?" Olivia said in polite interest and Jarrod smiled in a patient manner.

Sammy pegged them both from the videos at once. Yep, Jess was here. "Eh, Shannon and Brett showed me up for the amateur that I am," Sammy demurred. Olivia laughed and Jarrod suddenly looked kindly on him.

Sammy's acute hearing told him that the theater door had opened again; when Alex looked up stiffly, Sammy dropped nonchalantly into a seat on the first row out of the stage lights. Alex said coolly, "Can I help you?"

A slightly condescending voice replied, "Yeah, I'm looking for one Jessica Threlkeld." Sammy kept his head down to study his manicure lest Reardon Smith, of the execrable Dunbar & Smith, recognize him.

"I'm sorry; I don't know anyone by that name," Alex said righteously. He was transparently lying and angry about it.

Reardon paused. "Yeah, well, her grandmother is offering a cool five hundred grand for her safe return," he said, extending a business card up to him.

Alex took the card. "We'll keep that in mind. Please excuse us; these are private rehearsals."

"Sure," Reardon curled his lip. He glanced at the actor on the shadowy first row who was intently studying a script he had found one seat over.

As Reardon walked out, Sammy watched over his shoulder to make sure he departed the doors and didn't just slide into a seat.

Then Sammy turned back to say, "Yeah, whoever he's working for, that's Reardon Smith. He's a crooked PI who lies like a dog and colludes with the cops. If there's a reward, he'll make sure he gets to it first."

The others looked down at him uncomfortably. Sammy was uncomfortable. Hellier had said nothing about a reward, but Sammy could imagine Dolly's offering one on the spur of the moment, which complicated everything a hundredfold.

Alex checked the card in his hand, then quickly looked at Sammy. "You know this guy?"

"I've had run-ins with him. You didn't see me jumping up to shake his hand," Sammy said bitterly. After absorbing that, Olivia turned her back to him to speak in a low voice to the other two, and Sammy took up the script again. He'd just have to play off whatever they decided. The iffy part was, as far as Jess knew, he was still a cop—one who was sympathetic to her grandmother, at that. But Jess also liked him, and he thought she might even trust him.

The three on stage finished their conference and just watched him for a minute. Sammy snickered at the dialogue. "This'll be fun to watch, even if I'm not in it."

"Well, come on back to the relaxation room for a minute, Chase," Alex invited.

"Sure." Sammy got up, bringing the script.

Lounging in the relaxation room backstage were two other actors, to whom Sammy was introduced (as Chase). "Wow, this takes me back," he said, sniffing the room, which reeked of stale cigarettes. "I was trying to quit smoking. Had to keep trying for the next two years afterwards." That provoked a little light laughter.

He threw himself into an old, frayed armchair while the others settled around the room. "Hey, whatever happened to the New York bigwig—Montpelier?"

"Montblanc," Alex laughed. "Who knows? Went back to New York, I imagine."

"I don't know why you'd need him. There's plenty of money in Dallas, and lots of support for the theater. They love this kind of play. Vintage, witty, and just a little naughty. You just need to get the attention of the right people," Sammy mused.

"Like the Threlkelds?" Olivia murmured.

Sammy glanced at her, thinking that she said that a little too casually. He raised his shoulders. "I don't know."

Sammy looked at the advertising posters for PU's theatrical productions along the walls. Most of these posters featured cast members in costume. Although it had been two years since he had last seen Jess, Sammy recognized her right away in the poster for *The Merchant of Venice,* which had run for a week in October. Her hair was a light crimped blond (possibly a wig); her makeup theatrical (obviously); and her weight 20 pounds less than it had been when he saw her at her grandfather's funeral—but he'd know her anywhere. She'd given birth barely eight weeks prior to this photo, assuming that it was taken shortly before opening night. Now *that* was dedication to the arts.

To not show undue interest in the heiress who was the object of a $500,000 reward, Sammy applied equal scrutiny to several other posters, even rising from his chair to stand before the one for *Noises Off.*

"Hey, I remember him," Sammy said, pointing to a dashing fellow with admirable eyebrows. "He stepped in as Charles the Wrestler when Seth died. His name is Matt, uh. . . ."

"Horton. Matt Horton, that's right," Alex said.

"He was good. Surely he's in *Earnest*," Sammy said, stepping back to glance over the posters again.

"As a matter of fact, he's John Worthing," Alex admitted, pleased.

Sammy turned around, blowing a raspberry. "*Pbbbbt*. What am I doing here? You don't need me. Maybe I can run the light board."

Everyone in the room relaxed and a few laughed, seeing that he was not out to filch anybody's part or show anybody up. But there was a strong undercurrent in the room, as if they were all trying to communicate over his head. Sammy, wishing to facilitate their communication, sat down and leaned over the script again.

At last Alex said, "Chase, you seem to be . . . resourceful."

Sammy looked up a little quizzically. "I've gotten out of a few scrapes."

"And you seem to know something about private investigations," Alex continued.

Sammy straightened. "Let me give it to you straight, Alex: I'm an ex-cop. And I didn't leave on the best of terms."

They all glanced at each other. "Who do you work for now?" Alex asked uneasily.

Right off, Sammy answered, "Fletcher Streiker."

"The billionaire?" somebody murmured.

Sammy turned to nod, though he was uncertain who spoke. After another hesitation, Alex said, "So you're . . . paid well, I assume?"

Sammy hesitated. "If you want the honest truth, I'm pretty well set for life."

"Then why are you here?" Alex asked.

Sammy lowered his head, but found that he was unable to lie in the face of a direct question. He looked at Alex to reply, "Streiker is concerned about Jess. He asked me to bring her to one of his offices in Fort Worth."

They stared at him. "For how long?" Olivia asked, flushed either in anger or strong emotion.

Sammy inhaled. "Knowing Streiker—not well, but enough—I'd say that depends on her. I also know that he wouldn't ask me to bring her if it weren't to help her."

"What do you think she needs?" Olivia asked. Her face had gone from fierce red to stark white.

"I don't know anything but what Streiker asked me to do. He saved my hide, and I owe him," Sammy said bluntly.

Again there was an uncertain silence. "Well . . . we'll talk to her—"

"Please let me talk to her," Sammy interrupted. "She'll want to talk to me."

"Why?" Olivia asked, now smiling slightly.

"Because I spanked her," he said virtuously. At their faces, he insisted, "And she was glad I did. *Ask her.*"

Olivia turned to Alex, who said, "Chase, we need to talk about this. Please go sit in the audience until I come tell you what we decide."

There was no point in doing anything but what he asked. Reluctantly, Sammy nodded and turned out, after picking up the script on his way.

In the auditorium, he faced the seats, hands on hips. Was she here? Streiker had said that his people had lost touch with her entirely. Since Sammy had to assume they were competent, there must be a reason for that. Why would she go into complete hiding like that?

Since his instinct was to search—for her, Reardon, or anybody else who might be hiding here—he did that. From the stage, he walked up the outer aisle to the very back of the (small) auditorium. Starting there, he walked down a side aisle, looking down the row of seats on either side. This would enable him to see anyone crouching down in a seat. Once he got to the front, he canvassed likewise up the other side aisle clear to the back. No one was here.

Just as he arrived back at the stage, Alex came out. He descended the stage to meet Sammy, then gestured him over to the auditorium exit stage right. "Okay, Chase," he said in a low voice, "Jess has agreed to meet you—ONLY you—here tonight. This door will be unlocked, and the seating lights will be on." These were very dim lights that enabled late patrons to find their seats. "She'll be here by nine o'clock."

"Nine?" Sammy said in dismay. "Oh, come on, Alex, don't make me wait—" he glanced at his watch —"eight hours to get her help."

Alex clenched his teeth. "She doesn't want to be seen. She insisted on waiting till after dark."

Sammy regarded the strange passion in his face. "Okay, okay. I'll come to this door at nine."

"Don't knock; don't make any noise. Just come in," Alex instructed.

That set off an array of klaxon warnings inside Sammy's head. He studied Alex, but could see no reason for him to summon violence. If he really talked to Jess, and she agreed to meet him, then Alex would know he was a friend. If Alex suspected that "Chase" had designs on the reward money, all he had to do was continue to disavow knowledge of her whereabouts.

Studying Alex, he suddenly wondered: What name had he given Jess for him? She would know "Sammy" or "Jim," but not "Chase." How could she then agree to meet him? He did not know.

Well, any assignment came with risks; Sammy wasn't going to let fear of the unknown prevent his following through here. "Okay. I'll be back at nine tonight." He glanced up at the stage, but none of the other actors had come out.

"Okay, Chase." Alex stuck out his hand, and Sammy hesitantly shook it.

He departed by way of the side door indicated, just to refamiliarize himself with the layout. It opened into the back alley behind the stores. To accommodate deliveries, the alley was broad, with loading docks. There was plenty of room to park right by the door, he noted.

He walked clear around the block of stores to return to the lot in which he had parked, and he waited to place a call until he sat behind the wheel of the Mustang.

"Hello."

"Mr. Streiker, this is Sammy Kidman. I may have located Jess Threlkeld. Supposedly, she's going to meet me at the theater tonight at nine. So I need to know how to get to this warehouse in Fort Worth."

"All right. Are you familiar with the warehouse district on the Trinity River?" Streiker asked.

"Not really," Sammy admitted.

So Streiker gave him clear directions to the

warehouse in question, adding, "When you get there, the automatic sensors should turn on the driveway lights and open the gate on the right. Drive through it around the building to the ramp. The rear door will automatically open for you to drive right into the warehouse."

"Got it," Sammy said. "Mr. Streiker, I . . . do not have good feelings about this. Alex is lying about something, but I don't know what."

"As long as you do exactly what I tell you, you'll be fine. All right, Sammy?" Streiker said.

"Yes, sir. I understand. Ah, assuming I convince her to come with me, it'll take, oh, an hour and a half, at least, to get out there. Who'll be there to meet us?"

"I will, Sammy."

"You? Wow, okay. Great. Yeah, that helps. All right, then, look for us between eleven and midnight."

"Good, Sammy. Good-bye."

From there, Sammy drove straight to the Taylors' house. When he rang the doorbell, it was opened by his almond-eyed wife, who seized him by his jacket to drag him inside and kiss him. He ate her up, then sighed, "You don't know how much I needed that."

"Come tell me about it," she said, pulling him toward the kitchen.

Pam appeared from the area of the studio, also headed toward the kitchen. "Sammy, are you hungry?"

"Yes," he said, being inclined to accept all invitations. Then he paused in concern. There was no 90-pound dog blindsiding him nor any small person assaulting his leg. "Where are the guys?"

"Come look," Marni said. Pausing at the closed doors of the gameroom, she put a finger to her lips and gently opened the double doors. Brows elevated, Sammy looked in.

Clayton was snoozing in his lounger with Sam on his shoulder, also asleep. Clay was asleep in the playpen a few feet away. Bubba was stretched out in the space between them. He raised his head lazily to regard Sammy, thump his tail once or twice, then lie down again. Sammy shook his head, softly closing the doors. "What a crew. I fear to think what they might have been doing to wear themselves out so much."

"Don't ask," Marni advised. "But I promised my parents we'd pay for it."

"Don't tell me about it. Just write them a check," Sammy exhaled.

"Don't worry about it," Pam laughed, pulling out sliced ham, bread, and condiments. "What would you like on your sandwich, Sammy?"

He waved. "Whatever you put on it."

He and Marni sat at the table as she asked, "Did you find Jess?"

"Maybe," he grimaced in doubt. "According to Alex, she's agreed to meet me at the theater tonight at nine. He said she's anxious to not be seen, and if Dolly has really offered a five-hundred-thousand-dollar reward for her return, I guess I understand that. Anyway, I called Streiker, and he's meeting us at his warehouse in Fort Worth tonight. So there's that."

"Wow," Marni breathed. "Can I come?"

"Not by any chance in heaven, earth or the underworld," he said. "Something's fishy, and I don't know what that is. Streiker said that as long as I did exactly what he said, I'd be fine. So. . . ." He trailed off as Pam put a loaded plate in front of him, and then he picked up the sandwich without another word.

Marni watched him eat for a minute. "So what are you going to do for the next—oh, seven hours?" she asked, glancing at the wall clock.

Mouth full, he paused to look her up and down, then shake his head. "Not enough time for that," he mumbled. Marni rolled her eyes, but she was smiling. They were quiet while he ate.

Finishing the sandwich and wiping his mouth, Sammy asked, "Have you heard anything about Chris today?"

"Oh! Yes," Marni said, remembering. "Kerry says he's in so much pain, she relented a little on the narcotics—but not much. They've all been going over and over the videos, trying to see anything about the black angel. But there's nothing to see. She's allowing a few of his friends to come over for a little while."

"Is Pruett going in to the office today?" he asked.

"I don't know," she frowned. "Hey, aren't I the boss?"

"Well, you were," he said, thinking about Streiker. Then he stood. "Okay, I can't let them show me up. I'll stop by and pretend to do something."

Marni turned in her chair. "What are you going to tell them about this assignment?"

He paused. "Uhhhh, nothing, until I get it done. That is, if they don't see it on the news first."

Marni winced. "Sammy, let's pray about this."

"No," he said quickly. She looked at him in distress and he added, "I'm afraid to. I don't know what will happen. Thanks for lunch, Pam."

She stirred. "You're welcome, Sammy."

After he left, Marni turned to her mother to observe, "Well, at least he hasn't seen the painting. Mom . . . please pray for Sammy."

"Sure." Pam bowed her head, and Marni did likewise.

Sammy arrived at the office to find neither Mike nor Pruett there, nor evidence that they had been. Mike had left a message on the machine that he was working at home, which was fine. As much as Pruett drove them both crazy, it was hard to work here when he wasn't around.

So Sammy sat at his desk and studiously opened his laptop to find that it had no connectivity. After floundering around with the internet settings, he discovered that the problem was with their provider. Until they got it fixed on their end, there was no point trying to work here. He closed up shop again and left.

He went home to change into black clothes for tonight. To not draw attention to his dramatic Black Angel attire, he put on a tan jacket, as the weather was starting to turn cool. Then he drove back down to the shopping center to sit at a sidewalk cafe two doors down from the theater, where he could watch the front entrance.

As a cover, he bore a sheaf of random papers from the glove compartment to begin composing, again, his life story. To placate the waitress for ordering only water and chips, he handed her two twenties and explained, "I just like to people-watch while I work. Is that okay?"

"Sure," she said, accepting the tip. He was only a

little aggravated that she went off duty 30 minutes later, so that he had to repeat the payout with her successor.

All the rest of that afternoon, he watched the front of the theater while knowing that anything of interest would be taking place in the alley. But there was no place to surveille from back there until the surrounding stores closed for the day, which, as it happened, was at 8:30. Jess, if she was coming, would be in the theater before then.

By 7:00 he had to leave the cafe to make way for the dinner crowd. He went out to his Mustang to bring it in closer so that he could continue to watch the storefronts. Yeah, the car was conspicuous, but not unduly so: an Alfa Romeo 4C sat two spaces down from him.

At 8:00 he took a test drive down the alley, but it was no good—it was not only still busy, but too dark to see beyond the loading bay lights. The security light above the back door of the theater was out, he noted. Not a good sign.

So he drove back around front and parked in time to see Alex, Jarrod, Olivia, and the two other actors come out in a group. They made themselves conspicuous, broadcasting, *Hey, we're all the thespians, leaving in a group, all of us here together; nobody's inside!* Jarrod even caught the attention of a waiter at the sidewalk cafe, boisterously calling, "I've now realized for the first time in my life the vital importance of being earnest. So goodnight!"

"Ham," muttered Sammy. This demonstration was also an ill omen; it appeared they were making sure to have alibis for leaving the scene of a crime before it happened.

So, despite what Sammy had told his wife, he was praying, desperately and fearfully. Over the next 45 minutes, he watched cars leave the lot and stores go dark. And when his watch told him it was 9:00, he took off his tan jacket and started to get out of his car.

Then he paused. His inclination was to walk to the alley, to draw less attention thereby, but that meant he had to bring her to his bright green car in an otherwise empty lot. What if she didn't really want to come? He had no doubt, at this point, that he would force her. For that, he needed his vehicle close by. He also had duct tape in the trunk, by the way.

So, still with the top up, he cranked up the engine and drove back to the alley without headlights; only running lights. Everything appeared still and quiet as he crept to the theater door.

He cut the engine, listening, but heard nothing untoward. Then he swallowed and got out. He walked the few paces necessary to reach the theater door and stopped to listen again. Nothing.

So he put a hand on the door handle and turned, easing it open just enough to slip inside. Then he flattened his back against the wall to look around.

He saw her at once, sitting awkwardly in the next-to-last seat on the front row. Her head was tilted, braced on her hand, and her legs splayed. But she was sitting up.

Approaching cautiously, glancing around frequently, he drew up to kneel in front of her. She didn't move. She was dead.

TWELVE

In fact, Jess was so dead that she was in full rigor mortis, which meant that she had died at least 12 hours ago, probably closer to 24.

Heart pounding, Sammy studied what he could see of her in the dark. She was wearing jeans (that were stained but dry) and a loose shirt, undamaged. There was a bruise on the left side of her forehead, but no other obvious injury, such as a gunshot or knife wound. The only way to tell how she died at this point was an autopsy.

Standing, Sammy pulled out his phone and began to dial 911. As he did, his mind jumped ahead to the forensics investigation, which would prove inconclusive because she did not die here. He would be detained as the likely perp, with the theater group swearing that she was not here when they left, and that they had all left together tonight.

Even if her death had been an accident, such as a fall from the stage (which would account for the bruise) he would never be free of the suspicion. There was no statute of limitations on murder. Once again, he was facing the threat of a life-altering legal morass, "and all because I did what you asked," he muttered to the unseen Streiker.

Whereupon he remembered with a jolt that he hadn't done what Streiker asked, because Streiker had told him to *bring her to him.* He didn't specify that she had to be alive.

Sammy's fingers froze over the number pad on his phone. Then his shoulders sagged. *No. It's no good.* That was a hundred ways wrong, to move her. Even though her body had already been moved several times, it was a violation of half a dozen laws and morality itself to presume to take her anywhere.

He began to press numbers again. "Even if I weren't ever convicted of a crime, which I will be, I couldn't live with myself, or face Dolly, or Marni, or—" *As long as you do what I ask, you'll be fine.*

Sammy remembered that as clearly as if Streiker himself were standing beside him saying it. And he remembered Streiker sending him into that alley to save Chris.

Sammy suddenly looked down at Jess' body again. Her rigor had stiffened her into a sitting position, which is how they were able to make it look like she was waiting for him here. . . .

Before he could think any more about it, he stuffed his phone back into his pocket. Then he reached down to pick up her unyielding body and carry her to the door. Cracking it open with one hand, he peered out into the darkness. Seeing no one, he opened the door wide and brought her outside.

He had to set her down on the pavement to open the

passenger-side door. Then he lifted her just enough to maneuver her into the bucket seat. Her legs splayed awkwardly, but by pushing her back against the seat, he was able to get the seatbelt around her.

Sweating buckets, he came around to the driver's side, sat, and started the engine. Looking at her across from him, he sucked in a breath at her sightless stare. So he got out his sunglasses and fitted them on her face. He imagined explaining to the cop who stopped them: *"Shhh! Officer, she's trying to sleep and the headlights kept her awake."* But she did look more natural.

He wiped his sweating palms on his pants, then eased the car around, again without headlights. These he did not turn on until he had crossed the parking lot to the frontage road.

Once he got on the freeway going west, he relaxed just a little. With the Rubicon behind him—as well as the River Styx, for that matter—Sammy faced the road ahead as best he could. Jess rode quietly, without shifting when he changed lanes.

He drove very carefully, just about five miles per hour over the speed limit, because cops were trained to automatically suspect anyone being careful enough to not speed at all. And he stayed out of the HOV lane. He did not want any cops checking to see if that was a dummy in the passenger seat.

It was a long drive. Being Wednesday, there was not much traffic on I-30, but he did not allow himself to be lulled into complacency. He turned on the outside air vents because the smell was rather disagreeable. Then he drove and watched, watched and drove. A few people glanced over from their cars just because a classic green

Mustang convertible draws attention, but Sammy drove politely, yielding to everyone and declining, without hand gestures, to race.

When he took the exit Streiker had indicated, he had to circle tightly to his right. At the speed he was obliged to go to stay with traffic, his passenger shifted, leaning into him. He tried pushing her back, but could not adequately reposition her without stopping the car and getting out, which he was absolutely not going to do.

Having become dislocated from her original position, she was now unstable, so that he had to keep elbowing her off him while trying to drive. Finally, she slipped under the seatbelt to fall fully on him, one leg sticking up. Thankfully, her foot was caught on the dash.

He drove on, trying to read street signs through the sweat dripping down into his eyes. But every time he braked or turned a corner, he saw the foot slipping out from the dash inch by inch.

Finally it popped up, coming to rest up against the inside of the windshield. Near to panicking, he looked down at her head in his lap, the sunglasses skewed on her face so that she could reproach him with her one-eyed gaze.

About the time he felt himself close to blacking out, a bright light shone in his face. He reared up, soaking wet, to say, "Officer, I don't know what happened—" Then he saw that the light emanated from the security lights around a warehouse. A gate to the right was rolling open. He had made it.

Shifting, he promptly killed the engine, so he restarted it, shifted again, and drove through the gate, following the incline to his left as the gate closed behind him. Hampered by the sweat coating the steering wheel, he guided the car erratically through the opening. Then he stopped and cut the engine as the great warehouse door lowered behind him.

He managed to get his seatbelt unbuckled and the driver's side door open, then fell getting out from underneath his passenger. Streiker came over to give him a hand up. "Hey, Sammy. Glad you could make it."

Shaking and dripping, Sammy looked at him and said, "S-sh-she's d-dead."

Streiker looked over to his splayed passenger, foot planted on the windshield. "Are you sure?"

Sammy nodded with his whole body. But Streiker said, "Nah, I think she's just asleep." Sammy tried to explain what the man could see with his own two eyes, but his teeth were chattering too hard to make himself understood.

Streiker looked at him in concern. "You look like you could use some coffee, Sammy. It's there on the desk. I just made it myself. Go pour yourself a cup."

While Streiker leaned into the passenger side of the Mustang, Sammy turned to see a twin iron bed up against the wall of the warehouse. Next to it was a refrigerator, and a few feet away was a desk with a rolling executive chair pulled up to it. And on the desk was a coffee maker, plugged into a wall socket via extension cords. The aroma of fresh-brewed coffee filled his nostrils.

Sammy stumbled over to the desk. Exercising supreme self-control, he forced his hand to pick up the carafe by the handle, position the spout over an empty cup, and pour enough to fill the cup by about four-thirds.

Then he lowered his posterior to the chair in order to brace both elbows on the desk so that he could reliably bring the cup in contact with his mouth.

The first two sips steadied him greatly, besides burning his tongue. The second two sips brought his heart rate back within normal range, and he gripped a napkin to clean up some of the coffee he had spilled. Then he looked up to see Streiker walking Jess toward the desk. "Would you like some coffee?" Streiker asked her.

She pushed strands of tangled hair out of her face. "Would I ever! Ugh, I feel like death warmed over." Then she saw him. "Sammy! Where have you been?"

He did not speak, so Streiker said, "He brought you, Jess. I'm afraid he thought you were pretty badly hurt. What happened?"

"Oh, I tripped on that f——g catwalk. I thought I was falling—I must have hit my head," she said, fingering her forehead, which was no longer bruised. "Huh. It doesn't hurt any more, but I sure do want some coffee."

"Cream and sugar?" Sammy blurted, gazing at her.

"Tonight, Sugar, I'm taking it black," she said, plopping on his lap like she used to. Sammy looked down at the legs that were now crossed instead of splayed.

Streiker brought over two folding chairs. "Here, Jess," he invited.

Puckering her lips to mutter, "Prude," she lifted her derriere to sit in the seat indicated.

Sammy handed her a cup without spilling it and asked Streiker, "How do you take yours?"

"Black, thank you. See? I told you it would help," Streiker said.

"That, plus the fact that I'm dreaming," Sammy said. Streiker grinned at him but Sammy went on, "Since I'm in la-la land, where's Adair?"

"Running errands for me," Streiker said.

"At—" Sammy looked at his watch with the sweat-stained leather band—"one o'clock in the morning?"

"Oh, she's been pulling duty all day," Streiker murmured. He sipped his coffee, then said conversationally, "Jess, we need to get your baby out of your grandmother's house. Dolly is getting a little confused, and has forgotten she's there."

A look of tenderness came over Jess' face. "I want her back. I've missed holding her."

"That's a go, then. Sammy, I need you to bring Jess' baby here," he said.

Sammy blinked at him. "I'm not dreaming, am I?"

"If you are, that's not going to help Gussie any," Streiker observed.

Sammy sat up. "Okay. I can do that. They don't have any security anymore, so it would be nothing to break in tonight and—"

"Sammy, why don't you send Marni for her in the morning?" Streiker asked.

"Marni in the morning," Sammy repeated thoughtfully. "Yeah, that might work, too. Okay, then." He stood up, then looked down at Jess. He took her hand to feel the warm, healthy flesh, and brushed tousled hair off her spotless forehead. Looking in her clear eyes, he leaned down to hug her.

"Whew! You stink," she teased, waving the air in front of her nose.

Sammy looked at Streiker, and for just an instant

caught a glimpse of something profoundly powerful behind the eyes. Then Streiker blinked, and he was just a guy with vaguely Polynesian features. "I'll bring Gussie tomorrow after Marni springs her," Sammy said.

"Okay," Streiker said.

Sammy started toward his Mustang, then turned. "You keep giving me jobs because I do what you ask."

"That helps," Streiker said.

Sammy nodded, progressing another step. "Because," he said, turning again, "not many people would have brought her in the condition she was in."

"Probably not," Streiker admitted.

Sammy made it to the Mustang and opened the driver's door. "Are you sure I can't go get her baby tonight? It'd be fun to break in," he argued.

Streiker's face registered mild displeasure. "You're forgetting Yin and Yang, Sammy."

"The dogs!" Sammy slapped his forehead. "Okay, Marni in the morning."

He looked again at Jess, who yawned and plopped down on the twin bed. "Ugh, I'm just dead," she muttered, fluffing the pillow and burying her head in it.

Then Sammy looked back at Fletcher, who reiterated, "She was just asleep."

Sammy sat, starting the engine, and the warehouse door raised behind him. He turned the Mustang in a tight circle to peel out down the drive. Jess started up, then groaned, "Moron."

Fletcher smiled. "He's glad you're okay, Jess."

Circling back in front of the warehouse, Sammy slammed on the brakes. Adair, in dark pants and sweater, was opening the front door. On her arm were three or four grocery bags, plus a pack of disposable diapers. She looked back to wave at Sammy with her free hand before she slipped inside.

Thoughtfully, he drove back to Dallas, alert but detached.

He arrived home to an empty garage without surprise. He showered and shaved, ate Sam's leftover oatmeal from the refrigerator, and then climbed back into his Mustang to drive six blocks to the Taylors' house, parking next to Marni's Prius and blocking the drive.

Then he checked his surprisingly waterproof watch to find that it was four o'clock in the morning. Unwilling to wake the Taylors and unwilling to go back to an empty house, Sammy reclined the seat and crossed his arms over his chest to catch some z's.

"Sammy? Sammy!" He groggily came to at the gentle shaking. Blinking, he focused on Pam leaning over him in her bathrobe. "Sammy, what are you doing out here? Come in."

"Huh. Okay." After locating all of his arms and legs, he extracted himself from the bucket seat and put his feet outside the car on the driveway before attempting to stand. It was just sunrise, he noted.

Pam led him into the house like a child, sitting him at the kitchen table. "Do you want breakfast?"

"Yeah," he decided. "Uh, coffee and anything but oatmeal. Thanks."

While Pam was frying bacon, Marni came into the kitchen sleepily. "Sammy, that was you. I thought I heard you. When did you get back?"

"Uh." He focused on his watch. "About two and a half hours ago."

Marni snapped awake. "Did you find Jess?"

"Yes," he said, nodding. "Yes. She . . . had been hurt in a fall, but, I got her to Streiker okay. She's at his warehouse in Fort Worth now."

"His—warehouse?" Marni asked.

"Yeah, it's this warehouse with security lights and gates and everything. Listen," he turned to her earnestly. "Jess wants her baby back, and Streiker wants us to get her out of that house. He said Dolly has forgotten about her."

Marni gasped, "Is no one taking care of that baby?"

"I don't know. I offered to break into the house last night, but he suggested I ask you to go get her this morning instead," Sammy said.

Marni looked dubious. "I just—walk in and take the baby? Isn't that illegal?"

"Not nearly as illegal as what I did last night," he asserted.

"What did you do?" Marni breathed as Pam set a plate of bacon and eggs in front of him.

"Oh, man, thanks so much, Pam. You're heaven-sent." He proceeded to inhale breakfast while she brought him orange juice as well.

"Sammy! What did you do?" Marni exclaimed.

"Tell you what. Let's go get that baby, and then I'll tell you on the way to Fort Worth," he proposed.

Before Marni could answer, Pam cleared her throat. "I'm sorry; I know this is important, but your dad and I have an appointment with our accountant in two hours."

"Oh, yeah," Marni breathed. "They've bent over

backwards helping me with the guys. I can't ask them to take care of them all day today, too."

"Okay, let's break this down," Sammy said. "You get ready and go on out to the Threlkelds—I'll tell Hellier to expect you. The guys will hang with me while you snag the kid and bring her to our place. Then we'll figure out how to best get her to Fort Worth."

"You're tempting me to cancel our appointment," Pam said, eyeing him.

"No, Mom, you've done too much babysitting already. I'll tell you everything. I promise," Marni said.

So Marni had a quick breakfast and fed Clay. Before she went home to shower and change, Sammy called Hellier to set up her visit. "It's early, but Hellier never sleeps," Sammy told her and Pam.

"Threlkeld residence."

"Hellier! It's Sammy."

"Yes, Sammy! Have you had any success?" Hellier asked.

"Yes, actually, Hellier, more than I should have had. Ah, I found Jess—she had been injured in a fall from the catwalk, but she's okay now, resting at one of Streiker's places in Fort Worth. Hellier, she wants Gussie with her, so Marni is coming to pick her up so we can take her on out to Jess. Will you open the gate and let her in?"

"Certainly, Sammy," Hellier said warmly.

"Great, Hellier. She'll be coming to the back service entrance," Sammy noted, glancing up at Marni, who nodded.

"Yes, that's best," the butler agreed.

"Here's the hard part, Hellier—you can't say anything to Dolly yet. It's up to Jess to do that. If she hasn't already called her, she will. Can you keep a tight lid on it until Jess talks to Dolly?"

"I'll try, Sammy, but I can't help who might see Mrs. Kidman. Mrs. Threlkeld and Mr. Threlkeld are both here," Hellier warned him.

"Okay, we won't worry about that," Sammy said, a worried cast crossing his face. "Just let her in, and I'll hammer Jess about calling Dolly."

"All right, Sammy."

"Thanks, Hellier. Bye." He hung up, telling Marni, "Both Dolly and Stan are there, but—don't worry about them. You're authorized to take the baby, so get her and get out."

"Will do," Marni nodded. She left for home to get ready.

Sammy got Sam cold cereal for breakfast, then gathered up everybody and their gear. Since Marni had taken her car with the carseats, Pam had to lend Sammy their carseats for the guys. What with getting those secured in the Mustang, by the time they got home, Marni was gone.

The cohort was happy to be home, and Sammy needed some time to think. So he took his crew out to the backyard to play under the fruitless mulberry, whose leaves were just turning golden.

As the morning was crisp, Sammy put a blanket over Clay in his play seat, but Sam used his sweater to transport loads of landscaping pebbles to his various building locations. Bubba did his business in the shrubs, for which Sammy hollered at him without considering that it was incumbent on himself to pick it up.

Meanwhile, Marni was pulling through the open

gate to the Threlkeld estate. She drove down the long drive, noting the Rolls Royce Silver Shadow waiting in front, then continued around the mansion to park in back, as instructed.

Hellier was at the back door to meet her. "Mrs. Kidman," he said warmly, opening the door.

She gave him a big hug. "Hellier, it's so good to see you again. How is Mary?"

"Doing well, Mrs. Kidman. More relaxed than I've seen in a long while."

"I'm so glad. She's earned it," Marni said.

As they came to the back hallway, she paused. "Where . . . ?"

"Gussie is in the last bedroom down the right on the second floor, Mrs. Kidman." She nodded; that had been Morgan's bedroom. Hellier added, "Mrs. Threlkeld and Mr. Threlkeld are preparing to leave for a Dallas Arts Council breakfast in twenty minutes." Again she nodded: just enough time for her to get the baby and get out.

"Thanks, Hellier," she said, putting a hand on his arm, which he patted fondly.

She trotted briskly up the stairs, turning to the right to hurry to the end of the hall. She listened at the door for a moment; hearing nothing, she opened it and went in.

It was a beautiful, spacious nursery, beautifully appointed with expensive furnishings and designer fabrics. It took a moment for Marni to find the crib in all the glory; having finally located it, she approached and looked down.

A small, shriveled infant lay on her back on a

stained spot in the spacious crib, eyes closed. Dropping her purse, Marni raised the tiny feet to look at the leaking diaper, and the eyes barely opened. Marni picked up the baby, who thrashed slightly, and took her to the well-stocked changing table, where she stripped her, washed her down, and applied ointment to her raging diaper rash. Then she put her in a fresh diaper and a very cute fall onesie.

Finding herself attended, Gussie uttered a weak cry, which caused Marni's heavy breasts to let down as surely as if Clay were demanding to be fed. She paused; Sammy had told her to get the baby and get out. But Gussie was telling her differently. So Marni sat in the rocking chair and opened her shirt to Gussie.

The baby thrashed excitedly, rooting wildly at first to find the nipple. Marni got her settled and Gussie closed her eyes to drink deeply. After only five minutes or so, she began fussing at the lessened flow, so Marni switched her to the other side.

Eight minutes later she was asleep, full and rosy. Marni detached her gently, wiped herself down, and lifted Gussie to her shoulder to see if she needed to burp. Apparently, she hadn't sucked in much air with the milk, as she slept quietly on.

So Marni put her down in an infant car carrier and turned back to her changing table. Someone had spent a great deal of money on a layette, but Marni packed only the most essential items that she could cram into one bag. Aware that time was short, she hurried.

Slinging the bag over one shoulder and her purse over the other, Marni picked up the carrier with the baby lying loosely in it. Despite the pressure to hurry, she made herself stop. She dropped her purse and bag, and set the carrier back down to strap Gussie securely in.

Then she picked everything up again and left the room, balancing the carrier on her hip to reach out and close the door. She strode down the hallway toward the stairs, watching Gussie smile faintly in her sleep.

As Marni descended the stairs, she was aware of the purring of a motor nearby, but, concentrating as she was on keeping her balance with the additional bulk, did not stop to think about what it was.

She had reached the bottom of the stairs and turned toward the back hallway when the elevator door opened for Dolly and Stan Threlkeld to emerge practically in her face.

Thirteen

Gripping the carrier, Marni stopped dead. The Threlkelds also paused in surprise. But Stan merely glanced at her, never seeing what she carried, and continued his stride toward the front door.

Dolly, however, turned to coo, "Oh, my baby! You've brought my baby."

Marni opened her mouth to make some explanation, some excuse, some wild prevarication to get Gussie out, but Dolly went on say, "Why do you always have to be running off? You never stay and visit."

Marni paused. Dolly was talking just as she used to when Marni would bring baby Sam over to visit. Dolly always complained that they never stayed long enough.

At the door far across the foyer, Stan turned back to chide, "Mother! Don't dawdle; we'll be late!"

"I'm coming, Stanley; don't rush me!" she bristled. Then she raised a wrinkled, manicured finger to stroke Gussie's cheek. "Oh, sweet thing," she purred. "He looks just like Sammy, doesn't he?"

Marni glanced down at Gussie's wispy brown hair, but still said nothing.

"Mother!" Stan called angrily.

"I'm coming, Stanley!" she shouted back. Patting Marni's cheek, she said, "Do come back when you can stay longer. Good-bye, darling baby." She puckered red lips beside the baby's cheek, then turned to walk stiffly toward the front door.

Marni watched her, then turned to see Hellier looking on from the back doorway. He lifted his eyebrows meaningfully; she let out her breath.

Wordlessly, he opened the back door for her and she nodded good-bye. Then she tossed Gussie's bag on the floor behind the driver's seat. Since the guys' car seats filled up the back, she strapped Gussie's seat into the front seat beside her, facing backwards. She gazed down momentarily at the blissful sleeper, then started the engine.

Marni crept around the corner of the mansion to make sure that the Rolls carrying Dolly and Stan was gone. Seeing that it was, she drove down the long driveway and out the gates herself.

Arriving home, she had just pulled into the driveway and opened the garage door when the gate to the back yard swung open. Sammy appeared, carrying Clay, and at once so many bodies were clustered around her car that she cut the engine and set the brake.

Still holding Clay, Sammy opened the front passenger door and dropped to one knee to look at Gussie. "Is she okay?" he asked the baby expert, glancing up. "She looks tiny, but maybe I'm just comparing her to our brutes. Did you have any problems?"

Sam crowded up next to his dad to look around the

front seat and wonder what all the fuss was about.

"Not really." She opened her door to get out and retrieve Gussie's bag. "Let's go in and talk. Here, let me get her; you've got Clay. Hello, Bubba. Get down."

They got everyone relocated into the house, then put both babies in the playpen out of reach of a curious dog and older sibling. Throwing himself onto the couch, Sammy opened his arms and said, "Okay, spill it."

Marni snuggled up next to him. With a disapproving shake of her head, she said, "She was definitely neglected. I didn't see any trace of a nanny, and there's no telling when the last time she had been changed or fed."

"Oh, well, you can take care of that," he grinned.

"Already did," she smiled back. "That took so long that I ran into Dolly and Stan coming off the elevator."

His grin vanished. "Oh oh."

"They—" She paused in some bewilderment. "Stan didn't even look at her, and Dolly thought I was bringing Sam! She griped at me for leaving so soon."

Sammy studied her. "Do you get the sense that she's getting senile?"

Marni frowned thoughtfully. "Confused, certainly. But . . . it sure seems sudden."

They thought about this for a minute, then she said, "Your turn. What happened with Jess?"

He dropped his head into one hand, then raised his face to the ceiling, stroking the stubble on his neck. He cleared his throat and said, "She was dead when I got to the theater."

"What?" she whispered.

"Her—good buddies in the theater posed her dead,

193

rigored body in an auditorium seat to meet me," he said bitterly. "I started to call nine-one-one three times, and then remembered that Streiker had told me to bring her, period. So I—loaded her into my car and took her to Fort Worth."

Marni watched him wide-eyed, and he continued, "I drove her to his warehouse, and he was there to meet us, just like he said he would be. 'Oh, hai, Sammy,' he says. 'How'd it go?'

"'She's dead,' I says. 'Oh, no, Sammy. She's just asleep. Have some coffee while I do something.' And the next thing I know, he's bringing her over to get a cup of coffee, too. She's fine, not even a headache. And she was able to tell us that she tripped and fell off the catwalk."

Marni continued to stare at him. "You're *sure* that she was—?"

"Baby, she was in *full rigor*, which means she could have been dead for a solid day. I know a dead body when I see one; takes me just a glance to look and say, 'Ho, that guy's dead.'"

"And then she's okay and decides she wants her baby," Marni said, glancing toward the playpen.

"Almost. Streiker told her that Gussie needed to come out of her grandma's house, and Jess got all sentimental over her, said she missed holding her, so Streiker said, 'Okay, Sammy, go get her and bring her here.'"

"To the warehouse?" Marni said.

"Yes," he confirmed.

"I want to go with you to take her," she said in that voice of utter determination.

Sammy looked around at all the little bodies and the big furry body and said, "Okay—you know what? We're going to do this. Everybody come on."

Marni managed to hold him up long enough for her to change everyone's diaper, then he herded everybody out to the Prius. Diaper bags were tossed in the trunk; Gussie's car seat was wedged in between the guys', then the little people were strapped in.

Making Bubba fit was the challenge, but as he seemed to realize that not fitting meant staying behind, he squeezed beneath three car seats on the floorboard. Marni helped by moving her seat up as far as she could.

Sammy climbed behind the wheel and looked in the back. "All righty! Here we go." He felt his shirt pocket for his sunglasses before remembering that they had last graced a corpse's face. "Eh. I needed new shades, anyway." Marni located an old pair in the glove compartment, and they set off.

Although traffic on I-30 was far heavier today than last night, it was a far easier drive. Sammy pointed out notable milestones along the way: "Here is where she slid out of the seatbelt to lie across my lap with her feet in the air"; "Here is where I almost passed out."

As they approached Streiker's warehouse, they saw the gate standing open. Sammy drove through it and up the curving incline with the blasé confidence of a tour guide. The warehouse door was also wide open, so Sammy pulled in with considerable more finesse than he had 12 hours ago.

He and Marni got out, looking at the strange furniture grouping where two people sat. Streiker, sitting in the executive chair at the desk, was writing on a sheaf of papers. Jess slowly got up from the bed as Marni began unstrapping bodies and Bubba wriggled out from confinement. He shook himself thoroughly, then bounded over to plant his front feet on Streiker's lap, knocking his chair five feet back from the desk.

That would have been fun to watch had Marni and Sammy been looking at him instead of Jess. She came over hesitantly, as if fearing what she might see. "He said you were on your way," she whispered. "I didn't believe him."

Having released Sam from his seat, Sammy was the first to reach Gussie. He unbuckled the seatbelt, then lifted out her carrier. He presented it to Jess with, "Is this one yours? I'm not sure."

Jess unbuckled the baby from the carrier, which she left in Sammy's hands as she held her daughter, stroking her. "Oh, she's so beautiful," she sobbed. "She's like a little princess. The princess of a fairy tale."

Tenderly, she put Gussie back into the carrier. Then with tears shimmering in her eyes, she looked at Sammy and said, "Thank you." He received her grateful kiss on the cheek, then he watched as she turned around, walked to the far door of the warehouse, opened it, and left.

Sammy stood there holding Gussie in her carrier for the next 300 seconds. Bubba and Sam were having a blast running amok in the wide-open space of the warehouse, yelling and barking and chasing each other. Marni stood by the car, holding Clay in his car seat.

Finally, Sammy turned to Streiker to say, "She just went out for a pack of gum, right? Then she's coming back to take care of her baby, right?"

Streiker sighed, but said nothing. He looked down at

his hands folded contemplatively on the manuscript, then looked back up at Sammy.

Sammy turned to his wife. "Can I have your take on this?" he asked.

She blinked. "I'd say she's not ready to be a mother, Sammy."

He looked back to Streiker in alarm. "What do you want me to do?" When Streiker did not answer, Sammy became almost angry. "Look, I brought her out here because you told me to. Now I'd really appreciate your opinion on what I should do with her."

"You have to do whatever's in your heart, Sammy. Jess didn't have it in her heart to take care of Gussie. You have to look in your own heart to see what's there," Streiker said.

Sammy looked up at the warehouse lights and saw what was in his heart. He saw that this cherished fantasy of himself as desiring lots of babies was a lie, even to himself. Sure, he was happy to give generously to church programs benefiting orphans, and he was conscientious in taking care of his own sons, but when it meant babysitting and changing diapers and losing sleep on behalf of someone else's unwanted child—never mind. It was an act; it was all an act.

Stung to bitterness by his own hypocrisy, he looked at Sam and Bubba rolling on the concrete floor, looked across at Marni, then turned back to Streiker in vehemence. "My wife is already taking care of a toddler and a five-month-old. I can't ask her to take care of a three-month-old, too."

Marni looked past Sammy to Streiker still seated at the desk. "Mr. Streiker, regardless who takes care of

Gussie—whether it's us or someone else—unless they get legal custody, the Threlkelds can come back at any time and claim her, can't they?"

"Yes," he said.

Marni came around the car to put Clay in his carrier at Sammy's feet, then pulled out her phone, walking away. She stopped forty feet from them across the warehouse, well out of earshot, to put the phone to her ear and talk.

Sammy sagged. "She's calling her mom." Still angry, he looked back at Streiker. "So you knew Jess wouldn't man up for her own kid and sent my wife to fall in love with her so *we'd* take her in."

Streiker smiled faintly. "It's the stuff of fairy tales, Sammy. Like winning the lottery."

Sammy stared at him. The message in those lightly humorous brown eyes could have been: *I send good fortune and bad; I make weal and create woe; the good man uses what good he has received to offset the evil of others.*

Marni put her phone away and returned to the car. Sammy said almost despondently, "Pam and Clayton are going to take her" *to confirm what a jerk I am.*

"They're going to help us take care of her until we know of a better solution," she corrected him, reaching out to take Gussie from the carrier and nuzzle her. The baby emitted a tiny, happy squeal.

Left holding the empty carrier, Sammy stared at his wife in admiration. She was going to help him turn this big lie of his into the truth.

Streiker lazily inclined his head toward a pile of groceries and diapers on the floor—the same ones Adair had brought in last night. "Feel free to take the formula and diapers."

"Why doesn't Adair take Gussie?" Sammy asked.

Streiker smiled. "You don't know how many kids she's caring for already. You saw some of them Saturday."

Sammy dropped his head. "I'm sorry; that question was out of line."

"Only because it's not the question you wanted to ask," Streiker noted.

Sammy looked at him sharply. "Did Adair die?"

Streiker leaned forward. "Did you?"

"That's not the issue," Sammy argued. "I want to know if I'm being helped by a ghost or a spirit or what."

Marni was the first to see the figure walking up the incline to enter the warehouse. While Sammy and Streiker eyed each other, Adair came over to sit on the desk. Dressed in a slouchy sweater and jeans, she was eating chocolate mint cookies from a package.

"Hi, Sammy," she said easily. "Want one?" She extended the open edge of the package toward him.

Sammy tossed down the carrier and came forward. He studied her at close range as she finished one cookie and reached into the bag for another. He took the bag, touching her hand in the process. Taking out a cookie, he popped it in his mouth, chewed it, then looked at the package and said, "You should try the cookies from Mara's Kitchen. They're better."

Without warning, he kissed her on the lips—not aggressively, or even sexually, but he definitely made contact. Her blue eyes glinting, she wiped crumbs from her lips and said, "I have my own; I don't need yours."

He licked crumbs from his mouth, smiling in relief. "Okay, that answers my question. Thank you," he whispered.

Lip curling slightly, Streiker asked, "So, are you satisfied that my wife is alive?"

"I—" Sammy shook his head. "There's no explanation for a bunch of things. First, I saw all the news reports about the fact that, yes, she was dead," he said, aggrieved.

Streiker shifted in his seat. "An old enemy of mine instigated the attack that put her in the hospital. That is, he goaded her boss into the blind rage that caused him to choke her. When she was still in danger after a year in the hospital, I took the next step, and allowed many people to think that she died, including her boss, the police, and her friend who sat by her bed so long and so faithfully."

"Her former boss is being charged with murder," Sammy pointed out.

Streiker observed, "His intent was to murder her. Because I stepped in to prevent that does not mitigate his guilt. Besides, I'm not through with him."

He looked back at Adair, and the air seemed to vibrate between them. "Even before the attack, she—suffered a great deal because of her relationship to me," Streiker went on, and for the first time he appeared grieved, distressed. "She proved her loyalty to me when it almost killed her. So after it happened, I . . . cocooned her to prevent further attacks. And when she was ready, I brought her out of her cocoon to live with me and work with me."

Sammy thought about this, glancing at his son and

dog careening around the large, echoing space. "Okay, I don't really understand that, but we'll go on to—all this supernatural stuff. Orchids that don't wilt, and my arm that wasn't broken—"

Streiker laughed so suddenly that Marni started with Gussie and Sammy crushed the package of cookies in his hands. Adair bit her lip guiltily; her husband glanced at her as he said, "I warned her that dropping orchids on someone through thin air was going to create a commotion, but it really did seem to help you understand that you were not alone. She, uh, fell in love with the orchids after our first trip to Hawaii together."

"I did learn that from my betters," Adair admitted to Marni, who recalled her mother's mentioning Saint Thérèse's fondness for roses.

"As to your arm," Streiker resumed, "My wife pointed out that an injury like that would prevent your following through on the assignments I had for you. She asked me to take care of it, which I did. As a matter of fact, I did whatever she asked me to do for you, because that was the surest way to get you into my employ."

Sammy felt chastened, humbled, and honored, but mostly embarrassed. He opened his mouth, but a *thwomp* followed by a yelp from Bubba and a wail from Sam signaled the end of the discussion. Sammy pushed the crumpled package back onto Adair and trotted to where Sam was crying on the concrete floor. Bubba was folding his ears in contrition.

Picking Sam up, Sammy noted the small cut on his chin. But he said nothing, just bounced Sam until the toddler decided that he wanted to get down again.

Carrying him to the car instead, Sammy leaned over

to put him in his car seat. Bubba jumped onto the back floorboard without waiting for everyone else to load. Marni began strapping in Gussie and Clay while Sammy opened the trunk and walked over to pick up the grocery bags. "Pam and Clayton will appreciate these, at least," he muttered, still feeling like the cad he was.

Streiker said nothing, but leaned forward to start writing on the papers again. Sammy paused, feeling Streiker's approval like a—wait, he remembered something that described it perfectly: *"whence the waters flow in healing mercy to souls in torment."* Where was that from? He paused, thinking.

"Clothier!" he gasped, dropping a bag. "I'm quoting Gordon Clothier!" he cried. Then he saw the title on the front page of the manuscript. Sammy dropped another bag, exclaiming, "Hey! That's my—"

"I'm not finished with it," Streiker said, withdrawing it out of sight.

Looking a lot like Bubba when he was corrected, Sammy picked up the dropped bags and turned away, glancing at the beautiful Adair.

She grinned at him, folding the top down on the bag of cookies to stuff it in one of the grocery bags he held. He smiled weakly in response as he took the bags to the trunk of the Prius. He dropped them in, then suddenly stopped as something occurred to him.

Slamming the trunk, he said, *"Why?* Why would you —do what you did for Jess only for her to turn around and walk out on her own helpless baby?"

Streiker laid down the pen and looked at him. "I didn't help Jess because she deserved it, Sammy. I did it because you brought her."

Sammy stared at him as if he were speaking Aramaic, so Streiker explained, "I told you to bring her and you did, in the face of all contrary reason. If you have enough faith in me to do what I ask when it seems hopeless, what else can I do? Besides, I can't have dead bodies littering up the warehouse. I use it all the time." Eyes glazed, Sammy stood there a minute, then went to the driver's side door.

"Sammy," Streiker said suddenly. Sammy turned, attentive but fearful. "If I did that much for someone who was ungrateful, wouldn't I do as much and more for someone who was deeply grateful, and showed it?"

"Yes," Sammy said instantly. Streiker leaned back.

Marni had everybody loaded by now, so Sammy climbed behind the wheel and started the car. To avoid backing down the incline, he made a tight circle in the great empty space of the warehouse.

He stopped, opened his mouth, and then shook his head. Exiting, he lifted his hand to the Streikers, and they both waved in response. Adair kissed her fingers to Marni.

Descending the incline toward the open gate, Sammy said, "Like with Chris."

"What?" Marni blinked.

Sammy guided the Prius out of the gate, checking for traffic. "Jess was probably already dead by the time Streiker called me and asked me to find her," he said.

"Ohhh," she said in illumination. "Like he called you before the thugs started beating Chris."

"Right." Then he glanced at her. "Hey, Adair said good-bye to you specifically."

"I know," Marni said.

"She didn't want you to be jealous," he chatted.

Marni nodded, smiling. In fact, what he took for a token gesture on Adair's part, Marni knew to be a heartfelt expression of love. For reasons that escaped her, Streiker's wife loved the Kidman family.

To cover her silence—and not have to explain to Sammy once again that a beautiful woman wasn't in love with him—she asked, "What was that you saw on his desk?"

"My life story!" he exclaimed, putting a hand to his chest. "I couldn't see the title, but the subtitle was, *The Life of Samuel James Kidman.*"

"He's still working on it." She grinned at him.

"Yeah," he sighed.

They were silent for a few minutes, then as Sammy had to change lanes abruptly to get on the access road to the freeway, Marni looked in alarm at his watering eyes. He'd gotten about two and a half hours of sleep last night between two exhausting and emotional events. "Sammy, exit here and let me drive home," she said.

He shifted in the seat. "No, I'm okay, really. Talk to me; that will help."

She thought for a minute. "Okay. I can see why we had to bring Gussie to Fort Worth. First, we really did have to get her out of that house; she was just invisible there, but we wouldn't have known it without seeing it firsthand. And, I wouldn't have gone into that house to kidnap her and neither would you."

He considered that. "Maybe. You don't know how anxious I was to break in."

She continued, "Back to Fort Worth: We had to get Gussie to Jess, to give her the opportunity to do the right thing, even if she didn't take it. It would be one thing for us to kidnap Gussie and then Jess cry foul six months or three years later; it's another thing for us to bring her daughter to her and then for Jess herself to walk away."

"That's right," Sammy agreed, changing lanes competently.

"Okay, then. Where were we going to meet her? At the Threlkeld mansion, after she'd had this big blow-up with her dad? At our house? How was she going to get there from Fort Worth? Does Mr. Streiker bring her?" Marni asked.

"Right again. But, you know, that's mind-blowing, that after Streiker—did whatever he did for her, that she turns around and abandons her baby. What kind of gratitude is that?" he scoffed.

She shook her head. "How is she going to learn gratitude, Sammy? Good heavens, look who her mom is."

"Yeah." He shuddered at the remembrance of Linda Threlkeld-Rains. "I wonder if she's still in prison."

"I have no idea," Marni said, looking to the back seat.

So Sammy looked in the rearview mirror at the car seats lined up. Sam was poking Bubba with his foot while Bubba was trying to catch his toes in the act. Gussie was asleep, but Clay was awake, exercising. "Well, I . . . hope I can demonstrate enough gratitude for Streiker stepping in and paying off Clothier, but, I'm gonna make Pruett pull babysitting duty with Gussie."

Marni eyed him. "Before or after he sits with Chris?"

Sammy groaned, "I forgot."

"You, of all people," she chided.

Shortly thereafter, they arrived home. Marni called her parents to alert them of that fact. After hanging up, she told Sammy, "Their accountant had an emergency and had to cancel on them, but we were gone by that time. Can you believe it?"

"Huh," he said. "I guess Streiker wanted to see the Complete Kidman Cohort again."

She rolled her eyes, but set about getting everybody fed and changed. Bubba took care of his own needs in the back yard (where he had a second food and water dish) but, when the time came to leave again, he looked totally disinterested in climbing back into any car.

Marni paused in the driveway while Sammy stood at the gate issuing ultimatums to Bubba. "You know what?" she said. "Let's walk."

"Gotcha," Sammy said, turning from the gate, at which point Bubba agreed to come on out.

They geared up: Marni put Clay on her shoulder while Sammy piled the grocery bags, diapers, and Gussie's bag in his stroller. Sam was given charge of Bubba's leash, and Sammy took up Gussie in her carrier under one arm while hauling the packed stroller with the other. Marni guided Sam with her free arm, and the Complete Kidman Cohort Plus One set out.

Clayton answered the front door. "Well, here is a sight. Come in to the kitchen; Mother's cleaning up from painting. She'll be right with us."

They all trooped in, gathering around the kitchen table. Swinging Gussie in her carrier onto the middle of the table, Sammy said, "Grandpa Clayton, meet Augusta Mellon Threlkeld."

Clayton put on his glasses and leaned over the carrier. "Well, well, well," he said.

And then Pam came in, rubbing lotion on her hands. "I'm so sorry, I had to—"

Clayton turned around, giving her a clear line of sight to the table, and Pam stilled.

FOURTEEN

"That's it, kid," Sammy muttered in a stage whisper. "Now if you really want to get in good, give her a little wave, or maybe a smile."

They were appropriately stunned to see Gussie turn her little head toward the standing adult and spread her tiny lips in a smile.

Pam sat weakly at the table while everyone watched. Deliberately, she unbuckled Gussie from the carrier and lifted her out to her shoulder. Gussie turned her head, then fell back into Pam's hand for trying to look her in the face. Pam complied, holding her out a ways so they could gaze at each other.

Marni and Sammy exchanged wide-eyed glances. Clayton heaved a sigh and withdrew a pen and notepad from his shirt pocket. "What is the baby's name, again?"

"Augusta Mellon Threlkeld," Sammy said.

"And when was she born?" Clayton asked, writing.

"Uhh, that would be August fifth," Sammy said. He could hardly take his eyes off Pam and Gussie. The baby waved her little arm until her hand rested on Pam's face, and there it stayed.

"Where?" Clayton asked.

"Pardon?" Sammy turned back to him.

"I need the city of birth and the name of the father," Clayton said patiently. Marni put her hand to her mouth, hardly daring to hope, much less ask.

Sammy stood abruptly. "Wait," he said, extending a hand. "I have everything you need in the Mustang. Wait right here." With a short hop, he turned and ran out, inadvertently slamming the door even before Bubba could make it out behind him.

Marni turned back to her parents. "Daddy . . . ?"

He shook his head sadly. "I know that look in her eyes. It means she wants something that she's going to get no matter what I think about it."

Flushed, Pam glanced at him. "Don't be silly." Then she cuddled Gussie on her arm, cooing quietly.

"Now, sweetheart," Clayton continued matter-of-factly to his daughter, "I'll need an account from you of the conditions at the Threlkeld's house that might indicate abuse or neglect. Be as specific as you can, because this will be a legal deposition."

"Oh, you bet," she exhaled. "First, take a photo of her diaper rash. It's horrific." Then she began talking rapidly.

She was still talking when Sammy reentered without ringing the doorbell, evidently having run both ways. He laid Hellier's file folder in front of Clayton. "Here is everything you need. If you need more, I'll arrange an interview with Hellier."

"Uh huh. All right," Clayton said, opening the folder to peruse it. "Um hmmm. Okay, good. Aha," he murmured, flipping pages.

Marni got up with the grocery bags to start unloading them into the kitchen pantry. "Oh, Mom, this is THE best formula. And, I can pump some breast milk for you to have on hand, just to get her antibodies up. I'll leave the diapers here on the table until you know where you want them." Marni paused over the fresh, new, undamaged package of cookies, then stuck that in the pantry as well.

Within the next five minutes, Sammy's eyes had glazed over and he swayed a little. "Okay, we're going to leave you folks to get acquainted. I'll just . . . go, ah. . . ."

Marni put Clay in his stroller and hooked Bubba back on his leash with Sam. She leaned down to kiss her father on his cheek, murmuring, "You're such a great dad."

"We'll see," he said, reading a long sheet in the file.

Pam mused, "Oh, dear, we'll need a crib, and—"

"Gosh, Mom, just use the bassinet that Clay outgrew for now. We'll go shopping for a big one later," Marni said, backing Clay's stroller away from the table.

Pam glanced up, smiling. "No one could object to a little shopping."

Clayton cleared his throat and Marni laughed, kissing her mom. "Squee! I'm going to have a baby sister!"

On the way back to their house, Marni exulted, "Oh, that's just too perfect! Can you believe it? And I don't care how many lawyers the Threlkelds have, Dad will get Mom whatever she wants. He always has."

"Especially since they don't appear to want Gussie," Sammy said. "Whoa, partner. We're going home." He put a restraining hand on Sam's head when the toddler tried to direct Bubba to the park.

Meanwhile, Sammy had pressed a contact number on his phone and put it to his ear. "Mr. Streiker? This is —wait a minute. This is the Streiker Corporation number. You're at the warehouse! . . . Aren't you?"

"Call forwarding, Sammy," Streiker said.

"Okay, well, we just dropped Gussie off at my in-laws', and it looks like they want to adopt her! Marni's mother just melted into a pile of goo all over her."

"That's good, Sammy," Streiker said.

"You sound so shocked," Sammy noted.

"I'm glad you thought to tell me," Streiker said.

"Yes, well, I'm going to go pass out for a little while, and then I'm available," Sammy said.

"That also is good to know," Streiker said.

Sammy grappled with the appropriate words while he was fighting to stay on his feet. "Mr. Streiker . . . thank you for letting me be a part of this. And thank you for telling me about Adair."

"You're welcome, Sammy."

"Okay, then. Bye, now." He clicked off his phone as they turned up their front walk. Ten minutes later, all of them were sacked out on the queen-sized bed, including Bubba.

Sleeping for an hour in the afternoon disrupted everyone's sleep that night, except Bubba, who could sleep on demand for any length of time. Despite feeling haggard and grumpy, Sammy got up to get ready for work by eight o'clock the following morning, Friday. (He didn't have it in himself to run as well.) All he had to do to brighten up, however, was remember that he could have been awakened repeatedly during the night by a crying infant, as his in-laws undoubtedly had been.

Climbing into his slacks, he told Marni, "Call me when you find out how your folks got along last night. Shee, I hope that doesn't put a crimp in their plans to acquire her."

Sipping coffee, Marni murmured, "They're not new parents, Sammy."

"Yeah, but it's been a while. You forget that kind of thing. Okay, I'm off," he said, taking up his sports coat.

"Do you have your phone?" she asked.

"Uhh." He patted the pockets of the pants he had just put on, then leaned over to dig through the laundry hamper for the pants he had worn yesterday. Rifling the pockets, he brandished not only his phone, but his wallet, both of which he relocated to pockets of the current pants.

The little black detective notebook that he carried constantly was already in his shirt pocket. He kissed her enthusiastically, then headed to the laundry-room door that led into the garage.

Before he got there, he looked down at Bubba by his side, tail wagging. Marni waved. "Take him. I want Sam to rest today."

"Okay. C'mon, guy." Sammy opened the garage door and Bubba happily jumped into the passenger seat of the Mustang.

Backing down the driveway to the alley, he asked, "Is that better than the back of the Prius?" Bubba thumped the seat with his tail.

Arriving at the office with his usual coffee and

breakfast biscuit, Sammy was surprised to see both Mike's Toyota and Pruett's Firebird already there. He even found the door unlocked, which was convenient since both of his hands were occupied.

Entering with Bubba, Sammy looked at Mike going through mail that had piled up over the last few weeks and Pruett just hanging up the phone. "Wow. I seem to have entered a time warp to three months ago," he noted. Bubba went over for a head-scratching from Mike, who obliged.

"It would be great to back up and avoid a few potholes," Dave admitted.

"How's Chris?" Sammy asked on his way back to his desk.

"Better," Dave nodded. "We took him to the dentist yesterday—she took x-rays and splinted two teeth that were loose, but said we'll have to wait a few weeks to see if he'll need a root canal. Still in pain, but it's not as bad. We're just grateful every day that that guy came along when he did."

"Yeah, good. That's good," Sammy said. "Maybe Chris'll be up for us to come by and see him this weekend?"

"Sure," Dave said.

"We'll do that, then." Sammy sat, placing his breakfast on his desk and opening the laptop. He paused to look at the three orchid sprigs in the top cup. They were still there, still unwatered, still fresh. He reached out to touch one, feeling the delicate petal. Dropped through thin air. He smiled inwardly.

Dave said, "Ah, are you working the Edmondson case, Sammy?"

"Not very hard," he sighed, reaching into his desk drawer for the file. Opening it, he recalled, "I did manage to determine that he's renting the house on Bayview, not buying."

"Would that be twenty-six thirty-one Bayview?" Dave asked.

"That's right," Sammy said, noting Dave's sudden penchant for detail.

After an extended period of silent industry, Mike asked, "Were either of you in the office yesterday?"

Dave shook his head and Sammy replied, "Just briefly. Why?"

"Just wondered if any more reporters came by," Mike said.

Sammy looked out front. "We should move our cars."

"Probably," Mike agreed, and none of them moved.

Dave suddenly sat up. "Okay, I may have found something on Edmondson. Can I have that file?"

"Sure." Sammy gestured at it, but Dave didn't move. So Sammy got up to place it on Pruett's desk, but to not be in violation of office protocol (which stipulated that none of the three did anything in the way of a secretarial nature for the other two) Sammy made that the halfway point of his trip to the kitchenette to put sugar in his coffee that he didn't want. He returned to his desk, sipping his coffee and grimacing at how sweet it was.

His phone rang; composed, he picked it up. "MK and associates; this is Sammy Kidman."

His wife said, "Hi, Sammy. I just talked to Mom—Gussie did fine last night; slept almost the whole night through. Dad's lawyer started on the adoption paperwork yesterday! He's got a private investigator looking for the father—"

"PLEASE tell me it isn't Dunbar and Smith," Sammy pleaded, and both Mike and Dave looked at him.

"No, it's somebody else—I can't remember the name right now, but it's not anybody you've griped about. Anyway, they need to find Jess, and wondered if you knew where she'd be," Marni said.

"No," he said, "not unless she was stupid enough to go back to the theater."

"Which one was that? White Mountain Theater?" she asked.

"It's where White Mountain used to be, but they're calling themselves Prometheus Unbound now."

She objected, "No, that's a play by Shelley."

He snorted, "They knew it rang a bell. Uh, Alex is still there, and Matt Horton, who played Charles the Wrestler, but I sure don't want you going out there. For all I know, someone could have pushed her off that catwalk." Mike and Dave were openly eavesdropping by now.

"Oh, I'll let Dad's PI handle that; never fear," she said. "Besides, Mom and I are going to shop for a layette. I wasn't thinking clearly and packed the bag with diapers that can be bought anywhere instead of the clothes that she'll need."

"Uh huh," Sammy said, zoning out.

"Talk to you later," she laughed.

When he hung up, Mike and Dave were staring at him. "Uh, yeah," he said. "Mr. Streiker called me; asked me to find Jess Threlkeld and bring her to Fort Worth. I did that, uh—day before yesterday? So she wanted her baby; so he told me to bring her baby, and when I did, Jess decided she wasn't cut out to be a mom and split. So now Marni's parents want to adopt the baby, and they're trying to find Jess again."

There was a space of incredulous silence. "Mr. and Mrs. Taylor are adopting Mrs. Morgan Threlkeld's great-granddaughter?" Pruett asked in a moment of sterling clarity.

Sammy paused. "Sounds rather different when you say it like that."

"And what does the baby's grandfather, Stanley Morgan Threlkeld, heir and CEO of Threlkeld Enterprises, controlling billions of dollars, say about that?" Dave continued.

"Oops," Sammy whispered.

Mike added heavily, "They may not care anything about the baby herself, but they'll eat your in-laws alive to prevent bad publicity that could cost the company millions, Sammy."

Sammy's heart began hammering in his ears. "Streiker told us to get that baby out of the house, so Marni went after her yesterday morning. She said the baby was alone and neglected—that Dolly had completely forgotten about her. So when Jess rejected her, the Taylors told us over the phone that they'd help us with her. . . . And when we took her over there to see them yesterday—it was like love at first sight. The baby *smiled* at Pam. It was epic. You could hear the orchestra music swelling in the background."

Dave slowly shook his head. "How does the welfare of a baby measure up against market share? Do you know what the Threlkeld lawyers will do? They'll dredge up every tiny little incident that your in-laws have ever been remotely involved in and blow it up all over the internet. Your wife's parents will wake up to news stories about things that happened forty, fifty years ago, twisted to prove that they're unfit guardians—and that's before the lawyers even start on *you*," Dave hooted. Sammy wilted.

"Then, of course, the Taylors will be accused of attempting to adopt in order to get their hands on Threlkeld money. Your father-in-law's finances and business practices over the last forty years will be microscopically inspected and found wanting. Do you know that the statute of limitations on some types of securities fraud doesn't begin tolling until the fraud is 'discovered'?" Pruett's fingers made air quotes to emphasize that the discovery could be real or manufactured.

"They'll crucify him," Sammy whispered.

"To start with," Dave snorted. "And let me tell you another specialty of this kind of lawyer," Dave said with relish. "Your mother-in-law is a nice-looking lady for her age. Have you ever kissed her?"

"What?" Sammy scowled at him, as the answer to that was, *Yes*.

"You ever been at a restaurant with them and put your arm around her? Ever made a joke around friends about hitting on her?" Dave continued with merciless accuracy.

"What are you getting at?" Sammy cried.

"Inappropriate and unhealthy family relationships, Flea Brain! Oh, they love this tactic, because they can spin something so incredibly damaging out of thin air,"

Dave whispered, illustrating wisps of smoke.

Sammy put his head in his hands. "I can't let them do this," he groaned.

"Sure. Say, are the Taylors going to let you drop that baby back into oblivion?" Dave asked rhetorically, turning back to his computer. "Or are they going to fight until they, and you, have nothing left?" He looked totally disinterested at this point, already knowing the answer.

"Oh, God," Sammy whispered. "Oh, Jesus, he's right. He's—" Sammy broke off, staring at the orchids on his desk.

A whole array of differently colored orchid sprigs now filled his tall paper cup with no water. Besides the original three, there was a little pink one, a large orange one, and a deep purple one. *Dropped through thin air.*

When he could breathe again, Sammy muttered, "Okay, that means there has to be a way to deal with this." So he picked up his phone to dial Streiker, noting, "You can help me now."

To his amazement and consternation, a busy tone filled his ear. He stared at the handset. "Busy? It can't be busy!"

"Shut up, Sammy; I'm on the phone," Mike said.

Sammy put his head in his hands. "Help. Help," he whispered. "I need help. I need ammunition. I need. . . ."

Slowly, he raised his head. "I need blackmail material. And I think. . . ."

Hardly breathing, he opened his laptop and drew out his small notebook. He accessed the website of the monitoring system that McConnico had installed at the Threlkelds'. On the login field, he entered their phone number and passwords from his notebook. Then he watched as the system dashboard appeared on his screen.

"I'm in," he whispered. Then he noted, much to his surprise, that the system had been reactivated—from *inside* the house. Someone there now had turned the system back on. Which meant he had a very narrow window of opportunity wherein to get what he needed and get out.

Quickly, he navigated to the videos of last January 18. When he saw his father come on screen talking over his cell phone, Sammy threw back his head and laughed.

"What are you doing?" Pruett demanded. Mike looked over.

"In Texas, if you blackmail us, we will blackmail you right back," Sammy sang. "Come look."

FIFTEEN

Mike and Pruett sent their desk chairs flying back to come look over Sammy's shoulder at his laptop. And Sammy played for them the security video of his dad calling his girlfriend from his bedroom. Sammy prefaced the video with, "This is the day before he died in the car accident. This is proof that Mrs. Morgan Threlkeld had secretly married her chauffeur."

After watching it, Sammy's coworkers stood in thought. Mike said, "That is potent. But, Sammy . . . that would be most damaging to Dolly. I thought you liked her."

"I do," Sammy said. "I don't want to hurt her. But this would never have been possible if she hadn't lied about it so consistently and repeatedly. And if push comes to shove, I'd shove her over a cliff to make sure the Taylors have a chance to save that kid."

As Pruett was still silent, Sammy turned to him. "See, Pruett? All we need to do is show Stanley this video—"

"No, STUPID," Pruett barked, pantomiming a slap upside the head while Sammy flinched. "Load your ordnance and acquire your target before entering nego-tiations!" Bubba watched from the floor, then yawned.

"He's right," Mike observed complacently, returning to his desk.

"Show me what to do," Sammy said meekly. Vindicated in his battle prowess, Pruett yanked his chair to sit beside Sammy and plot out strategy.

An hour later, the phone rang. Sammy plucked it up. "MK and associates. This is Sammy Kidman."

Marni said, "Hi, Sammy. Just wanted to update you with some good news."

"Give it to me," he said, nodding as Pruett pointed to something pertinent on the laptop.

"Dad's PI found Gussie's father and got him to sign off on the adoption for nothing except release from all financial obligations. He was relieved to sign off because he thought Jess had had an abortion," Marni related.

Sammy looked up. "Cretin and maggot."

"But that's not the best news. The PI found Jess!" she exclaimed.

"At the theater?" Sammy asked.

"Yes, but not the one in Dallas. She's with a theater group in Fort Worth! Turns out she knew somebody there already, so when she left Mr. Streiker's warehouse, she called this other guy who came and picked her up. *She's* signed off on the adoption, too!" Marni exulted.

"Wow, that was fast work," Sammy muttered enviously.

"No kidding. So now Dad and his lawyer are going out to see the Threlkelds—"

"No!" Sammy exclaimed, standing. "Marni, stop

him! He can't go out there without me! I have something he needs!"

"Well, hold on. I'm at their house. Let me see if he's left yet—"

Sammy waited tensely on the phone as Marni left to go find her dad.

Minutes later Sammy heard Clayton say, "Sammy? What is it?"

Breathing out in relief, Sammy sat again. Pruett was swiftly typing on the laptop. "Clayton, don't go yet. You need me to go with you to talk to the Threlkelds."

"Jerry's meeting me out there, Sammy," Clayton said, referring to his lawyer. "He's competent in all areas of contract negotiations."

"I know he is, Clayton, but I have information he doesn't have," Sammy said.

"Well, give it to me, and I'll relay it to him," Clayton proposed.

"It's not that simple. It's visual evidence that I need to show to Stanley in person for maximum impact," Sammy said.

Clayton paused. "That sounds a little like blackmail, Sammy," he said reproachfully.

"You don't know anything about it, and if Jerry is smart, he won't even show up," Sammy maintained. "Do you have the forms for Stan and Dolly to sign?"

"Yes," Clayton admitted.

"Okay, bring them. And, uh, put your PI on to Linda Threlkeld-Rains, Jess' mother. Last I heard, she was serving time at Carswell, Fort Worth," Sammy said.

"I got a call a few minutes ago from his associate at Carswell, Sammy," Clayton said. "Ms. Threlkeld-Rains is demanding five thousand dollars for her signature, which of course we'll pay. She's destitute."

"Dang, who are these guys?" Sammy demanded, stung by the efficiency of his competitors on his in-laws' behalf.

"They're the Dante Agency, Sammy. They were engaged by Mr. Streiker on this case, since he knew you were busy," Clayton said.

"They sure got on it fast," Sammy muttered.

"Apparently, just in time. The agent told me that the Threlkeld butler and his wife had a few hours off this morning, so when the nanny came in and found the baby gone, she panicked and called nine-one-one," Clayton relayed.

Sammy's intestines froze to solid ice. He asked quietly, "How was that call disposed, Clayton?"

"I don't know. The agent said that the police did speak with Mr. Threlkeld. Would that be a problem? I thought they knew that Jessica had asked for the baby."

The ice spread to Sammy's lungs as he saw what could be the steep downside of taking Gussie without permission from her guardians. Of course, had Sammy pursued the correct course and told Stanley up front that Jess wanted her baby, he would have insisted that Jess come home to get her. Since Sammy was sure that Jess would not have returned for the baby, Marni would have lost the opportunity to rescue her.

Moreover, the fact that Stanley did not question Marni when he saw her with Gussie in her carrier was irrelevant; Marni had been a trusted visitor on many previous occasions.

Turning away from the phone, Sammy said with

difficulty, "Mike, see if there's a warrant out on Marni." Mike's head snapped back in alarm, then he picked up his phone.

Everyone waited until Mike turned back to say, "Two are pending, Sammy: unlawful entry and kidnapping."

Hand shaking, Sammy said into the phone, "Okay, Clayton, listen to me carefully. There are two warrants pending on Marni, so tell her to leave Sam and Clay with Pam and Gussie. Call Jerry and have him come pick up Marni and escort her to the Frank Crowley Criminal Courts Building downtown. He's to tell them that she is turning herself in for warrants pending, but she is admitting nothing and making no statements. Jerry will know not to let her say anything. Okay?"

"Yes, Sammy," Clayton said heavily.

"You wait right there for me. I'm coming to take you to meet Stanley and his lawyers. Don't leave without me. All right?" Sammy said.

"I'll be here," Clayton said.

"Bye, then." Sammy hung up and looked at Pruett.

Dave smiled with eyes of cold malice. "We're all ready here."

"Okay." Exhaling, Sammy bent down to stroke Bubba. Then he straightened and went out to the Mustang. Whining, Bubba looked after him, but didn't attempt to follow.

In twenty minutes Sammy was pulling up to the curb at the Taylors' house. He noted Marni's Prius in the driveway. As he opened the driver's door and stood, he saw Clayton come out of the front door and down the walk. Pam waved to Sammy from the doorway and then quickly shut the door when Sam came up to it.

"Whoa, power suit. This is a man dressed for battle," Sammy said, eyeing Clayton's attire respectfully. In order to transport Clayton in unruffled condition, Sammy raised the top on the Mustang.

"I've been in a few," Clayton grunted, sitting with his briefcase on his lap as he reached for the seatbelt.

"Is Marni okay?" Sammy asked casually, with a long glance at the house.

"She's fine. Jerry picked her up not three minutes ago, and her attitude was that it is all a mistake that will get cleared up quickly."

"She is correct," Sammy said with grim undertones. Pulling away from the curb, he glanced at Clayton's briefcase. "Did Jerry leave you with all the forms that Dolly and Stanley need to sign?"

"Oh, yes. He said that technically, Dolly's signature is not required, but it shows good faith for us to acquire it," Clayton said.

"Oh, we're nothing if not in good faith," Sammy breathed. He had been wanting to physically damage Stanley ever since the lecher gave Marni his old clothes for her husband. While it may not be possible for Sammy to beat on Stan today, he was willing to take whatever opportunity was presented to express his deep feelings. Only—

Seeing a crimp in his plan, Sammy said, "If Hellier was gone this morning—Clayton, your PIs need to talk to him, too."

"Oh, they got a notarized statement from him last night," Clayton said.

Sammy turned to stare briefly at him, jerking the

wheel. "Are you serious? That is the fastest investigative work I've ever seen. Still, I wish Hellier would be there. I'm gonna need him."

Clayton glanced at his watch. "He should be there by now. Yes, Mr. Streiker personally lit a fire under the investigators. He was apparently unwilling for the baby to be returned to the Threlkelds for any length of time. Without the agency's involvement, we would have had no choice but to relinquish her."

"Ah," Sammy said in illumination.

"He went so far as to send a pediatrician to our home yesterday to look at her, along with a notary for the forms," Clayton added.

Sammy squinted in wonder, murmuring, "When he moves, he does not mess around." Clayton nodded.

They drove in silence for a while, then as Sammy turned on to Royal Lane, he said, "Clayton, I appreciate that this is your life we're primarily talking about, but I want to do the talking."

Clayton replied, "Sammy, I appreciate that you want to do the talking, but this is my wife and daughter we're talking about. I will do the talking."

"Dam'," Sammy muttered under his breath, and Clayton smiled.

Belatedly realizing the imperative of having their own unedited record of this meeting, Sammy took the phone out of his pocket. "Listen, Clayton, Stan is going to be recording everything."

"Sammy, I am wearing a wireless video recorder. The lens is in my lapel pin," Clayton said.

"No lie? Awesome," Sammy grinned. His hand dropped the phone back in the direction of his pocket. It slid right past the fabric to the floorboard, unnoticed by either man.

Turning a corner, Sammy pulled up to the closed gate and tapped the horn. "Yes?" Hellier's voice said.

Knowing that Hellier was following orders, Sammy looked benignly into the surveillance camera. "Hi, Hellier. Sammy Kidman here with my father-in-law Clayton Taylor, who has an appointment with Mr. Threlkeld."

"Very good, Mr. Kidman. You may drive on through." Technically, Sammy couldn't, but the gates rolled open a minute later to give him access.

Sammy parked in the front circular drive, then he and Clayton mounted the steps as Hellier opened the door. "Hellier!" Sammy exclaimed, reaching out to shake his hand warmly. "Hellier, this is Clayton Taylor," Sammy said, an arm around Hellier's shoulders as he indicated Clayton.

"Yes, I remember Mr. Taylor. How do you do, sir?" Hellier said, shaking his hand.

"Very well, Hellier; thank you."

Still on the front porch with his back to the house, Sammy leaned into Hellier's side to whisper, "Where is Dolly?"

"Mr. Threlkeld sent her out shopping, Sammy," Hellier replied. His use of Sammy's first name indicated his willingness to be a conspirator.

"Can you call her?" Sammy asked.

"I can call the chauffeur," Hellier said.

"Good. Have him tell her that I'm at the house for a visit and asked to see her," Sammy said. "Whenever she gets here, send her in to wherever we are."

"Certainly, Sammy."

"Thanks, Hellier."

The butler led the visitors to an office on the second floor—a room that Sammy had never seen before. He guessed that Stan had told McConnico in no uncertain terms that this room was not to be monitored, and McConnico had respected that. Today, of course, that all changed.

As Sammy and Clayton entered, two people in the room looked up. One was Stan, and the other a woman. A glance at her made Sammy's heart leap for joy: he had a woman lawyer to play with.

Now, some of the toughest lawyers and judges he had ever faced were women—but those women were too scholarly and serious to make themselves look cheap. This woman, on the other hand, was young, not out of her 30s, and dressed a little too stylishly, wearing a skirt that was a little too short. Her careful hair and makeup job indicated that she relied too heavily on her appearance in her work.

Being pretty could be an asset in the short-term, but was rendered ineffective as the years began to take their toll. And this kind of vanity was a weakness that Sammy could exploit with abandon.

Stan was making introductions: "Scarlett, this is Clayton Taylor, whose daughter gained illegal entry to kidnap my granddaughter. And this is his son-in-law . . . what's your name again?"

"Sammy Kidman," he said, reaching out to shake Stan's hand, which had not been offered. Clearing his throat, Sammy turned to the woman. "And you are—?"

"Scarlett Cotton, Mr. Threlkeld's attorney," she said

with a smile of condescension as she shook Sammy's hand. She received Clayton's handshake with a little more professionalism.

"Please have a seat." Stan indicated two chairs opposite his desk. Sammy and Clayton sat in those while Scarlett sat in another at the corner of Stan's desk—not behind it, beside it or in front of it, but just sort of floating in the area.

"So," Stan said, clearing his throat. "When are you going to return my granddaughter?"

"Mr. Threlkeld," Clayton said, opening his brief-case, "I have evidence that your granddaughter was suffering neglect after your daughter vacated the premises. Upon Jessica's request, my daughter and son-in-law retrieved Augusta from this house and brought her to Jessica.

"After consideration of the responsibilities she faced with the child, Jessica decided that it was in Augusta's best interest to give her up for adoption. All that is spelled out in considerable detail in these affidavits." He laid several sheets on the desk in front of Stan.

During this speech, Sammy had his head down as if listening, while he was actually studying Scarlett's crossed legs. She was quite aware of this, for when she shifted, accidentally hiking her skirt an inch or two, he immediately glanced at the fresh display of flesh before earnestly turning his attention to his father-in-law.

Stan picked up the sheets to hand them to his lawyer without looking at them. She, in turn, wadded them up and tossed them over her shoulder.

"We'll do our own depositions," she told Clayton coolly.

Like a kindly father, he asked, "Are you incurious as to our allegations?"

Dropping his purported interest in Scarlett's anatomy, Sammy glanced at Clayton's astute blow. In a nice way, he was calling attention to her rookie error in remaining willfully ignorant. True, she might shred their complaints in court, but not if she wouldn't condescend to read them.

Sammy then began ogling her chest, but so discreetly that not even Stan noticed. Sammy would eye her assets, then look thoughtfully over her shoulder, or turn around to regard Clayton. Then when she moved or spoke, he would look at her again—in the chest.

A surveillance camera would never catch it; he would only appear a little restless. But it was truly unnerving to any woman other than a Hooter's waitress to have her chest so closely monitored. An honorable woman subjected to this treatment would bristle with indignation. The fact that, upon noticing his interest, Scarlett faced him and arched her back put her squarely in the Hooter's category.

On the other side of the negotiations, Clayton gravely continued, "We have had Augusta examined by a pediatrician, and his opinion is that her physical condition indicates recent neglect. Combined with your butler's statements as to the habitual, prolonged absences of the nanny, it is his recommendation that Children's Protective Services be called in to conduct an investigation."

At Stan's suddenly slack face, Sammy almost applauded. Getting CPS involved was seriously hardball. It would unleash not only the rabid hounds of bad publicity, but the unending bureaucratic nightmare that all such government entities inflicted under the guise of public service.

In support of this, Clayton laid another sheet in front of Stan, turning to advise Scarlett: "I, personally, would not discard that before reading it."

Sammy almost blew snot out of his nose at Clayton's patient fatherly manner. He was patting Stan's high-dollar attorney on her head: *Dear, sweet child.*

Stan skimmed the sheet, noting only the medical legalese, the signature of the pediatrician affiliated with an accredited hospital, and the notary's seal. He looked up to ask in a tight voice, "What do you want?"

Clayton nodded, extracting another sheet. "Here are our terms, which are: My wife and I want to legally adopt Augusta and change her name to ours. We neither desire nor require any monies or property from you in support, ever.

"We have no expectation of her receiving any bequests or gifts from you, although the decision to confer such is not ours, of course. We are willing to give you and the mother supervised visitation rights, if you desire. We wish to keep this transaction completely private. And we will tolerate no subsequent challenge of the legality of the adoption."

Blinking, Stan scanned Clayton's list of demands. Sammy looked at Scarlett's lips and licked his own, unconsciously, of course. Or so it seemed. Stan said, "Jessica really didn't want her?"

Clayton nodded to one wadded-up form on the floor. "That affidavit is in her handwriting. As for the father, he had assumed that the child had been aborted, and was thrilled to hear that he would not be required to pay child support."

Stan sank back in his seat. "Well, [expletive]. I'm sorry to hear that."

"As a grandfather myself, I understand that, Mr. Threlkeld. We only want what is best for Augusta, and we don't wish to cause you any further distress or inconvenience. If you and Mrs. Threlkeld will sign those two forms, we'll be on our way."

With a sigh, Stan picked up a pen to sign. But then Sammy, as occasionally happens, overplayed his hand. He took one last longing glance at Scarlett's midsection. She, in turn, decided that he was not getting away without paying toll.

Scarlett stood, unconsciously thrusting out her hip. Sammy stood; Clayton and Stan did not. "Mr. Threlkeld, I'd advise against your signing that right away," she announced. Sammy, breath quickening, parted his lips and looked her up and down.

"What's the problem, Scarlett?" Stan asked. Clayton looked on calmly.

"I'd like to clarify a few matters with Mr. Kidman in private," she said, chest out.

"Well—use the library downstairs," Stan said, gesturing with his pen.

She turned on her high heels and marched out, Sammy quickly following. The two men in the second-floor office were still, listening to them retreat down the stairs.

"Eh, she likes your son-in-law," Stan muttered, signing the form anyway and handing it over. "This other one will have to wait until Mother gets back. As long as I don't tell her what it means, she'll sign."

"Thank you Mr. Threlkeld," Clayton said, delicately receiving the piece of paper to place it in his briefcase. "She is welcome to come see the baby, if she wishes."

"She won't know who it is," Stan murmured, tapping his chin thoughtfully with the pen. "Well," he said, perking up. "Let's see what Scarlett wants with Sammy."

Turning to a cabinet behind him, he opened a pair of doors and slid out a desktop computer with monitor. Waking it, he typed in instructions which brought up a video on the monitor. Stan scooted his chair out of the way so that Clayton could see, then turned up the volume on the surveillance camera in the library as Scarlett and Sammy entered.

Sixteen

As Sammy and Scarlett entered the library, she closed the door and shoved him up against the wall. "Hey," he smiled, hands in the air to demonstrate his innocence. "What gives?" Glancing up, he saw that they were out of view of the camera, so he slid to an adjacent wall as if trying to get away from her.

She pushed him flat against the wall again and brought his head down to kiss him open-mouthed. He lifted his head back out of range. "That's assault, baby. I just might press charges."

"Shut up," she breathed, pressing up against him. She was making really close contact that he knew he had to stop post haste.

So Sammy brought up his wrist to look at his watch over her head. "Better hurry. We've only got fifteen minutes."

"Why's that?" she grunted, unbuttoning her blouse.

"You want to see?" he grinned, holding her arms up by her wrists, bondage-style.

"Uhmm." She went slack in submission.

Sammy turned her around to place her hands on the security-system console. She stuck her posterior up in the air, and he briefly covered a silent laugh. Then he leaned over her to begin inputting on the keyboard in front of her.

"What're you doing?" she muttered, displeased, and attempted to relocate his hands to a more personal area.

But he breathed, "You want to see this."

She pouted, "What is it?"

"It's a preview of video that is going live on three big gossip sites in—" he checked his watch again —"thirteen minutes. Watch."

He hit "play," and they watched Sam say over his phone, "Hi, Carla. I've made up my mind. I'm gonna divorce Dolly so that we can be together like we were always meant to be. I . . . I've been prayin', Carla— yeah, I've been talking to God, trying to figure out how to make my life right, and—yeah, it's gonna be okay. I have somethin' to take care of tomorrow, then I'm coming out to your place. Okay. Bye."

The video stopped and Scarlett went glassy-eyed. Sammy leaned around her right side, then remembered where the hidden camera was and leaned around her left side instead, so that his face and words would be clear in the recording.

"That's surveillance footage of my dad when he was Dolly's chauffeur—see all the coded notations? Anyway, it's also proof that Dolly had married him. Mrs. Morgan Threlkeld married her chauffeur. Now, if my colleague doesn't get a call from me in—" he consulted his watch—"eleven minutes, he's going to send this video to the North Dallas *Expositor*, the *National Inquisitor*, and *BuzzTalk*. I really don't want to see that happen, do you?"

"That's blackmail!" she hissed.

"Duh. It wouldn't be effective if it weren't. We're down to ten minutes," he noted.

"What do you want?" she spat.

"I want you to let Stan and Dolly sign the adoption papers so that Jess will be happy, Gussie will be happy, and my wife's parents will be happy," Sammy said.

Clayton's disembodied voice said, "Sammy, Mr. Threlkeld has already signed, and promises to give the form to Mrs. Threlkeld. You can call Dave and tell him to lay off the joke."

Without being told, Clayton somehow knew who Sammy's colleague was. Gasping, Scarlett frantically re-buttoned her suit blouse.

Sammy turned to bare his teeth savagely at the hidden camera. "Oh DEAR," he said, making a show of checking his watch again. "EIGHT minutes until this excruciatingly embarrassing knowledge goes viral—"

"Sammy—"

"Unless Stanley gets on the phone with the DA and I hear that all charges against Marni Taylor Kidman are dropped," Sammy uttered.

There was the creaking of a chair and the clicking of buttons. There was a voice speaking rapidly; the tone indicated that it belonged to Stanley, but the words were not discernible.

A minute later, Sammy detected a change in speakers; Clayton was talking now. There was a definite conversational end, then Clayton said, "Sammy, I just talked to the assistant district attorney. The warrants on Marni have been voided."

"Okay, then. I'll call my colleague and tell him to abort the transmission," Sammy said righteously, digging in his pocket. "Hmm. Clayton, have you seen my phone?"

"No, Sammy."

"When did I last change pants?" he muttered, searching his pockets. He heard Stan saying something, but Scarlett grabbed Sammy by the lapels to shake him furiously, screaming at him.

"Calm down," he huffed, removing his jacket from her grasp. "Hey, Clayton, have you got Pruett's number in your phone?"

"No, Sammy."

Scarlett began screaming at him again; he turned to her to chide, "That isn't helping." Addressing the hidden camera, he said, "Well, you have our office number, don't you?"

"Yes, Sammy."

"Okay, try that," Sammy advised.

"All right, Sammy; I'm calling," Clayton said. While they waited, Scarlett clung to Sammy in an agony of suspense. Again, they heard Clayton's voice but not his words.

As Clayton continued to talk, Sammy called up, "Is there a problem?"

Clayton replied, "He thinks it's a trick."

"HERE'S A TRICK FOR YOU IDIOT SCUMBAG IF YOU DON'T ABORT THAT VIDEO I WILL COME HUNT YOU DOWN AND HURT YOU SO BAD!" Scarlett screamed up at the corner with misbuttoned blouse, runny mascara, and brandished fist.

An instant later Clayton said, "Okay, he killed it."

There was a moment of quiet in the library, then Sammy smirked to Scarlett, "There, you see? That wasn't so—" She fell on him with a cry of guttural savagery, knocking him clear over the console and falling (inadvertently) on top of him.

The door to the library opened and Dolly wandered in. "Why, Hellier, I don't see—oh, there you are, Sammy! What are you doing down there? Who is that? That's not Marni," she bristled.

"Dolly! Good to see you," Sammy said, springing up to kiss her cheek. "Stanley, bring the form down to the sunroom," he said to the corner of the room. Dolly looked up distractedly, then allowed him to walk her down the short hall to the sunroom in the back of the house.

Sammy set her gently on the glider as she complained, "Marni was just here and didn't stay two minutes!"

"They're always running off somewhere or other," Clayton agreed, entering with the form. "Mrs. Threlkeld, you may not remember me—I am Clayton Taylor, Marni's father."

"Of course. Have a seat. You drank beer, anything but lite, is that right?" she said.

"That's correct, Mrs. Threlkeld," he said in surprise. As she turned to call Hellier, he interposed, "But I'm sorry that I can't stay for a drink today. I'm just here to ask you to sign this. Mr. Threlkeld has already signed one like it." Clayton offered her a pen. She took it and began scrutinizing the form.

Her son, having entered the room behind them, explained, "Now, Mother, this is nothing. It's just something that—"

"It gives Marni permission to take care of my baby," she said, laying the form on the rocker arm to sign unsteadily. Clayton and Sammy glanced at each other.

Stan looked back to his lawyer, standing outside the room in torn hose and general disarray. "Would you like to make yourself useful and get your notary ledger?" he asked, restrained.

She limped away, returning in a few minutes to notarize Dolly's and Stan's sheets. Clayton, the picture of courtesy, said, "Thank you very much," upon receiving them from her hand. Sammy, sitting next to Dolly, opened his mouth but Clayton added, "I think we'll be going now. Mrs. Threlkeld."

Clayton leaned over to gently shake her hand, but Sammy kissed her cheek. She ordered, "Come back when you can stay longer, Sammy."

"Sure, Doll," he murmured.

Clayton shook Stan's hand and Hellier escorted them to the front door, smiling. Sammy, exultant, emerged into a glorious fall afternoon. "Okay, Clayton; hold on to your hair piece; I'm gonna lower the top," he announced, opening the driver's side door.

Clayton, who did not wear a hair piece, smiled. "Go right ahead, Sammy."

"Well, there it is!" Sammy exclaimed, bending to retrieve his phone from the floorboard. Clayton sighed mildly; Sammy sat, started the engine, and laid rubber down the Threlkelds' drive.

On their way home, Sammy suddenly veered into a

shopping center. Clayton grasped the arm rest and glanced at him. "Sorry about that. I just remembered. . . ." He pulled into a parking space next to an outdoor cafe and a theater.

Getting out of the Mustang, Sammy reached into his pocket. "Clayton, will you—get me a coffee and maybe a roll or something from here?" he said, indicating the cafe. "They have really good . . . rolls."

"I have money, Sammy," Clayton said, glancing at the theater, which was obviously Sammy's object of interest. But Clayton went into the cafe while Sammy opened the theater door.

He strolled down the aisle, gratified to see Alex, Tony and Olivia on stage. The three of them turned to watch him advance. While Alex and Tony remained frozen in place, Olivia threw down her script and ran backstage.

"Hey," Sammy said, drawing up to the edge of the stage. "That was a mean trick."

Alex, sweating profusely, opened his mouth, but Sammy went on: "Why didn't Jess show up? You could have at least left a note that she had changed her mind about meeting me. I sure didn't appreciate looking for somebody in a dark theater at night. It was spooky. Anyway, do you have any idea where she might have gone?"

Alex and Tony gaped at him in near terror. "No," Alex croaked.

"Well, darn," Sammy said in disappointment. "Do you think she's still in the area?"

"No!" Alex cried.

Sammy muttered something in disappointment, then

said, "Well, okay. If you see her again, please ask her to contact me."

"All right," Alex gasped.

Sammy walked back up the aisle, grinning. "Forgive me, Mr. Streiker, for I have sinned, and it was fun." On top of that, it was satisfying to contemplate PU's loss of Threlkeld funding.

With all this running through his head, he didn't even see the coffee and sweet roll that Clayton held as he stood beside the car, waiting. So on the way back, Clayton enjoyed them himself.

SEVENTEEN

What with getting Marni sprung from the criminal courts building and finalizing adoption matters with Jerry, MK's associates had little opportunity for a group hug that afternoon.

So the next day, Saturday, Sammy ordained a meetup at the Fletcher Streiker Arboretum. The Kidman Cohort, including Bubba, was to be the advance guard; Clayton, Pam and Gussie were to attend, as was the entire Masterson Gang (Mike, Charisse, Lacie and Todd) and the Pruetts (Kelli in a stroller; Chris in a wheelchair). Sammy called the Hawkinses to beg them to come, but Sarah said that Les was not feeling up to it and she declined to come without him.

So, as soon as the Arboretum opened that day, the various squadrons met up in the entrance plaza to set exploratory parameters and regroup times, but the Masterson teens kidnapped Chris, spiriting him away in a wheelchair wheelie. Charisse raised her mighty voice after them, but they had disappeared down a path.

That left adults with toddlers, babies, and one dog. Kerry Pruett admired the sling carrier in which Pam was carrying a contented Gussie. "Wow, Pam, that's elegant. You look so happy."

In fact, everyone noticed Pam's glow. "I've hardly seen you smile so much," Marni murmured.

Sammy sang, "Oh, man, your dad was masterful. He was King. By the time he got done 'splaining matters, Stanley was crawling on the floor, crying."

Clayton turned a grave eye on his son-in-law. "Then what was the need for the performance in the library?"

Sammy gestured defensively, "You heard Stanley's lawyer! She was going to muck things up but good."

Pam said, "You weren't really going to release that video, were you?"

"No, of course not, Mrs. Taylor!" Pruett said energetically. Sammy studied his fingernails, then hissed something to Pruett, who snapped something back. Then Pruett added, "But there was also the matter of springing Mrs. K from illegal detention."

Everyone looked at Marni, who shrugged, "It was no big deal. I got a chance to catch up with Jerry, and the bailiffs were very sweet. I don't think there were ever any warrants."

Mike, who knew differently, distanced himself from the possibility of disclosing that. "Would you care for some mango shave ice?" he asked his wife. She consented, and they walked off toward the shave ice stand.

Not knowing exactly what "shave ice" was, Sam nonetheless recognized an opportunity for treats. So, accompanied by an eager dog, Clayton took Sam to get him some shave ice, too.

The others looked around at the brilliant trees and fall-blooming shrubs. Pam and Marni, pushing Clay in a stroller, began wandering up one path toward a fountain. "I'd love to carry Clay in a sling, but he's getting too heavy! Gussie's enjoying it," Marni observed.

"We're going to change her name," Pam mentioned. "I'm seriously thinking about 'Adair.'"

Marni quickly looked at her. "I think that's a beautiful name." After a pause, she said, "Mom, I never knew that you wanted another baby. I always thought, since you only had me. . . ."

Pam sighed, looking at the fiery purple sage bushes lining the walk like sentinels. "In the five years after your birth, I had two miscarriages, the last one at five months along. It was so—terrible, I had my tubes tied and started painting."

Marni gaped at her. "You never told me this," she whispered.

"I just couldn't talk about it. I picked up the pieces and went on with my life," she said, laying a hand on the snoozing little ball on her chest. "And then later on, I didn't want to burden you with that, especially after you told me that Sammy couldn't have children." She glanced at Clay ironically.

"Oh, Mom," Marni breathed, reaching out to hug her shoulders.

Back at the plaza, Sammy, Dave and Kerry stood idly watching Clayton and Sam bring a carton carrier of various shave ices to Marni and Pam. Bubba followed to catch drips. "Well?" Kerry said to her husband.

"Ma'am?" he returned, slightly startled.

"Are you going to get me a shave ice?" she asked.

"Yes, of course," he said. But he didn't move, and Sammy looked at him in mild disgust.

But Dave was thinking. "I should take some shave ice to Chris, too, if I can find him. He seems to have wheeled off somewhere. Yeah, he doesn't really need the chair, but the RN required it"—referring to Chris' mother, of course.

"Do not argue with the powers that be," Sammy said, suddenly distracted by someone entering the gate.

"Wouldn't think of it," Dave continued airily. "But we were wondering how to appropriately thank you for coming to his aid in that alley."

Sammy waved dismissively. "It's nothing that you wouldn't—" He broke off, suddenly focusing on Pruett.

Kerry breathed, "Sammy, it *was* you! Why didn't you tell us?"

He looked annoyed, then worried. "Oh, sh—. There *is* a video. Is that how you found out?"

"No," Pruett said, studying him. "Chris couldn't sleep for reliving the attack over and over, and we finally prayed about it. The next time he fell asleep and started reliving the attack again, he saw your face on the black angel, and woke up knowing it was you. He slept much better after that."

"Ah ha," Sammy said, glancing down.

Kerry began, "We just can't thank you enough—"

Sammy cut her off: "Kerry, you know good and well that Pruett would do the same thing if he passed by and saw somebody getting a beatdown. I didn't know it was Chris. Please, please don't tell *anybody*." Then turning to Pruett in aggravation, Sammy said, "You wanna take your wife over there for some shave ice, Romeo?"

Smiling vaguely, Pruett escorted her, pushing Kelli in her stroller, to get them all some refreshment.

That left Sammy free to turn his attention to the new arrival. Apparently having come alone, she had paused in the entryway, looking around. She was something of the mousy type, with dark hair and large glasses that he recognized from news photos.

He approached her with extended hand. "Hi! I'm Sammy Kidman."

She tentatively accepted his hand. "Sharon."

"Want some shave ice?" he said, nodding toward the kiosk.

"Not this early in the morning, thank you," she said cautiously.

"I'm an employee of Fletcher Streiker," he said. While she evaluated that, he went on: "And I thought I recognized you from the newscasts."

She looked back over her shoulder in alarm. So he said, "If you want to avoid the reporters, we might just walk down the path a ways."

Again she hesitated, but there were so many people coming in that she decided to accept his invitation. They started off down one path into the trees. Neither spoke for a while, as Sammy deliberated the best opening. "Still working at the bank?" he finally asked.

"Not The Rivers Bank, no," she said quietly. "There was just too much—" She broke off, but it was unnecessary for her to finish the thought. "Mr. Whinnet found me another position."

"That's good," he said. "Good man. He could have taken my head off for a stupid mistake, and didn't."

She smiled a little, looking at the masses of bronze

mums along the path. "This is a nice arboretum. I can't believe I've never been here before."

"What made you come today?" he asked.

She turned to him in wonder. "I got an invitation in the mail!" She suddenly dug in her purse to pull out a stiff card and hand it to him.

"It's engraved," he said in surprise, running his thumb over the embossing. "I did not know they still made these." He and she were still walking, following the path.

"I know!" she exclaimed. "But there it is, addressed to me, for today, so I thought, 'Well, why not?'" she laughed. Looking at her drained face, listening to her strained laughter, Sammy saw how very wounded she was.

"I'm glad you came," he said. "Streiker seems to do a lot of people good."

"Maybe," she sighed. "But, you know, after you pray and pray for something, and then see that it was all for nothing, you wonder if there's any use in it at all." She had come to a stop, blinking back tears. "I think I need to go back now."

She started to turn, but Sammy caught her arm, smiling. "Hey, you can't go yet; you just got here! There's lots to see. There's a koi pond. They go nuts for the pellets; you'd think it was doughnuts or something. C'mon," he urged.

"Well . . ." she sighed.

"Please come," he whispered.

She relented, allowing him to nudge her down the path. But she was reluctant and restless. Undeterred, he looked up to the golden birch canopy overhead. "I love the fall. After a blazing summer, it's like everything relaxes, lets out its breath. . . ."

She dropped her head, tears rolling down her face. "My grandmother died in the fall. She was the one who raised me. When she died, I felt I had no one left in the world. She . . . had been a ballet dancer when she was a young girl. She tried to teach me to dance, but I'm such a klutz, I could never do it. . . ."

Sammy kept very quiet, and eventually she went on, "The teller who worked in my bank—maybe you saw the news accounts," she said tentatively, glancing at him, but he still said nothing. "She was a dancer. But she was also terrible at math, so I tried to help her keep her accounts straight, and she showed me some steps now and then, like at lunch or after work. When she'd take my hands to dance, I swear I could do it! We'd laugh and laugh. She was so sweet. It was almost like—having my grandmother back, young and healthy. . . .

"And then she . . . fell in love. She got obsessed with this man that no one had ever seen, and everyone thought she was going insane. I think that's why Duane did it," she said vehemently, turning on him, and Sammy watched her.

"Duane was jealous because she wouldn't even try to play up to him anymore. She knew he could fire her, and she didn't care. That's what made him attack her—it was his own jealousy." She cut herself short, tossing her head.

They continued walking. Sammy remained silent. Eventually she resumed, "I sat with her in the hospital because I could see she was still alive, still—I don't know. There was so much going on that I couldn't see.

Every now and then, I'd catch glimpses of her dancing, or shopping, or walking with a little boy under some palm trees. And there was a man with her. But, when she died, all that stopped. She left, and left me behind." She stopped to cry bitterly.

It took every ounce of willpower for Sammy to refrain from holding her, as he instinctively knew that to do so would interfere with some better consolation at hand.

Raising her head in sudden rebellion, she said, "There's nothing here for me. There's no one who cares." She planted her feet, refusing to go farther down the path. When she blindly turned back, Sammy went so far as to block her from retreating.

Hearing music, they looked toward the same place at the same time. On the other side of a brook spanned by a footbridge was a large gazebo which was very similar to one Sammy had seen before. Only that one, where Streiker and his wife had been dancing, was in another part of the Arboretum where there had been no brook and no bridge.

Around this gazebo, children were rolling in the grass, digging in the dirt, or dancing, as the ballerina was dancing. Sammy watched the beautiful black-haired dancer pirouette in joy in the gazebo. A few other people leaned on the rails, watching or talking.

Sharon gasped, watching. Sammy regarded her pale face and open mouth. "That's—" She caught herself, then asked in a whisper, "Do you believe in ghosts?"

"Ghosts?" Sammy repeated, glancing back at the dancer. "Nah. I believe in angels and saints." He quickly looked to the side of the stage, where Streiker had appeared from the back. Sammy straightened. When seeing Streiker or speaking to him, it was always his impulse to straighten. Strange. But Streiker was coming this way.

At something Streiker said, the dancer turned, throwing her arms out to Sharon in joyful recognition. Sharon clasped a hand over her mouth, crying. She turned as if to run away, but she couldn't get around Sammy.

Then Streiker walked up to the middle of the footbridge, a mere fifteen feet away. "Hello, Sharon. It's good to see you again."

Her curiosity piqued, she looked at him, then breathed, "I know you. You were there, with Adair. . . ."

"That's right. I'm no stranger. Come on over," he said, extending his hand. The dancer, still in the gazebo, was bouncing up and down in anticipation, her arms still outstretched. Sammy noticed that she never even attempted to cross the bridge, as if understanding that it was impossible.

Sharon looked longingly at the dancer, then tore her eyes away to look at Streiker. To Sammy's astonishment, her mouth hardened in anger. "I won't blame you for my precious grandmother dying. But where is Adair? You left her lying there like a—a—pile of rotting meat! She couldn't eat; she couldn't talk—she withered down to skin and bones and bedsores! She suffered horribly for a year! And then you let her die!" she cried.

"Sharon." The soft voice from the path to the left of them caused Sharon and Sammy to swiftly turn. And there stood Adair, dressed in the bodysuit and tulle she wore when Sammy had first seen her at the park.

Sharon cried out, clutching at Sammy's sleeve without regarding him.

Adair approached, holding out her hand. "Sharon, darling, come talk to me." From that point on, Sammy could hear nothing they said between them, though he was only a few feet away.

"You're dead! I saw you die!" Sharon cried.

Adair took her hand. "No, darling, you didn't. Let's talk about what you did see that night."

Frowning in concentration, Sharon pressed Adair's hand between hers. "I was sitting by your bed as usual. I was almost asleep—it had been a very trying day."

"True," Adair said sympathetically.

Sharon's dark eyebrows gathered tightly. "You began gasping. I pressed the call button for the nurse. No one came." She choked back a sob, and Adair nodded. Sammy watched intently, attempting to read lips, but Sharon's back was to him.

She went on, "You stopped breathing. I was screaming into the intercom by that time. Then the—the light—there was the light all around the bed—"

"And who did you see in the light?" Adair asked leadingly.

Sharon glanced back at Fletcher waiting patiently on the bridge. Sammy looked back at him, too, noting peevishly that *he* seemed to be hearing them just fine. "The light scared me," Sharon admitted, "so I ran out looking for the nurse. I . . . didn't see what happened after that."

"You missed the good part," Adair chided. "But what did you see when you brought the nurse into the room?"

"That you were gone," Sharon whispered.

"But they issued a death certificate and performed an autopsy," Adair tossed off carelessly, as if reading from a news report.

"They were lying," Sharon said darkly. "I told them what I saw and they wouldn't believe me. They pretended to do the post-mortem so they wouldn't have to answer any questions about what happened to your body.

"Then the funeral home 'cremated' you and presented your family with some leftover ashes. They charged your parents for it, too! I heard them talking about it. I wasn't supposed to, but I did," she said defiantly.

"Then why didn't you believe what you saw and heard, silly girl?" Adair cried.

"You suffered so much," Sharon whispered. The way she kneaded Adair's hand reminded Sammy of how Marni had felt his arm after the unbreaking. She was demanding proof through her sense of touch for what she could hardly believe with her eyes.

Streiker crossed the bridge to their side of the brook, but did not come close. By his restraint, Sammy realized that he wanted to draw her, not coerce her. It was all Sammy could do to not pick her up and throw her across the bridge.

Streiker said, "Adair's suffering is what brought me to her side, Sharon. And when it had served its purpose of equipping her, I brought her out of it." Sammy, hearing him, quickly looked at the women.

Uncertainly, Sharon reached out to touch Adair's face, then gripped her in a tight hug. "Someone is waiting for you, Sharon," Adair whispered, stroking her dark hair.

Wiping her eyes, Sharon looked back at the dancer in the gazebo, who was watching anxiously. Seeing Sharon look over, she said something to her companions, who began gathering at the near railing to watch.

"Sharon, *everybody's* waiting on you," Streiker said in mildly humorous irritation.

Trembling, she began stumbling down the rocky path toward the bridge. Then she stopped to complain, "I can't see! Where is it? Where are you?"

"Take off your glasses. You don't need them anymore," Streiker said, leaning back on the bridge railing.

In great hesitation, she removed her aid, her crutch, her defense against anyone who tried to get too close. When she looked up without them, she cried out in surprise. Flinging them down, she ran toward the bridge, straight into Streiker's arms.

Sammy glanced at Adair as she joined him on the path to watch her friend with misty eyes. Then he looked back to the bridge as well.

Streiker held Sharon only a moment, because the partyers in the gazebo were beckoning. In her excitement, she stumbled a little getting past the first step on the bridge. But Streiker steadied her, and she clung to him as she made her way to the top of the bridge.

From there it was all downhill. As he led Sharon down the incline to the other side, she came to life, running up into the gazebo to hug her grandmother. The others rushed to embrace them both, and Sharon was engulfed.

While Sammy and Adair watched, one of those quirky morning fogs settled on the grounds, blocking their view of the gazebo and its occupants.

With a sigh, Sammy started to turn away, but something on this side of the footbridge caught his eye. He went over a few steps, then bent and picked up her great black eyeglasses, almost lost in the grass where she had tossed them away. She'd never need them again.

Tucking them into his pocket, he glanced through the mists at the empty patch of grass where the gazebo had stood. Then he looked at the invitation he still held. It was addressed to "Sharon Betschelet," and engraved with a blooming orchid spike. He stuffed that also in his shirt pocket, wondering what he would see in the news about her. Finally, he raised his eyes to Adair, who was watching.

"There's still a lot I don't understand," he began as he would to a suspect caught trying to spin a fishy story. "That first day, when I saw you in the park dancing, we heard the music, and saw the children, but when my mother-in-law came by minutes later, she saw . . . nothing."

Adair smiled at him. "The old divines called them 'visions,'" she said softly. "Fletcher sent everything you saw and heard, but, Sharon is not the only one who associates the fall with loss. That Saturday, your mother-in-law had been grieving a terrible November loss of her own, and Fletcher chose not to inflict unnecessary pain on her by allowing her to see what you saw."

Sammy's brows drew down in a scowl. "What loss? How would seeing you dance hurt her? Oh yeah, and there were—the kids. Lots of little kids," he added. He hesitated on a new thought that had crossed his mind.

"Marni will tell you about it," she said.

"Guess I'd better go find her." He started to turn, then paused. Hesitantly, he extended his hand to her.

Adair laughed as she shook it. "I don't have any more cookies to prove that I'm real, Sammy."

"What? None to drop down through thin air?" he scoffed. She squinted in sudden mirth, and he felt a little chastened. "Yeah, okay," he said, turning down the path toward the plaza. Glancing back, he saw that she was gone.

As he regained the central plaza, he spotted a special attraction that had just been set up to the side, and was already drawing a lot of attention. Large signs proclaimed that the Dallas Cowboys' new starting quarterback would be signing photos and souvenirs FREE for arboretum visitors up to 17 years old.

Sure enough, sitting behind long tables under awnings were Jon Ramey and six or eight cheerleaders signing autographs. Chris was being wheeled away from the tables with an alarming load of autographed photos, gear and clothing. Todd and Lacie were likewise carting great bags of football souvenirs.

Sammy rushed to the front of the line to pound on Jon's table. "What did you say in that interview?"

Ramey squinted up at him as he tossed off an autograph to the kid eagerly waiting. "Aw, you're not sore about that, are you, Mick? He just asked about my last game with the Guns."

Gleefully, the kid told Sammy, "He said, 'Between the owner and my offensive specialist, I had a real clown show going on.'"

Sammy's mouth hung open, then he snapped it shut and thanked his young informant.

"Hey, get in line and wait your turn!" a kid behind him cried.

"He just wanted to know what Jon Ramey said in the interview about his last arenaball game," the first said on his way out.

So as the youngsters pushed ahead of Sammy one at a time, they each informed him, "He said that the owner and his offensive specialist turned the whole thing into a clown show."

"He said the owner and his number-one receiver made the game a clown show."

"He said he should've worn big floppy shoes, 'cause the whole thing was a clown show."

"He said he had to keep checking for little cars and cream pies in the clown show."

"He said—"

"Thank you, thank you, THANK YOU," Sammy said, throwing up his hands.

"Peace out, Mick," Jon said, grabbing something from down the table to scrawl on with his thick pen. Then he handed Sammy an autographed package of chocolate mint cookies.

Sammy inhaled sharply, but the line of kids nudged him aside. He escaped the special attraction to look around for his family.

When he couldn't find them, there was a sharp bark, and he looked down at a big ol' grinning dog. "What're you standing there for? Where are they?" Sammy said, waving the cookies in exasperation. Bubba barked again, moving away, so Sammy began following.

He paused at a kiosk filled with orchid plants. A sign on the side of the kiosk read, "Each kit is equipped with everything you need to grow your own!"

Equipped! He felt the invitation in his pocket. "All that was about being equipped! Yeah, I can get into this helping business," he murmured.

Remembering what Streiker had said about Adair's being equipped through her suffering, Sammy winced. "*I* don't have to suffer to be equipped, do I? After all, working with Pruett is suffering enough for anybody. And it's not like there are monsters in Dallas, or anything."

Satisfied with that and his cookies, he turned to follow Bubba down the path.

The story continues in *Abby's Monsters*.

A Reader's Questions

Who is Streiker? He is an imperfect representation of the resurrected Jesus Christ.

But you already mention Jesus in the story. How can you have Streiker, too? Streiker is the analogy; Jesus is the reality. They had better be compatible. If they're not, I've screwed up badly.

In the original Streiker Saga, I omitted the mention of Jesus Christ to avoid confusing readers about the analogy I was trying to make. This distressed some readers, and over time I began to realize that it was possible to incorporate both in the same story.

Also, prior to Streiker's appearance in the Sammy Series, Sammy and Marni are Christians who pray to Jesus. It seemed rude to cut Him out now. So I decided to structure the analogy according to various aspects of our relationship to Christ. The bottom line is, if Streiker's dealings with the other characters help encourage your faith, great; if not, Jesus is still the Rock, still the Cornerstone. Streiker is just a character in a story.

Who is Sammy? He is exactly what he appears to be: a Christian trying to do the right thing in all circumstances. In varying degrees, this also applies to Marni, Pam, Clayton, Mike, Dave and their families.

Who is Sharon? She is a weak Christian who makes it to the finish line—death—with help from other Christians (Sammy and Adair) and the personal intervention of Jesus Christ. I want to emphasize that Sharon's lack of understanding about what she saw and heard did not impede her salvation. Reaching out to Fletcher was enough.

Who is Adair? As the Bride of Christ (Eph. 5:31-32) she is my idea of a Christian who has grown so much in love with Jesus that He, in turn, is highly receptive to her requests, i.e., her prayers. Because her love of him has held up even in her suffering, He confers on her the ability to do some astonishing things to help others in their faith.

My authority for this comes from verses such as John 14:12-13: "Whoever believes in me will do the works I have been doing, and they will do even greater things than these, because I am going to the Father. And I will do whatever you ask in my name, so that the Father may be glorified in the Son." (NIV)

Let me clarify that Adair is not dead. I attempted to foreshadow this not only by Streiker's reviving Jess, but in the conversation in the warehouse when Sammy and Marni bring Jess's baby:

Sammy looked at him sharply. "Did Adair die?"

Streiker leaned forward. "Did you?"

"That's not the issue," Sammy argued. "I want to know if I'm being helped by a ghost or a spirit or what."

In fact, that's exactly the issue. Before Sammy even knew him, Streiker raised him from the dead (in *Sammy: Dallas Detective*). This is an illustration of Ephesians 2:1-2—"And you he made alive, when you were dead through the trespasses and sins in which you once walked" (RSV).

Whether Adair had actually reached the point of death or not, I don't know, but Streiker did the same for her. However, since she already knew him in marriage, he endowed her with special gifts that he didn't give Sammy at the time of his "resurrection."

Here are a few other Scriptures relating to Adair (all from the RSV):

"We were buried therefore with him by baptism into death, so that as Christ was raised from the dead by the glory of the Father, we too might walk in newness of life." Rom. 6:4

"[W]e suffer with him in order that we may also be glorified with him." Rom. 8:17

"The Spirit of the Lord caught up Philip; and the eunuch saw him no more, and went on his way rejoicing. But Philip was found at Azotus. . . ." Acts 8:39-40; see verses 26-40 for context. This is in reference to some of Adair's movements.

"Many signs and wonders were done through the apostles." Acts 2:43

What do the orchids represent? They are visual

reminders of the truth we must keep in our inner being. To me, personally, they are representative of the whimsical creativity of a God who creates unimaginable beauty just for our enjoyment. See 1 Cor. 2:9-10: "'What no eye has seen, what no ear has heard, and what no human mind has conceived' [are] the things God has prepared for those who love him." (NIV)

I also think that because of their beauty, their variety, their long-lasting blooms, and their ability to root without soil, orchids are a wonderful symbol of eternal life.

Following are a few other verses that I had in mind with this story (all of which are from the Revised Standard Version):

Streiker (Christ) as First Cause:

"I form light and create darkness; I make weal and create woe, I am the Lord, who do all these things." Isa. 45:7

Sammy's father:

"When you make a vow to the Lord your God, you shall not be slack to pay it; for the Lord your God will surely require it of you." Deut. 23:21

Jessica Threlkeld:

"All were weeping and bewailing [the dead child] but [Jesus] said, 'Do not weep, for she is not dead but sleeping.' And they laughed at him, knowing that she was dead. But taking her by the hand he called, saying, 'Child, arise.' And her spirit returned, and she got up at once." Luke 8:52-55

FURTHER NOTES

Background information on some events and minor characters mentioned in this story can be found in these books:

Fletcher's meeting Adair; her dance background, and her work at the bank: *Streiker's Bride*

Adair's hospitalization: *Streiker's Morning Sun* (4th edition)

Officina Gentium: *His Strange Ways*

Sammy's meeting Marni; Jill and Mark; the play *As You Like It*; Sammy's shooting and hospitalization; Kerry and Chris: *Sammy: Dallas Detective*

The Threlkelds; Linda Threlkeld-Rains; Sam, Jr.'s birth: *Sammy: Women Troubles*

Sammy's modeling underwear: *Sammy: Working for a Living*

Dr. Joe Brodie; Lawdry and Jana: *Sammy: On Vacation*

Terry Sinclair; Channel 2: *Sammy: Little Misunderstandings*

Jon Ramey: *Sammy: Arenamania*

Janet Greer; Sammy's winning the lottery: *Sammy: In Principle*

The FreeWay Church; Vane: *Sammy: Grave Agreement*

McConnico; Sammy's father's marriage to Dolly and his death: *Sammy: Love Shouldn't Hurt*

Bubba; Jan Breemont; Great Deal Life Insurance Company; Clay's birth; Judge Evelyn: *Sammy: The Consolation of Bucephalus*

Books by Robin Hardy

The Streiker Saga
Streiker's Bride
Streiker: The Killdeer
Streiker's Morning Sun
(Fletcher and Adair's story continues in the Sammy/ Streiker Salmagundi, below.)

The Annals of Lystra
Chataine's Guardian
Stone of Help
Liberation of Lystra
(first published as *High Lord of Lystra*)

The Latter Annals of Lystra
Nicole of Prie Mer
Ares of Westford
Prisoners of Hope
Road of Vanishing
Dead Man's Token
Games of God and Men
In Extremis
All Mirrors and All Suns
The Laughing Side of the World

The Sammy Series
Sammy: Dallas Detective
Sammy: Women Troubles
Sammy: Working for a Living
Sammy: On Vacation
Sammy: Little Misunderstandings
Sammy: Ghosts
(continued on the next page)

Sammy: Arenamania
Sammy: In Principle
Sammy: Grave Agreement
Sammy: Love Shouldn't Hurt
Sammy: The Consolation of Bucephalus
(Sammy and Marni's story continues in the Sammy/ Streiker Salmagundi, below.)

The Idecis
Unknown Name, Unknown Number: A Wimsey Reade Mystery
Padre and its sequel *His Strange Ways*

The Sammy/Streiker Salmagundi
If Only for This Life
Abby's Monsters (coming 2015)

Edited by Robin Hardy

Sifted But Saved: Classic Devotions by W.W. Melton